wicked little thing

MYRANDA RAE

Publisher: MyrandaRae.com

Author: Myranda Rae

Email: connect@myrandarae.com

Website:myrandaraebooks.com

Cover Art by: Melvin M.

Illustrations by: Anita & Myranda Rae

Please direct all inquiries to the author.

To all the wicked little things that just want a Ringmaster of their very own.
Get on your knees, baby.

preface

This book is 25.6% smut. Yes, I did the math.

Playlist

Bad Intentions - Niykee Heaton
Burn Alive - The Last Dinner Party
if u think i'm pretty- Artemas
Black Out Days - Phantogram
bad decisions - Bad Omens
Black Milk - Massive Attack
Good Girl (Praise) - Nation Haven
Good Girl - SLOWBURN
Talk - Hozier
Dream of You - Elita
Put Me In A Movie - bulcadoshow
Too Close - Sir Chloe
Beautiful Boy - The Last Dinner Party
I Feel Like I'm Drowning - Two Feet
Long Nights - 6LACK
Lovers - Anna of the North
I Want It - Two Feet
Do It For Me - Rosenfeld
Fuck You - Silent Child
Show Me - Black Atlass
Worship - Ari Abdul
Figure You Out - VOILA
Eat Your Young - Hozier
Teeth - Mallrat
Cornflower Blue - Flower Face
Sex and Candy - Alexander Jean
Want It No - Lo Nightly
underwater - Amelia Moore
The End of Love - Florence + The Machine
HELLGIRL - Ari Abdul
obsessed - zandros, Limi

touchin' me - Chandler Leighton
Need You Like Oxyfen - NIGHTSYN
Primal Calm - Nox Averill
Lick Me - EVE'S LUSTER

Search WICKED LITTLE THING on Spotify
for the playlist!

CHAPTER ONE

court-mandated counseling

"CAN YOU EXPLAIN THAT, please? Delve deeper." Dr. Kim taps her stylus against her tablet.

I can keep my eyes from rolling, but I can't stop the heavy, irritated sigh. I simply can't.

"I don't know how to explain it." I lean back against the armrest of her plush, oversized sofa.

"Well, you said you've always felt this way. Tell me more about that." Her voice never gives anything away. She's a goddamn professional. If I'm getting on her nerves, she never lets it slip.

"I'm just bored. Chronically bored." I pick at a bit of lint on my sweater. "I spent a lot of time alone as a kid; you know, 90s latchkey and all that. I read a lot. It started off with kids' books, and then I started reading some things that I probably shouldn't have been reading. I was always drawn to the excitement and the adventure. I guess I just assumed I would have that in my life." I shrug. "What's it called when you're disappointed in your life because you always thought that it would amount to something greater—something more?"

"Delusions of grandeur." Her mouth doesn't move, but her eyes sparkle a little bit. I think she's making fun of me. Maybe I don't hate her.

"I mean, when you're a kid, things seem so possible, and then you grow up, and everything's just so fucking mundane. It's just work and rules all day long, every single day. It's hopeless—like a never-ending loop that plays on repeat until we die."

"And do you think that's what led to the incident?" She leans in slightly.

I don't mean to chuckle, but I do. It slips out. "The incident? Is that what we're calling it?"

"What would you rather call it?" She's tapping her stylus again.

"Do you have my arrest record? What did they call it?"

"Aggravated battery." She looks up at me over the top of her glasses.

"I'll be honest with you. I don't really know why it happened. Linda pisses me off. Every fucking day, she comes into the office and treats everyone there like we work for her. Just in case you don't have it there in your notes, I don't work for her. She's not my supervisor. She isn't even a manager or trainer. She's been there one month longer than me!" My fists clench just thinking about her. "She acts like she's mother-fucking Teresa just because she chose to have kids. When she came over to dump her work on my desk because her kid had a dance recital, I lost it."

"Does this happen often?" Her eyes are trained on my face, so I keep my expression neutral.

"Yeah! She pawns her work onto other people all the fucking time! She acts like-"

"No," she cuts me off. "Do you 'lose it' often?"

"Oh, um, no. I don't. This was the first time." I tell the lie with ease. It doesn't even taste bitter. Once you start, it gets so easy to do. Sprinkle them in anywhere. It's a wonderful tool to have at my disposal.

"Do you remember what was going through your head at the time?" Her voice is calm, neutral, but I can feel her watching me, waiting for a crack so that she can pounce.

"Not really. I remember the moments before, though. The lipstick on her teeth as she grinned at me, so smug, like she'd already won."

My stomach tightens, and deep in my chest, that familiar simmer starts—the slow burn of something darker. A little tickle of irritation that I press down hard. Ignore it. Always ignore it.

"This is your first offense; you have no record of violence. Have you had violent thoughts before this incident?"

I might not have a record, but I definitely have violence in my past. My last three boyfriends will attest to that.

"Nope." I meet her gaze, unwavering. My hands rest casually in my lap, as if my whole life isn't a ticking bomb waiting for the next trigger. I'm not going to give that information away for free. As far as she knows, I'm a squeaky-clean first-time offender.

"Really?" She must sense my bullshit.

Her doubt prickles at me, but I don't flinch. "Oh, look at that—time's up!" I jump out of my chair and rush for the door. "See you Thursday!" I'm already halfway down the hall before she can respond.

This is only my second session, and I already hate this place—the sterile walls, the quiet judgment. It's better than jail, but also, fuck. Maybe jail would've been easier. Thirty days in a cell, no one poking around in my head. No one asking questions I don't want to answer.

I rush home, eager to sit in my bed with sugary snacks and watch trash television for the rest of the day.

Dr. Kim's office is only a few streets away from my apartment complex. I could walk the distance. But I drove. And now I get to sit in crawling downtown traffic.

My fingers tap against the steering wheel. Looking at the cars stopped between me and the stoplight, I wonder if all of these people are here specifically to irritate me.

I wonder what she would do if I were really open and honest with her.

I think she would have me committed if I told her the intrusive, greedy, awful things that run through my mind all day.

When I get bored, the darkness starts to close in around me. A violent rage that sits in my chest where my heart should be. I want to do something, anything, to feel alive. Life doesn't feel real. It's just a simulation of misery and trauma. I didn't even ask to be here, now I have to work every day to afford overpriced shit like rent and electricity? Things get dark when I'm bored.

And right now, I'm bored.

The best thing for me and society at large is to sit in my bedroom with the curtains drawn and watch the dregs of humanity backstab each other on TV for money.

As soon as I make it through the door, my heart sinks. "Why are you getting ready?"

"There is a carnival in town. Go change out of that. You're coming with me!" Janie points toward my room, the very room I planned to hibernate in for the rest of the day.

"Oh, darn. I can't! Liam is coming over, and we-"

"Bullshit, Sasi! He's out of town." She rests her hand on her hip. "Go get dressed. You can't wear that to the carnival."

Damn. I forgot that I told her that he was out of town this week.

"What's wrong with this?" I look down at my business casual clothes. I was hoping to look put together enough to trick my therapist into thinking I'm not such a hot mess.

Her response isn't verbal, just a dramatic eye roll.

"I don't want to go to a carnival. Aren't those for little kids?" I whine.

"No, they aren't." She turns on her heels and starts to look through the shelf that holds all of our shoes. I guess that's the end of the discussion.

Pouting and dragging my feet, I stomp back to my room.

Why did I tell her that Liam and his shitty band are out of town? What is wrong with me? That was a perfect excuse to stay home.

"What does one wear to a carnival?" I call out to her.

"I'm thinking sexy-casual. I'm in desperate need of some dick." She leans against my door frame. "Be my wingwoman tonight?"

"I'm always the wingwoman! Why can't I be the catch tonight?" I pull out my tiny leather skirt.

"Um, hello? You have a boyfriend!"

"Oh, yeah." Him.

"He's so hot, Sasi." She has to remind me of this often.

He is. He is so hot. But he's also so, so stupid. And if that isn't bad enough, his band is truly awful. They are going to be waiting a very long time for their big break. Every time they talk about it, I have to keep myself from either laughing or gagging. The delusion runs deep.

Instead of listing all of the reasons I hate Liam, I drag lip gloss over my lips.

"I'm so excited! A few of the girls from work went last night, and they said it was amazing!" She bounces on her toes.

"We'll see about that." I pull my boots on. "I can't think of a single thing at a carnival that I would describe as amazing. Elephant shit and screaming children? Oh, goodie! Where do I sign up?"

"Oh, shut up." She waves her hand, ignoring me. "Let's go have dinner, then we can head over."

"I want to be back here in my bed no later than ten!" I shout after her as she leaves. "I'm serious, Janie! Ten!"

I want to say no altogether, but I owe her. She's been covering my share of the rent ever since I lost my job. The idea of being out on the street doesn't exactly appeal to me, and I know she's doing me a favor. It's probably best not to rock the boat. If she wants me to go to a carnival, then I guess I'll be going to a carnival.

With a sigh, I drag myself into the living room, watching her as she bounces around, pulling her jacket on like this is the best night of her life.

Sometimes, I just stare at her, trying to understand. How can anyone be that bubbly and carefree, especially someone who spends their day working in the insurance department of a bank? She screws people over for a living, denying claims and enforcing policies from her little office in that dingy strip mall. How can she still act like life's some big, happy adventure?

The only explanation is that there is nothing bouncing around up there—her brain is asleep.

"Come on!" She squeaks.

"Yeah! Better beat the rush!" I plaster on a fake smile and follow her out the door.

CHAPTER TWO

is it just me, or is this carnival hornier than most?

EVERY PERSON in the state of California is here.

It took thirty minutes from the time we turned into the lot for her to find a parking space, and then we had to trek three miles from said space to the ticket line, which is longer than should be legal. This line is the kind of long that would have me turning around and heading home if the choice were mine.

Unfortunately, I'm stuck here.

To make matters worse, we're flanked on either side by groups of loud, prepubescent girls.

God, strike me down.

So far, I've gathered that they are here to meet with a group of prepubescent boys. I never liked teenage boys, even when I was a teenager. Older, wiser, richer –that's more my style.

Janie babbles excitedly, and I try to listen, but something more interesting catches my attention.

A guy on a motorcycle just pulled to a stop, parking and jumping off of his bike right in front of us. As he grabbed his jacket from one of his side-saddle compartments, his wallet fell to the ground. He didn't notice, and apparently, neither did anyone else.

No one but me.

My eyes follow him as he disappears into the crowd. My fingers itch. It's less about whatever he has in his wallet and more about the excitement of the unknown and the thrill of taking it right under the noses of so many people.

I have to play this cool. If I'm too obvious, someone will see what I'm doing. I can't have any witnesses.

Humming, I take a step toward the curb.

The line hasn't moved in over ten minutes. I should wait until we start walking to do this. That's the best plan. That way, when he comes back to look for it, I'm not still standing here in front of him.

Patience, Sasi.

"Oh, we're moving!" Janie pulls my arms.

"Cool!" I cringe. Too much –too obvious.

Very casually, I drop my bag. It falls off the curb into the gutter and spills open.

Perfectly executed. Ten out of ten, no notes.

"Oh no!" Janie bends down to grab my lip gloss as I scoop up the rest of my belongings, plus one new edition.

The line shuffles forward slowly. When we finally round the corner, the carnival comes into view in the distance.

I'm impressed despite myself. The front entrance looks grandiose and magical. This is the kind of place I would have liked as a kid. There is a buzz in the air. The atmosphere of this place is tangible.

The lights twinkle in a pattern, white to red to purple, shining down on the crowd. It's mesmerizing.

Billowing sheets of multicolored fabric hang down around the ticket booths, making tents that reach up into the sky. They're being held up by hot air balloons. At least a hundred of them dot the sky, hanging above like glowing lanterns.

It seems structurally impossible. As I search for the cables that must be holding them up somehow, a sweet smell—sugar and vanilla wafts through the air.

Breaking my gaze away, I dig around in my bag until I find the wallet.

Shielding it from Janie, I open it. The driver's license belongs to one William Ford. Sorry, William, this thirty-two-dollars and fully-stamped sandwich shop reward card are mine.

Dumping his wallet in the garbage as we step up to the ticket counter, I slip the money into my pocket.

"Two, please." Her voice is soft and breathless. She can't tear her eyes away from the magical spectacle.

"Have a lovely evening." The man slides our wrist bands toward us with a strange smirk on his face. His gold teeth glint in the white light. As it shifts to red, he looks more sinister.

"Come on!" She links arms with me, somehow unaware of what a creep that guy is.

As we step through the gate, the lights, sounds, and smells intensify immediately.

"What do you—" The words die in my throat, all coherent thoughts screeching to a stop.

Right there, in the center of the entrance, on a small circular platform for all to see, three clowns are...performing. This might be a normal occurrence at most carnivals, but these clowns aren't tying balloon animals.

They're having a threesome.

Dicks out.

I'm speechless as I watch them. Three grown men dressed as clowns, absolutely railing each other. This isn't just sex; they are really going at it.

"What the fuck?" I gather my jaw from the ground.

"What, you don't like clowns?" She quirks her brow and laughs.

"Are you serious?" I look between her and them, unable to look away for long.

"They aren't scary or anything!" She's still laughing at me like I'm the crazy one here.

For a split second, it occurs to me that this might be some kind of prank, but there are kids here.

"I mean, I'm not scared of them! I just wasn't expecting to see them." Why is she looking at me like that? My surprise is not unwarranted. I'm not a prude by any means, but I wasn't expecting an orgy before we even made it past the entrance.

She starts to walk away, but I can't leave yet. Maybe her life is more wild than I thought. She's not even batting an eye at this.

One of the clowns reaches forward, grabbing the exaggerated collar of the one in front of him. He wraps it around his fist and tugs tightly. I watch, my breath catching as his eyes widen, then roll back into his head.

Holy shit.

This is, without a doubt, the strangest thing I've ever witnessed. It feels wrong to watch, but I can't stop.

Clowns. In full dress and face paint –big shoes and all– pounding each other in a train formation. When the one in the front starts to honk a colorful clown horn, I can't hold back my laughter. This is absurd.

The families gathered around the stage cheer for what I can only assume is the final act.

A huge balloon pops open above the crowd, raining down confetti and smaller balloons twisted into the shape of a penis.

"Sasi?" Janie calls, waving me over. I don't understand how she's being so nonchalant about this. "Look, there is a trapeze show! It starts in thirty minutes. I grabbed tickets for us!"

"Yeah, ok," I barely hear her. I'm not even sure what I'm agreeing to. Now that we're deeper in, I can see more and more things that are just slightly off.

There are food vendors, games, rides — typical carnival stuff.

The glow of the lights, the music, the laughter, all of it blends together in a dizzying mess. I feel like I'm spinning. My gaze catches things, little flashes of people in elaborate costumes or decorations that look so life-like I would bet my life that they are. Shadows move in ways I've never seen before. They snake across the ground like they're alive. The eyes glow unnaturally. The workers here are too tall, too short, too stunningly beautiful. Each looks like something masquerading as human.

The further in we go, the heavier the air feels. It crackles around me, touching me, assaulting all of my senses. There is darkness, like a current, blowing through the breeze. This place is dangerous. A raw, frightening, powerful sexuality wraps around me, exciting me, choking me, flustering me.

My breath catches in my throat; each new thing I look at is more fascinating than the last.

A black fog creeps across the ground. I thought it was just machines—something to add to the mystique and atmosphere. But it's not.

Fog doesn't move like that. This mist dances and curls, twisting around people as they walk through it.

What is this place?

We walk past a tarot card reader, her cards scattered on the ground as she spreads another woman out on her table. As I walk by them, she looks up from feasting, licking a long, slow strip as we make eye contact.

My feet stutter against the ground as I stop to watch, just for a second.

"Is it just me, or is this carnival hornier than most?"

"What?" Janie stops, already several steps away. "You want to have your fortune told?"

"Huh?" Whatever she says misses me completely. The sound of my blood rushing pounds in my ears, drowning her out completely. She doesn't see it.

I'm looking right at them. She's watching me from between a woman's legs, and Janie doesn't see it.

Is this hell?

Purgatory?

Was I drugged, and this is all a fever dream?

"Come on, we're going to miss the beginning of the show!" She pulls my arm, forcing me away from the show already happening, only for me apparently.

The tent for the trapeze show is gauzy blue chiffon that is dark enough to dim the lights outside but not enough to obscure it. It feels like a dream –a hazy, altered state that I've never felt without the help of pharmaceuticals.

Sliding into one of the bench seats, I watch the people around me. They don't seem to be affected by this place. There are families, children, and regular, everyday people who are spending an evening enjoying themselves. No one looks like they're finding the earthy scent of sex in the air intoxicating. No one is blushing after watching a clown orgy or a woman going to town on pussy right outside the entrance.

I wonder what sexual show is in store for me here.

The lights dim, leaving only the soft flickering glow of candles. The audience is buzzing, I can feel it in my chest. The excitement is tangible. A woman with fiery red hair and a flowing gown steps into the middle of the circular stage. She looks like an angel. Her bare feet sweep across the ground like she's floating.

"Good evening, my lovelies!" Her voice sends a hush over the crowd. "I'm Thalora Baine. Welcome to The Reverie of Dreams. Tonight, we're going to thrill you! Open your hearts and your minds! This is what dreams...and nightmares are made of." She bows with a flourish, her gown swirling around her before vanishing into the shadows.

A haunting melody begins to drift from the shadows, low and melancholic at first, its notes winding through the crowd. It seems to come from everywhere and nowhere at once, its eerie sweetness pulling at something deep inside me.

Overhead, the lights begin to shimmer, shifting into pinpricks of starlight that dance above us, transforming the tent's ceiling into an endless night sky. A single beam of light cuts through the darkness to focus on the center of the tent, high above the ground.

The fog rolls in, swirling at our feet but moving upward, dissipating as it rises around us. A chill that wasn't there before bites at my skin, but I hardly notice it.

In the center of the tent, she appears. A woman drifts down from the ceiling–floating, levitating. Her dress billows around her like feathers. She spins slowly in the air, her movements languid and dreamlike, her body floating effortlessly as if she's part of the fog itself.

“Wow.” Janie leans in. She says something else, but it’s muffled and distorted.

"Where are the cables?" I whisper, leaning forward. Squinting, I search for any sign that she isn’t somehow actually flying. There are no cables, no harness, no safety nets. Just her.

She starts to spin, slowly at first, then faster and faster. When she reaches the top of the tent, she stops.

No one in the crowd moves. No one breathes. Collectively leaning in, eyes wide and hearts pounding, we wait.

And then she drops. My heart leaps into my throat. A collective gasp ripples through the room. My pulse races. She falls so fast it seems like the only possible outcome is her slamming into the ground.

Another woman—this one as dark and fluid as night—appears from nowhere, catching her midair. Their fingers lock, and they tumble, head over feet in perfect synchronicity.

Then Thalora returns.

Suspended upside down, her knees hooked around a swinging bar, she swoops down from above. Seamlessly, she grabs both women by the ankle, her arms outstretched like wings. Together, they become one, twisting and twirling, bodies entwined in impossible formations.

The audience gasps, some clutching their chests, others with their hands over their mouths. It's dangerous, hypnotic. There’s something about the way they move. Like everything else here, it feels erotic.

I can’t look away. None of us can. It’s not just a performance; it’s magic, raw, and visceral.

It’s enchanting.

They move in perfect unison, never missing a beat. Time stands still. This show has been going on forever. We’ve been here for an eternity.

Suddenly, a scream. It echoes through the tent. The music stops, the twirling and soaring screech to a halt.

A man, the ringmaster, appears in the center of the ring. A mask covers the bottom half of his face, a golden mandible glinting in the light. His eyes give nothing away, steely and cold.

He stretches his arms out, up into the air, and I brace myself.

One of the women falls, her eyes fluttering closed. She's completely at peace.

He catches her, cradling her body. The crowd goes wild, cheering and clapping, a standing ovation.

I can't move. I'm rooted to my seat, staring at him.

His eyes catch mine from beneath the brim of his tophat.

He sees me.

CHAPTER THREE

run, little darling.

"W-WE HAVE TO GO." My voice trembles as I grab Janie's arm. I can't tear my eyes away from the exit, my heart hammering against my ribs.

She scowls, pulling her arm from my grip. "What is wrong with you?" Her annoyance is crystal clear. "The show's not over yet!"

I don't have the words to explain. Hell, I don't even understand what's happening to me.

It's like something inside me shifted and twisted the moment I locked eyes with him. That man. The pressure in my chest feels like a weight, growing heavier with every second.

His stare wasn't just a glance; it was an invasion. Like he reached inside me and saw everything. We had a whole conversation in that single moment. His gaze ripped me open, laid me bare, exposed every raw nerve, every buried thought—and then it lingered there, touching everything.

My breath catches in my throat, and I shudder. I can't tell if I'm violated or exhilarated. Maybe both.

This feeling—this unfamiliar pull—whatever it is, it isn't safe. It's like standing on the edge of a cliff, staring down at the abyss, knowing it's about to swallow me whole.

"I need to go," I choke out, more to myself than to her. My body feels on the verge of flight, every instinct screaming at me to run. I don't know what the hell that was, but I need to get the fuck out of here.

Rushing outside, I inhale the sweet, syrupy smell of candy in the air. All of the laughter, crowds, and blinking lights make me feel like my head is in a fishbowl. I can't think straight. Everything is distorted. There are people everywhere, walking around me, bumping into me, blocking my way.

My head spins as I try to remember which way we came from. It's all the same, in every direction.

"You look lost." A silky woman's voice from behind me makes me freeze. I know it before I even turn to look. Thalora.

"I'm fine." I wave her off, but I know it's not going to be that easy. There is no realm of possibility that she's here coincidentally.

"Don't play hard to get, love. He wants to see you." She takes my hand in hers, leading me away like a lost child.

I don't have to ask. I know who 'he' is. He told me he would come for me the moment his gaze met mine.

We walk through the tent, where the show is still mesmerizing the crowd.

Whatever this feeling is—this heart racing, immobilizing feeling—I don't like it. I'm normally so sure of myself. My heart is racing, and I feel too warm.

A long, smoky hallway in the back has doors all the way down on both sides. The last door glows red like a beacon, beckoning me toward it. My mind is in fight or flight, ready to turn and run, but my legs move, walking me toward him.

I hardly feel the ground.

"Go on in, love. He's waiting." She presses her hand to the small of my back.

The room glows with different hues of red and pink, pulsating almost like standing inside a womb. It feels psychedelic and completely unnerving.

I sense him as soon as I step through the threshold into the room. My eyes dart around, searching the dark corners.

His top hat is sitting on a small vanity table, positioned carefully, like it's guarding the room somehow. I take a single step, then stop.

The reflection is wrong.

"Where's the hat?" I whisper, my breath leaving a puff of white in the cold air. My mind is playing tricks on me, but it isn't.

Not a trick. Not an illusion.

The mirror isn't really a mirror at all. I step in front of it, and my reflection isn't staring back at me. It ripples, like water, but shows a dark room with a crackling fire in the hearth that looks older than time itself. Shelves of books line one wall. A desk. It's an office, kind of.

"You catch on quickly," his voice a low murmur that seems to seep through the glass like smoke. His eyes, sharp and gleaming, peer from the darkness. "Come here."

A hand clad in black leather emerges from the mirror, extending toward me.

Even in the light, he's a shadow. Strands of dark hair fall forward into his face, the golden mask still covering his mouth. He could be anything.

Time stops as I reach out, sliding my hand into his. A chill runs over my skin, not fear but like the fresh, crisp cold of mountain air. It fills my lungs as I step through the mirror into the other room.

It doesn't feel like just another room, though. It's as if I've stepped out of the world entirely into something else.

"There she is." His voice coils around me like smoke, deep and ancient. Just hearing him makes my insides tremble. His grip on my hand is firm and grounding, yet I feel like I'm floating. His other hand cups my face with a strange tenderness, his thumb brushing my cheek in a way that feels both intimate and possessive. "Precious thing."

"Who are you?" My insides churn. Being so close to him is mesmerizing. Deep down, in the dusty, forgotten parts of me, it's as if I already know him.

"I'm the Ringmaster." His words are soft but rich, dangerous and mysterious, curling around me like dark velvet. It's like a melody to a song that I know, something deep in my memory.

"What?" I breathe, barely aware that I'm even speaking, ensnared in the sound of him.

He releases my face, but his grip on my hand tightens, keeping me close; his fingers are cold and unyielding. In the dim light, he pulls the golden mandible mask away, and my breath catches.

"I'm the Ringmaster." He smiles, his sharp canine teeth pressing into his lower lip.

His gaze rakes over me, and I feel it, cold and thrilling, all the way down to my bones—a penetrating darkness that feels like it's wrapping around my soul, coaxing it closer, peeling back the layers of everything I am. He's beautiful, yes, but it's the kind of beauty that promises wreckage. I'm transfixed, helpless beneath the weight of it, as if looking away isn't possible. He's a perfect storm. Something disastrous wrapped in pretty skin.

"I've been waiting for you." He steps closer, bringing our toes together, our chests separated by a mere inch. His hands weave into my hair, holding my head. "Wicked little thing."

In the sensible part of my brain, I feel like I should fight against this urge to melt into him. I should run away from this—whatever it is.

"My friend is probably looking for me." I fumble through an excuse, the words sticking to my tongue.

"You don't really care about that." His smile grows, and amusement flickers in his eyes. "Forget about her. Come with me; I want to show you something."

Nothing good can come of this. My own destruction is set out in front of me; all paths lead to ruin. For my own self-preservation, I should walk away.

But, oh, the intrigue.

What does he want to show me? What could it possibly be?

It might just be the hesitation written on my face, but it might be deeper than that. It's as if he can read my mind.

"You're thinking about it as if I gave you a choice." His thumb catches my lower lip, slipping up to glide over my teeth.

In one swift move, he suddenly pulls me forward, holding me, my back against his chest. The feeling of falling, my heart in my throat, and nothing beneath my feet takes my breath away. Shadows, like mist, swirl around us. The air is knocked out of me.

Before I can even scream, I see the ground below.

We're in the tent again, high above the crowd, floating. I can see Janie and my empty seat, the families watching in awe, and the fairgrounds outside. Below us, the women swing through the air. Everything looks smaller from here. Surrounded by stars, I feel free.

The monotonous, mediocre life I lead will burn to ash. That is what will be left in ruins. His arms wrap around me, and everything becomes crystal clear. My life will be scorched, but I don't really want that life anyway. I never have.

Is this the grandeur I've been waiting for? It's dark and mystical; it's otherworldly. I'd be lying if the thought that I might be having a psychotic break hadn't occurred to me.

"You can see every dark thing, all of the filthy thoughts and dirty deeds." His lips brush against my ear. "That's why you're here, darling; you see through the illusion."

"The illusion?" My breath catches as he wraps one of his arms around my neck, just tight enough to make it harder to breathe.

"Look." He points across the sky.

An inky black shadow, the same mist that seems to surround him, is swirling all around us. It's rising from the fairgrounds.

"You can have all of this. Come with me, let me show you how dark your heart really is. Let me show you all the wicked things you've fantasized about." He runs his hand down over my body, stopping over my fluttering stomach. "My wicked little Sasi." He hums before suctioning his lips to my neck—that place just below my ear that leads me to make very poor decisions.

Leaning into his chest, I tilt my head, giving him better access.

"I have a boyfriend." I whimper, not because I care at all about him, but because I want to know what he will say.

"Fuck him." He growls, slipping his hand down to the hem of my skirt. He pulls it up to my waist.

"Can they see us?" I look breathlessly at the crowds below as he yanks my fishnets and panties down my thighs. The idea excites me. Thousands of people below us, all they have to do is look up.

"Only people like you, only the ones that see beyond the illusion." He releases my neck. "Let's give them a good show."

A tremor runs through me, rattling my bones. I've had plenty of one-night stands. I've fucked losers in nightclub bathrooms. I've carried on salacious affairs with married men. I've seduced people as a game, just to see if I could. He is different. It's not the sex that makes me hesitate.

"Give in to me." He dips his hand between my legs.

"No." I thrash against him.

He spins me around, pressing our chests together. "Your soaking wet cunt is giving you away. Why deny me?" His eyes glint, power and mischief swirling together.

"I don't think you've earned it." I taunt him. I've given it away to lesser men, but I want to see what he'll do for me. Will he play?

He slams his lips to mine. Rough and painful, he slips his tongue into my mouth, and I bite it hard.

The metallic taste of his blood hits my tongue, and I feel a rush of adrenaline. Shadows swirl around us, like smoke.

When he bites my lower lip, breaking the skin, I whimper but don't pull back. His sharp teeth sink into my skin, puncturing it until my mouth fills with blood –both his and mine.

"Give it to me." He growls, his hands roaming over my body.

"No." I grit my teeth. I want it. I just can't give it up so easily. He's too worthy an opponent not to play with.

In a whirlwind, we fall until we're back in the backstage room behind the tent, my feet on solid ground.

He pulls his lips from mine, blood smeared all over his face. A wicked smile tugs at his lips. "Run, little darling."

Without hesitation, I spin around, running out of the room. I have to yank my tights up. He's got me tangled up and unable to move quickly.

"When I catch you. You're mine." His voice floats on the wind behind me, a warning, a promise.

CHAPTER FOUR
soaked in sin

"MOVE!" I run into a man standing in the doorway.

He yells some expletives after me, but I don't have time to care. Pushing through the crowds, I search for the exit. I feel like a mouse being stalked by a cat—if a mouse could be thrilled by the possibility of the cat catching up.

Which way did I come from?

This place is a labyrinth, a twisted maze of people and shadows. Everything around me almost feels like a hallucination. It's just off enough to seem like a fever dream. My vision blurs, and the masses of people tilt to one side, then the other. The misty shadows slip between my legs, crawling up my skin.

"You're not playing fair." I whisper, the fog wrapping around my throat like a hand.

"I never said I would, my darling." His voice sweeps over me, his breath hot against my ear.

Spinning around, he's not actually there. He's just toying with me.

My eyes dart around, searching for a way out among the madness. My brain feels chaotic and confused, shadows are creeping in at the edges.

Running into the moving sea of people, I can still feel him hot on my heels.

"Come out, come out, wherever you are." His voice taunts me, blowing through the air.

It's almost as if he's in the mist that clings to my skin, woven into every shadow, every brush of the cool night air. He's everywhere. His presence wraps around me like invisible chains, hooks buried deep beneath my skin, urging me to give in and to stop running. But that's not in my nature. I've never been one to make things easy. I'm a pain in the ass.

"I love a good chase." His voice whispers in the wind, echoing like a bell.

"I bet you do." I squeeze through the crowd, my pulse thumping beneath my skin. I stumble into a tightly packed group and realize it's the girls from earlier. It seems they've met their horny, teenaged counterparts. They're laughing, leaning close, eyes glowing with that heady mix of eagerness and anticipation, ready to see what the night will bring. Anything can happen.

Excitement stirs in my belly—electric and dangerous. Maybe I'll get away. Maybe I won't, and he will absolutely fuck the life out of me. Either way, it seems like a win-win.

Ducking inside of a nearby tent, I slip through the crowds of people gathered around pens of strange animals.

Immediately, it's apparent that these aren't normal animals. They look almost normal, but something is just ever so slightly off about each one.

A huge snake slithers up, coiling around the wooden fence post beside me. Bright orange and yellow scales, it looks like a flashing neon sign warning of trouble. It's looking at me like it knows. It understands.

I don't have time for this. Everything in this place is fucking weird. If I stopped to look at all of it, this little game will be over much too soon.

Making my way through the tent, I come out on the other side.

There is chaos everywhere, but I can't blend into it. It's all around me, but like oil and water, I'm unable to mix.

Bright flashing lights and jovial music catch my attention.

The tilt-a-whirl.

A long line wraps through roped-off sections all along the outside of the crudely constructed metal deathtrap. Twelve rusty metal pods spin inside of a circular cage. Perfect.

He will catch me before I ever make it through the line.

"Shit." I search the faces for a lonely-looking single rider. I've seduced my way into more difficult situations than a carnival ride.

As I inspect the people in front of me, the unusually tall, pale man operating the ride makes eye contact with me.

A ghost of a smile spreads over his face, and he beckons me with one of his long, bony fingers.

Well then. That was easy.

"Excuse me." I weave my way up to the front of the line, ignoring the grumbles from the people I'm cutting in front of. This is urgent!

"Thank you," I smile as he stiffly opens the gate at the top of a small wooden platform.

He's definitely odd. He moves like rigor mortis has set in. His thin, gray lips twitch. "Most people don't get a chance to ride solo. Lucky you."

I give him a tight-lipped smile. This is a bad idea. Even the operator knows, he's taunting me.

Moving through the ride, I find an empty ride car and plop down in the seat. As the metal creeks to life, the base starts to slowly spin before the individual cars do, and I hear a laugh. It's quiet. The echo of laughter in the air. It's him.

"The tilt-a-whirl? It's like you didn't even try." His voice washes over me. "You filled this place with the sweet, needy smell of desire. I could have tracked you anywhere, but you made it too easy." A cool, misty shadow creeps up over my legs, a hand that comes to rest on my throat.

As the ride starts to spin faster, so does my head. My heart is in my throat as his hand comes up, fingers creeping into my mouth.

In the span of a blink—he's here. Not just mist and shadow, but really here. I was alone, and now I'm not.

The shadows that rise out of him are still around me, pinning my shoulders back, fingers in my mouth, hiking up my skirt. They're more like tentacles now, splitting and multiplying to do the work of many hands at once. His actual hands slide up my thighs, taking my fishnets in his fists and ripping them right at the seam.

"Oh, fuck." I'm usually the aggressive one. I feel like a whimpering, quivering harlequin romance heroine in his hands.

He presses his fingers into the easy-access point he created in my clothes. With no warning whatsoever, he shoves them inside of me and curls them.

My breath catches, and a sinister smile stretches across his face, a Cheshire grin that seems to grow larger than possible. "Soaking wet. I knew it. My perfect little darling."

He pulls his hands away just as the rhythm starts to get good.

"I'm going to fuck your soul." He yanks his pants down, and a giggle escapes my throat. Not humorous, but a toe-curling, kicking my feet, and clapping my hands kind of giggle.

"Is that for me?" I can't take my eyes off it. Long and thick—perfection. A piercing through the head makes me want to pump my fist in the air.

"Once it's inside of you, I own you." One of his shadowy hands grips my chin tightly, pushing it up and forcing me to meet his gaze. "Understand?"

"No one owns me." I'm already panting. I've never been this instantly, fully, completely, bone-deep drawn to anyone. The idea of him is such a turn-on. If he puts it down the way I suspect he might, he probably could own me. I might let him with very little persuading.

"I do. I've searched the world for you. Now that I've found you, I'm keeping you." He takes hold of my ass, pulling me up into his lap and thrusting up inside of me. "I caught myself a little mouse."

A scream wants to claw its way up my throat, but I swallow it. I can take a dick. I'm not going to give him the pleasure of knowing just how stretched I'm feeling.

"Scream for me." He groans.

Rolling my lips into my mouth in defiance, I close my eyes.

"It's not even all the way in." He whispers against my ear.

My eyes fly open as he pushes the rest of the way, punching the air out of my lungs.

The scream he asked for claws its way up my throat. I have to let it out.

He groans and drops his head back. "Fucking heaven."

I feel like I've just been thrown into the center of a frozen lake. My body is stuck—static. I can't breathe; I can't think. It's a shock to my system.

"Just breathe, darling. You can take it." He rolls his hips, the piercing at the tip of his cock hits something that makes my eye twitch.

Even with the dripping wet mess between my legs, his thickness meets resistance.

The ride spins, a strange kind of vertigo taking over, faster and faster. He matches the pace—brutal, unyielding. He'll have nothing left to own but my battered body.

It's almost as if his speed is pushing the ride faster. We're turning so rapidly that the cars are going to fly off into space.

Pinching my eyes closed, I focus my mind on what I feel. His hands are everywhere. Real flesh and bone, and misty shadows that feel cool against my flushed skin. He is wrapped around my throat, there are fingers in my mouth, unbuttoning my shirt, rubbing my clit.

He's everywhere at once.

I feel my shirt being tugged down. "Ah, what have we here?" He rolls my piercings in his fingers. I knew he would appreciate those. His piercing is doing amazing work.

"Your perfect little cunt was made for me." His raspy moan sends a chill of pleasure up my spine.

Spinning, everything.

The world is tilted off its axis, and I'm free-falling into unknown space. A black void with no beginning or end, I'm just here, alone.

A desperate kind of hunger, starving and insatiable, grows in my stomach. My fingers dig into his forearms; I need to hold onto something to stay in reality. The darkness is trying to take me.

All of the strange events of this evening didn't really faze me. I always thought there was more out there, whatever he is—an alien, a spirit, a demon. I don't care.

The chance to fuck a mystical beast from the underworld excites me.

What's scary is the way he's fucking me. So completely inhuman that I truly believe I might not survive it.

When his misty shadow fingers push down my throat, I wonder if this all might have been a huge mistake.

Too late.

He kisses me so hard that it breaks my lips against my teeth.

"Sasi," he speaks my name into the air, and it feels like power—raw and real. His voice rolls like thunder, rumbling and sweeping through the sky.

Then, as if he summoned it, lightning cracks above us, illuminating the sky before rain pours down. I'm soaked to the skin in seconds.

Outside of the car, the rain and the lights blur together into a kaleidoscope of chaos.

"More." He growls, gripping my hips with bruising force. Beyond the basic outward sex appeal, I know nothing about him. He's a shadow. It occurs to me that he might not be real. My mind finally snapped, splintering into factions—creating the excitement I crave in the form of a stunning sex demon. That's more plausible than his actual existence.

No matter the reality, I've never felt so wanted—so desired. He said he would fuck my soul, and he is. He's not just inside of my pussy and he's really in there. He's inside, like ink in my blood. I feel his shadows inside, taking hold, rooting themselves into everything.

They're taking hold of my organs, twisting in beneath my ribs, vines that suffocate.

"Give yourself to me," he begs against my lips. "I want your soul. I want your allegiance, I want your fear."

Aching, throbbing, clawing, gnashing, burning.

Arching forward, I pinch my eyes closed and give in—to everything. "Take it if you want it."

His laughter echoes around us like a gust of wind, I feel it on my skin. Thunder claps and lightning bursts through the dark. The world is breaking apart at the seams. Everything is ending…or beginning, I can't quite tell.

"Mine!" He grits his teeth, and his fiery eyes lock with mine. His breath vibrates through my bones.

Then it hits me. Something dark and unnamed, a force so strong it wrenches my spirit right out of my body. It's not just power—it's hunger, vast and consuming, pulling me from the ground, from the carnival, from my life.

It feels like a drug—poison injected directly into my veins.

I brace for my muscles to ache and spasm, but they never do. It spreads through me, like blood in water, swirling and moving until I can't separate the two—what parts are me and what parts are 'it.'

"I worship you." He sucks my neck, pulling the skin tight, biting down, piercing it. I can feel him coming, and it makes me come again. This one is longer, more drawn out, more powerful.

Pressure washes over me, and my mind goes blank—stark white, nothing. Peaceful. I'm soaked in his sins, they're burrowed inside of me now like a secret I'll keep forever.

My eyes close, my eyelids so heavy I can't keep them open.

He hums, pressing a kiss to my temple. He's holding me, and we're floating. "Rest, my darling. When you wake, we take the world."

CHAPTER FIVE
midnight train

"WHERE ARE YOU TAKING ME?" I hum against his neck.

"Away."

In the dark, dusty, long-abandoned place in my brain where common sense resides, I feel a twinge. It's trying to dig its way out of its hidden place. I should ask questions. I should care more about where he's taking me and what he plans to do with me when we get there.

But I'm sleepy.

"Let's get you in the bath." He sets me down, and I finally force my eyes open.

"Um, whoa." My eyes dart around the room, trying to put everything together quickly. It's dark, blacks and grays—a plush bed, high-backed armchairs, a thick rug, and a clawfoot tub. The ceiling is glass, and rain is pittering softly from the hazy night sky.

I register that we're moving, but I'm still missing pieces.

"Where are we?"

"The Midnight Train." He starts to fill the bathtub. "Come." He holds his hand out, waiting for me beside the bathtub.

"What are you?" I step forward, accepting his hand.

"An Umbramancer."

"And what exactly is that?"

"A manipulator of shadows and darkness. I command them, and they do my will." With gentleness and care, he removes my torn clothing. "I am darkness."

A little giggle climbs up my throat, but I swallow it down. It seems like his moral compass might be a bit screwed but "I am darkness?" Really?

I step into the tub and sit.

The warm water engulfs me, and for a moment, I forget my questions. Humming, I lean back against the side, letting my eyes close.

"Can you control the weather, too?"

"What?" His voice is caught in a laugh.

"The rainstorm, you did that, didn't you?" I peek one eye open.

"Technically, I suppose I did. You're a peculiar thing, aren't you?" He sits on the bed, stretching out comfortably.

"Why's that?"

"You're not the first person with darkness in them, but..." his voice fades, drifting off.

I let his words sink in, thinking about them as the water sloshes in a rhythmic pattern, back and forth.

I wonder if he's referring specifically to my lack of fear. I know I should be afraid. I'm just not, and pretending is exhausting.

"I have more questions." I roll in the water so that I can rest my arms on the side of the tub to look at him.

"I thought you might." He starts to unbutton his shirt. All of my questions are momentarily forgotten as I watch him strip the layers away. The jacket, the vest, the shirt. Damn.

My pussy is beaten to absolute shit, but that clench-y, empty, yearning feeling is back again.

"Careful, darling, we wouldn't want to break it." He licks his lip to cover his smile.

"Where are we going?"

"Oregon."

"Why?"

"Because that's the next stop for the carnival. Portland."

"How many stops are there?"

"Three in North America."

"Where?"

"You ask a lot of questions."

"I don't like to be ill-prepared."

"I think you just like to be in control." He yanks the belt from his pants in one quick motion.

"Don't we all?" I bite back a moan. God damn.

"Slide forward." He pushes his pants down.

Without hesitating, I roll back around and move forward to make space for him. Who am I? Normally, I would have a smartass reply and a bad attitude. I think he might have fucked it right out of me. After a good nap, I'll be ready to be a brat again.

He slips into the bathtub behind me, resting his arms on the sides as he leans back. His shadows move around in the water like ink; cloudy and murky, they creep toward me.

Closing my eyes, I lean into him, listening to the rain pinging against the glass ceiling.

As the silence settles over us, I realize something. The itch, that unreachable, always present, insufferable feeling that is always wiggling, tickling, growing darker and darker until I can't ignore it—it's gone. It's simply not here. It's never gone.

Sitting up slowly, I blink my eyes open.

I feel peaceful.

Careful not to hurt him, I turn around to face him. "What is your name?"

His shadows move around his neck like smoke; they crawl up my arms and chill my skin. "I don't have one. I did a long time ago, but that's long forgotten."

"Well, I'm not calling you Ringmaster. What should I call you?"

His lips tug up into a smile, a lopsided grin that makes my core tighten.

"Why won't you call me that?"

"I'm not into the whole 'master, daddy, sir,' thing." I set my hands on his thighs.

"Not your kink, huh?"

"Not at all."

"You can call me..." He pauses, tapping his long fingers on the tub while he thinks. "What about Steve? Or Harry. Do you like Jason or Daniel?"

"No." I cringe. "Those don't suit you. You're darkness and power. You need a name that evokes that."

He hums. "Darkness and power."

"Yeah." I shift my weight, coming up to my knees. "Shadows and magic."

"Stand up." His shadows wrap around my upper arms and pull me up to stand in front of him. Deep in his throat, he growls and sits forward. "Open." He taps my thigh. "I want to see it."

I'm not a wilting wallflower. There is no doubt or self-consciousness here. I know how fucking pretty I am. I use it to my advantage every chance I get.

But having this man so keen to look between my legs makes me blush.

Lifting one of my legs, I set it on the edge of the tub so he can get a good look.

"So fucking perfect." His shadows move around me, lifting me so that my feet are barely touching the ground. His fingers spread my lower lips open, and he studies it, like he's memorizing me. "A pretty little pink flower. So pretty and all mine."

Watching him stare at it—that dark, hungry look flickering in his eyes—makes me clench, my empty pussy desperate to grip around something.

"Shade," I whisper. "You're like shade. Cool and dark."

His fingers move in response, slipping inside of me but quickly sliding back out. He explores every part of me, my body suspended above him, his shadows forcing me open.

Every time he touches my clit, my muscles jerk, but he always moves his hand away.

A strangled sound, a moan mixed with desperation, chokes its way up my throat.

I know what he's waiting for. He wants me to beg him. I don't beg. Fuck.

"Tell me what you need. Ask for it. I'll never deny you anything." He hums and grazes his fingertips over my clit again.

"Lick it." I pant. "Kiss it."

"Gladly." He hums. His mouth falls open, and instead of his tongue, shadows emerge. They sweep through my skin. I feel them inside of me, moving in a way that makes me writhe and thrash against the restraining bonds around my arms and legs. It's heavenly torture. So good I can't do anything but shake and scream expletives.

Forcing my eyes open, I crane my neck to look down at him. He's got his cock in his hand, quickly moving it up and down.

"Fuck, you're delicious." He hisses, and the shadows move faster and deeper, the pressure in my stomach unbearable.

He leans forward, thrusting his tongue inside of me, pressing loud, wet, messy kisses to me—making out with my pussy.

I can't watch anymore.

I let my head drop back and surrender again. This is twice now in as many hours that I've given up and let him do whatever he wants. I don't even recognize myself.

This is the kind of sex that can quickly become addictive. The kind of sex a girl might find herself doing dangerous things for.

"Shade!" My hoarse voice scratches at my throat as I scream his name.

He groans against me, his hot breath hitting my clit as he comes. I can't see it, but I can hear it. He's not even a little bit quiet about it.

Slowly, the shadows bring me down, placing me in the water with him.

"Your shadows are amazing." I slump against the wall of the tub.

"My shadows?" He laughs. "They aren't shadows, precious. It's darkness."

"Potato, po-tah-to." I wave my hand.

"Come with me. I want to show off my new prize."

This gets my attention. "Who me?"

"Of course you." He smiles, stepping out of the water as his 'darkness' lifts me out and sets me on my feet.

I almost argue, but I'm too tired. Wow. He ate the argumentativeness right out of me. I can think of a fairly significant number of people who would have liked to know about this years ago.

He hands me a black gauzy dress. "Wear this. I want to see your body whenever I look at you."

"What brand is that? It's stunning!" I step into it, buttoning only a few of the buttons, just enough to keep it closed, not enough to actually cover up any of the good stuff. Let them feast their eyes.

He pulls up his pants and slides his boots on.

He hits a button beside the door, and it slides open. I knew we were on a train, but I was too busy to care before. Inside of this car is his room and a few seats. I follow him into the next car, then the next, they're all the same. A room and chairs.

In between each car, we're on a small, rather unstable-feeling metal bridge. It seems like one small bump would knock us onto the tracks below.

The air outside is freezing. It whips around us with so much force that I worry about being thrown off. It's too dark to see anything, so I have no idea where we are. I squint, but it's too dark. I almost ask, but I'm distracted when he opens the door to the next car.

The sound coming from inside immediately grabs all of my attention.

Sex.

It wafts through the air and vibrates in the floor. I feel it in my chest—a heavy, tugging feeling.

It's not just sex. It's an orgy.

"Holy shit." My eyes bounce around the room. There is too much to take in. The first thing I notice is that I appear to be the only human in the room.

Without thinking, I take a step forward, eager to see more. His arm comes out, stopping me. "Careful, precious. They'll eat you up."

Something about his tone makes me freeze. Somehow, I think he's being literal.

All manner of debauchery is on display in front of me. Jagged teeth, horns, wings, and forked tongues doing absolutely vile things.

"Ringmaster." A slithering voice steps out of the darkness. "Did you bring us a toy? She smells delicious." The thing, the... monster, runs his tongue over his teeth. As he does, the jagged edges slice it so that blood runs down the sides of his mouth. He doesn't have eyes, but his head tracks my movements, his nostrils flaring as I take a step behind Shade.

"She's mine, love. Didn't you have your fill already?" He rests his hand lovingly on the thing's shoulder.

"Just a little taste?" His chest moves more rapidly.

"Taen." Shade's shoulders square up. His voice dropping into a low, authoritative rumble. "Touch this one, and I'll make you wish you were never born. I will send you back to the hole in hell from whence you came. She's mine, alone."

"Yes, Ringmaster." He bows his head like a scolded dog.

"Now, go enjoy yourself. There is plenty of essence left in the air. Go have some." Shade smiles, patting his shoulder.

The monster slinks away, and I scoot closer to Shade's side, tucking myself under his arm.

"Not to worry, darling. They just need a reminder from time to time. No one will harm you." He squeezes me into him.

Something wet drips onto my face.

"Please let there be a leak in the roof." I cringe, looking up to see what it really is. It was too... warm.

The snake from earlier, the orange and yellow giant with the mesmerizing eyes. He's holding the tilt-a-whirl operator up in the air. It looks like some kind of strange torture porn. If his eyes weren't rolling back in his head, I would think he was in pain.

"What is this?" I try to shake the image that has now burned itself into my mind as I turn to Shade. He's watching some fairy-looking creatures bite a man with large red horns. Their tiny rows of sharp teeth leaving behind pinpricks of blood all over his body.

"It's the power." He chuckles. "It makes everyone a bit horny."

"Power?" My voice is distant and distracted.

"We're harvesting human energy—essence."

"Oh." The words float around in my mind, and I can't grab onto them. "So, everyone here is a demon?"

"Certainly not," a feminine laugh forces my eyes from the darkness. Thalora is standing beside us, watching the chaos. "She's so precious." She smiles at Shade. "What a lovely little darling. She's so calm. She belongs here." She turns to me, a wide smile on her face. "Have you been here before?"

"The train?" I'm still desperately trying to put the pieces together. I'm not entirely sure I wasn't drugged at some point. A hazy fog lingers at the edges of my mind, taking everything just out of focus.

They both laugh. "No, love, the spirit realm."

"No, I don't think so."

But deep down, I feel vindicated. I always felt it. There is more than just what we see.

"She's the one." He wraps his fingers around my throat and gently squeezes.

The sky above us is fading from black to a gentle blending of colors and light. Streaks of orange and pink sweep through the clouds. It's only now that I realize that we're not on the ground. The train is barreling, full speed ahead, through the sky.

Stepping to the window, I press my hands to the glass. It's stunning—a brilliant burst of magic in the sky. The sun on the horizon, the darkness behind.

Maybe I do belong here.

CHAPTER SIX

gods & monsters

THICK GRAY CLOUDS fill the sky, blocking out any view of the city below. He swears that Portland is down there somewhere. I guess I'll see it later. There are plenty of things inside to look at—like his bare chest or the way the outline of his cock shows perfectly in his briefs.

The train lurches and drops suddenly—that dizzying feeling of being in an elevator, and the floor feels like it's falling from under my feet.

Pressing myself against the window, I watch as we drop down below the clouds. The train falls out of the sky, smoke billowing through the air as we rush toward the ground at an alarming rate of speed.

My heart is in my throat. We either land or crash and burn.

Somehow, the train slides to a stop on a small sliver of land, water on both sides.

"I was pretty sure that was the end." I laugh, but it immediately stops, a choking sound coming out instead.

Everything is set up.

Everything.

In a blink, the smallest measure of time that could possibly be calculated, it's all there. It wasn't; now it is.

"How?" My breath fogs the glass.

"Magic, darling." He wraps his arms around my waist. "Here, I have something for you." He tugs his wardrobe open. There is another dress inside, a red one this time.

"Wow." I crane my neck to look up at the silky fabric tents and the lights twinkling above us.

Slipping the dress on, I run my fingers over the fabric. It's slightly scratchy. The kind of lace that rubs, not painfully, but just enough to feel it. The light friction is going to be there all night—reminding me.

"After my duties as master and commander are over for the night, I have somewhere I would like to take you."

"Master and commander, huh?" My skin pricks as he pulls up his pants. I've never been so affected by a man putting his clothes back on. He does everything with a kind of sexual flair that I can't help but notice. Putting on a belt shouldn't be that sexy.

His top hat and mask are the final touches and the nails in my coffin. He is sex in physical form.

"Later, precious." His deep voice is muffled slightly by the mask.

Sulking, I follow him through the mirror. We're in the back room again. The air is thick and buzzing with excitement. It's not the same as last night; it's anticipation now. They know what's coming, hundreds of people overflowing with essence, whatever that actually is. This place is going to be ripe—ready for the taking—in only a few short hours.

"Can I ask, just for the sake of my own sanity, what are other people seeing? The clown orgy, for example. I was seeing the raunchiest sex I'd ever witnessed, up to that point at least." My mind wanders back to the celebration last night. I'll never forget the sight of the snake swallowing that strange giant's cock. Not ever. I can't scrub the image away. "What are the crowds of people, the families, seeing?"

"They see whatever they want to see," he muses. "Probably just a silly clown show, jokes and jest."

"Interesting." My lips tug downward. I don't think I wanted to see the clown threesome. I'll never be able to unsee it.

"Clowns don't do it for you?" I can't see his mouth, but I know he's smiling.

"I think it's the face paint. I quite liked the contortionists."

"They're fantastic, aren't they?" He leads me down the hallway that seems less dark and creepy this time around. Maybe it's the daylight peeking in through the open tent flaps, or maybe it's him.

It's hard to feel afraid when you're walking around with darkness itself. What else could possibly get me?

"Can I ask you a question?" Now is as good a time as any.

"Come with me. We'll talk about whatever you want."

With our arms linked together, we walk through the carnival to the Ferris wheel at the center.

He gives the operator a gentle nod and a smile as we sit down.

The metal creaks to life, rotating to carry us up into the air in the metal bucket we're trusting to keep us safe.

"What happens now? You said forever. What does that actually mean? Am I just supposed to stay here with you?"

He wraps his arm around me, pulling me in closer. "Yes."

"Yes?"

"Yes, just stay with me." He says this so confidently—casual like it's not crazy to even consider it.

"But my life…"

He pulls the golden mask down, revealing his perfect lips and white teeth. The teeth that sank into my skin just a few short hours ago. "What life, precious? What would you be leaving behind to join me on the adventure of a lifetime—traveling the world through the spirit realm, enjoying the best of both worlds? There is nothing I wouldn't give to you."

"We're just going to travel around? No work, all play?"

"You say that like it's a bad thing." His hand rests on my hip, warmth biting at my skin.

"All play and no work probably makes Johnny something else entirely."

His brows furrow. "Does that hold some kind of meaning I should understand?"

"No movies in the spirit world, huh? Shame. That one seems right up your alley."

He doesn't laugh. His demeanor is suddenly very serious. I can feel the shift in him, it's palpable.

"If you try to leave me, I will find you." His hand slips down into the slit of my dress.

"Is that a threat?" I gasp as he quickly and with very little effort yanks me up into his lap.

"It's a promise, darling. There isn't anywhere that you could run that I can't follow. I will find you." Both of his arms come around my hips, reaching under my dress.

The Ferris wheel creaks to a halt with our cart at the top. All of Portland stretches out in every direction, as far as I can see.

"Look," he whispers against my ear. "It's starting."

"W-What's starting?" I whimper as his fingers touch my inner thighs. He's so close but not quite there.

"The feast." He practically purrs.

In the distance, the gates open, and crowds rush in. Almost immediately, like smoke rising from the ground, the fog rolls over everything. It sweeps through them, pulsating as it takes from them. I can see it.

Their laughter, joy, and excitement it wafts through the air—tendrils of human emotion.

"Can you taste it?" He digs his fingers into my skin.

"What does it taste like?" I watch it leave them, little pieces of their souls, their essence.

"It's delicious." He sweeps his fingers through my pussy. "Fucking fantastic."

My back arches up, and my ass presses hard into his hips. I can feel him through our clothes, hard as a rock.

"Will you ever deny me?" He circles his fingers against my clit, and my mind goes haywire.

"No!" I pant.

His fingers move faster, but he never adds pressure. He isn't just sloppily moving around—precision and attention exactly where I need them.

With his other hand, two of his long fingers press in.

My head falls back against his shoulder, and I let everything wash over me.

We've already had sex, but this feels dirty—crude even. He's merciless with his hands, in and out, curling his fingers so quickly that it makes my legs twitch.

Below us, a feeding frenzy has begun. They're taking from them—stealing their essence.

I can feel his smile, I can't see his face as his chin rests on my shoulder, but I know it's there.

"Look at them," he growls, his voice low and velvety, a whisper meant only for me. "They give it so freely, don't they? All that emotion, spilling over. It's beautiful."

And it is, in its own twisted way. The vibrant essence of joy, fear, and wonder shimmering faintly in the air, curling like smoke as it's siphoned away.

My heart beats faster, my mind as stimulated as my body. From up here, it was like watching art in motion—raw, unapologetic, and utterly captivating.

"Do you object?" His lips graze my ear.

"No." I whimper, moving my hips against his hand. "You're not hurting them. They don't even know it's missing."

His silky groan, the pleasure deep in his throat as he thrusts against me, is like fire in my veins.

"You have no moral objections to it?"

"Should I?" I pant, choking on a moan. "I don't see anything wrong with it."

He works his fingers in and out of me. "What's your limit?"

"I don't have any."

A whimper slips past his lips, the sound alone making me come. It's so soft and needy; I can't fight it.

"I just might fall in love with you." He finishes me off, touching against the sensitivity, pushing me through it to the other side. He freezes behind me, his cock jerking against my ass.

My body melts against his, my dress still bunched up at my hips, his fingers lingering between my legs.

Below us, the carnival spins on, the families oblivious to the predators walking among them. And up here, at the very top of the world, watching it all, I feel like a god. Everything belongs entirely to us.

Not just gods but monsters—free to do as we please with no one to stop us.

CHAPTER SEVEN

kneel for me

"I WANT A CORN DOG." I gather the sheer skirt of my dress in my hands to step onto the platform. The wooden planks feel slightly damp and cold against my bare feet.

"A corn dog?"

"Yes, there must be some here. No proper carnival is complete without it."

His lips tug down into a slightly disgusted frown, but he gestures down the walkway surrounded by colorful tents.

"Oh, look! Right there!" I bounce on my toes when a glowing neon sign of a hot dog on a stick comes into view.

We slip into line, and I revel in the way eyes follow him—part curiosity, part hunger. Everyone stares. The magnetism that pours out of him draws everyone in–impossible to ignore. A dark current of something thick and potent hums in the air around him, heady and sexual. He doesn't react, doesn't acknowledge the way people stare, but I see it. I feel it.

He's intoxicating in a way that makes me feel feral.

"Do you want one?" I glance back at him as we reach the front.

"I do not."

"Oh? Is darkness too good for carnival food?" My grin is syrupy sweet as I lean into him.

He hums, a soft sound that could be amusement, but I can't tell.

The slightly sweet, salty fried meat smell fills the air as they drop another batch into the deep fryer.

The bored teenager behind the counter barely looks at me as he shoves the corn dog into my waiting hands. I almost squeal.

Turning to face him, I bite into the end, sinking my teeth into the crispy coating.

His eyes darken.

"Don't tease me. I'll bend you over right here." He growls as I hold eye contact and take a bigger bite.

Chewing slowly, deliberately, I let out a quiet moan. Mostly to get to him, but a little bit because this is delicious.

His fingers flex at his sides.

"Are all the workers here...other?" I ignore him. I don't plan to stop teasing.

"No. Most of the food vendors are local. Why?"

"Just wondering." I shrug innocently.

"Inquisitive as ever." He wraps his arm around my neck, just tight enough to press against my throat.

"Get used to it." I drag the last bite from the stick, teeth scraping lightly against the wood.

He groans, quiet but full of promise, fingers tightening ever so slightly. "Do you trust the magic?"

"In theory." I recognize the edge in his voice.

"I want to take you into the center of the ring with me."

My heart rate picks up.

"Alright."

"No questions asked?" The excitement in his voice sends a shiver down my spine—thrill and anticipation.

"Whatever it is, I'm down." I couldn't possibly mean that any more. Whatever it is. I am in.

He leads me through the crowds quickly, dodging families full of laughing children and groups of teenagers.

The tent is set up in the center of everything–like the heart in the middle of it all. The grand spectacle.

The fabric shimmers like liquid starlight. Twinkling lanterns float above, casting warm, golden light that flickers on the crowd. Heavy curtains billow open, tethered to hot air balloons with golden baskets and deep red fabric.

It's magic.

The more I see it, the more convinced I am that it really is from some other world. This kind of beauty doesn't exist in reality. Unless this is a fever dream or a hallucination, he has whisked me away into something fantastic.

Inside, the tent is filling up. People excitedly take seats around the circular stage.

"Kneel in the center of the ring." He growls against my ear. "Wait for me."

He runs his hands over my body, touching me through the barely there fabric of this dress. I hum under his touch.

A lone spotlight shines down in the center of the dark tent. Walking out, I stand in it, squinting to make out the crowd hidden in the shadows.

I can't see their faces, but I can feel them. The weight of their gazes touches me, thick with anticipation. A hush ripples through them, a collective breath held in suspense.

I kneel, pressing my hands flat to my thighs. Waiting.

I wonder what they're going to see. What wholesome family entertainment will the magic put before their eyes? What beautiful deception will the magic weave for them tonight? Part of me wants to know, wants to glimpse the illusion for just a second.

"Portland!" His voice ripples over the crowd. "I have a treat for you tonight. Prepare yourselves. This will dazzle you. It will leave you spellbound and breathless. It will break your heart!"

The energy in the room shifts, the anticipation sharpening into something electric. They can't even see him yet, and they're mesmerized.

Then, he steps into the light.

His red and black jacket gleams in the dim light. The illusion is already working—he is larger than life, every movement slow and deliberate, as if he commands time itself. The crowd drinks him in, enraptured.

The golden mandible lets just enough of his face show to let everyone here know how fucking attractive he is. The dark, mysterious eyes and the piece of his hair falling perfectly over his forehead. He's unreal.

The audience claps, excited.

I'm excited for a different reason.

They don't see the way his fingers flex at his sides. They don't hear the way his breath drags just a little deeper.

But I do.

And my heart rate quickens.

As he approaches me, he yanks his belt like a whip. The crowd cheers. Maybe we're seeing the same thing after all.

The button on the front of his pants opens first, and then he unzips. When he pulls it out, the crowd cheers again–wild, thunderous applause.

I can't stop the giggle that bubbles up in my throat.

The piercing at the end of his cock stops my laughter immediately.

"I want you to swallow it. Take the whole thing." He holds it in his fist, rubbing his thumb over the shaft slowly.

Coming up on my knees, my stomach flutters. We'll see how strong the magic really is.

"And now," he growls, his voice booming like he's speaking into a microphone. "A tale of love and loss." He points upward, toward the two new spotlights illuminating women in sparkling costumes on tiny platforms high in the air. "A tale as old as—fuck," he growls, his voice fraying at the edges.

I suck him deep in one swift, merciless motion, swallowing him down to the base. No teasing. No build-up. Just raw, desperate hunger. I want him to lose control because of me.

I slurp on the end, and his hands fist into my hair, tugging hard.

"A tale as old as time." His voice is raspier now.

Rolling my tongue around the piercing, I bring my hands up around the back of his thighs, holding him close.

"You look so pretty taking my cock like this." He grunts down, caressing my head before tightening his fist in my hair again.

The feeling of his piercing in the back of my throat is a mixture of terrifying and thrilling. It's a big undertaking, and I do mean *large*. But I can do this.

I moan, the vibration sending another shudder through him. The weight of him on my tongue, the stretch, the salty taste of precum—I take it all, let him own my mouth completely.

His hips flex forward, thrusting deep, pushing past the tight resistance. My eyes water, but I hold steady, gripping his thighs, urging him to take what he wants.

"Fuck," he pants. "You like this, don't you? Let me hear it. Don't hold yourself back." Occasionally, I see something in the corners of my vision. A flash of light, the twirl of a dancer, a glimpse of their shimmering costumes.

The crowd is captivated. They gasp and clap in unison. The oh's and ah's aren't directed at me, but they spur me on.

His hips pump forward, meeting the thrusts of my mouth, pushing deeper.

"Fuck, you're beautiful." He chokes out. "So fucking beautiful."

He's getting close. I can taste it.

His voice rolls over the crowd, pulling them into the story the dancers are weaving with their bodies. I'm sure it's great, but I'm only interested in this.

The muscles in his thighs flex and jump. "Fuck, Sasi!" He groans. "I love your fucking mouth!"

I reach between his legs, rolling his balls in my palm, squeezing just enough to tip him over the edge.

"Fuck, Sasi!" His voice breaks, his whole body bowing forward as he comes hard down the back of my throat.

The guttural sound he makes, primal and wrecked, makes my pussy drip. Holy shit.

I suck him through it, hollowing out my cheeks and milking every spurt out of him. His body bows, arching slightly as every muscle constricts at the same time.

The audience gasps again before breaking into a long, passionate applause. The finale.

"Thank you, Portland!" He bows with a flourish, his cock in his hand.

He turns his dark eyes to me, yanking me up from the ground. Our bodies are flush as he kisses me so deeply, pressing his tongue into my mouth where his cock just was. "Let's go. I want to take you somewhere special. Then I'm bringing you back to the train and fucking you all night."

CHAPTER EIGHT

ghostly sightings

THE TAXI MOVES through the city, the hum of the engine blending with the distant sounds of night coming in through the open windows. His fingers drum against my thigh as we pass by groups of people. Food trucks gathered in small courtyards. Bars, restaurants, and tattoo parlors line the streets. The city is alive. It doesn't matter that it's midnight or that heavy gray clouds hang above us. They rolled in out of nowhere.

The neon glow of streetlights flashes through the windows, painting his features in streaks of gold and red. He looks like art. Chiseled and carved with care by a talented hand. Looking at him makes my stomach ache, in a good way.

The cab slows to a stop–Belmont Street. The pavement is wet, puddles of water filling every indentation with the remnants of the rain that only just stopped.

As soon as I step out, the chilly night air blows against my skin, sending a shiver down my spine. This dress offers no protection from the cold.

Before I can ask where we are, he takes my hand and pulls me forward. The world narrows. It's just us. Then, suddenly—he spins me.

Laughing and free, I let him guide me through the middle of the street. He catches me effortlessly, his arms strong but gentle. I feel like a ballerina in his hands, graceful and surrounded by magic.

"Where are you taking me?" I'm breathless–the city spinning around us like a dream.

He leans in, the corners of his mouth tugging up. "I know it's not in your nature, but allow me the pleasure of surprising you."

He takes my hand again, leading me up the dark street, where the unknown waits.

We cross the street, and a wall of green meets us. "Lone Fir Cemetery." I stop outside of the iron gates where a sign stands posted. "Shade, what is this?" I giggle as I read it.

"Please wipe your feet! Are you giving ghosts a free ride?
When you walk over their graves, the ghosts that reside
there can cling to your shoes.
- The Portland Bureau of Supernatural Containment."

There is a shoe brush attached to the bottom of the pole, ready and waiting to wipe away any unwanted tag-alongs.

He smirks and tugs me inside.

"Is there really a bureau of supernatural containment?"

"I hope not. I don't want to be contained." He stops, gently pulling me to walk in front of him.

"Wow." All of my questions are gone. Haunting and eerie but beautiful, the cemetery opens up before us. The air smells like damp earth and trees. Dotting the ground, the towering trees grow so high they disappear into the sky, guardians of the tombstones. The graves stretch into the darkness, their weathered stones jutting out of the ground at odd angles, some covered in ivy and moss. Some are broken or worn down so that their letters are unreadable now. I stop and pay extra attention to those ones, the nameless resting places of the people forgotten by time.

We walk deeper, passing tombs and crypts and crumbling mausoleums.

"I think there might be ghosts here." I'm talking more to myself than to him.

"Can you feel them?"

"It's like a cold hand on my neck."

He hums, walking purposefully through. We aren't just wandering; he has a specific destination in mind.

We leave the path, walking through the lush, wet grass, weaving between tombstones.

"Here." He slips a coin into my palm.

"What's this for?"

A stone statue of a couple holding hands stands just ahead of us. "That's James and Elizabeth Stephens. Place the coin in her handkerchief." He gestures with his chin.

"Seriously?"

"Yes, we have to pay our way."

Rolling it in my fingers, and I trace the grooves carved into the edge. This isn't like any money I've ever seen. It's crudely cut and heavy.

I place the coin in the carved knot of her scarf.

Almost as soon as I do, a voice crawls out of the dark. "Welcome back."

"It's been too long." Shade grins. "How are things in the land of the dead?"

"The same, centuries and centuries of nothing new. And the land of the living?" His voice is cold, like it's sucking anything warm, or light, into his darkness and killing it.

"Oh, well, you know how much fun we have on this side." His voice is cool and relaxed.

I spin around, looking into the darkness for who–or what–he's talking to.

"There, darling." He presses his hand to the small of my back and points toward a particularly dark corner.

Squinting, I step toward it.

He grabs my arm, pulling me back to his side. "Careful. If you get too close, he might pull you in with him."

"I still don't see him." I tilt my head.

"I'm here, precious." His voice curls around me, ice cold against my skin. "It's been a long time since I've seen something so lovely. Come on, Umbramancer. Let her come closer so I can have a better look."

He laughs, but his grip tightens. "This one is mine. I don't share."

"What are you?" My eyes dart around, still searching.

"Inquisitive, little thing!" He sounds surprised. "And I sense no fear in her! How exquisite!" A rush of cold air blows through my hair as he laughs. "I'm a ghost."

"Really?"

"Not what you pictured?"

"No, not at all."

"You thought I would be a levitating white spirit?"

"That's what movies show." I shrug.

"We aren't wispy, transparent beings. I am a soul left here to wander. I am darkness." His voice dips down into a sinister whisper.

"Oh, darkness? Does that mean you command him?" I turn to Shade.

His head drops back, and he laughs loudly. His shadows swirl around him, fading into mist at the ends.

"Oh, my darling." He holds me tighter.

The ghost grumbles something, another cold breeze hitting me. I think he did that one on purpose. "I suspect you're here for the gem?" His tone is sharper now.

"Yes." He steps in front of me, shielding me from the dark. His hand stretches out, and a necklace appears, floating in the air, hovering over his hand before dropping into it. "Thank you, old friend."

Shadows and mist move around him, taking the necklace from his palm and bringing it to my neck.

A deep purple teardrop stone is encrusted in a gothic pendant. The velvet band is tied around me tight enough to make me gasp.

"Sorry, love. The darkness gets overly excited." He smiles, touching the stone with his fingers before wrapping them carefully around my throat. "It looks good on you."

"What is it?"

"It's very old. And powerful." His tongue runs over his lower lip. "It will let you move freely in my world."

"Freely, huh?"

He hums, releasing my neck to wrap his arm around my shoulders. We walk slowly through the cemetery, leisurely. We came all the way out here to get this? For me?

The quiet is nice. It feels real, like we aren't filling the silence with bullshit just so that it's less awkward.

Shadows move around freely, untethered to people or things. They swirl around in the air–floating, drifting–they look alive. The trees creak, and the wind rustles through the leaves. We aren't alone here. I can sense things all around, watching us, listening.

When we reach the street, it's emptier now.

Sighing, I lean into him, running my fingers over the pendant. I feel full–content. "How do I do it?"

"You don't have to do anything. Just wear it. You can pass through the realms."

"This is romantic." I hug him tighter.

"Is it?" There is a hint of amusement in his voice.

"I think so."

"I'm going to show you the universe. The entire world. And everything in it." He turns, holding me close as he tips my head back. But he doesn't kiss me. He just stares, looking so deep I can feel him digging around again. He just steps inside like he owns it and looks around. And I can feel it–he likes what he sees. "You have no idea how long I have been looking for you."

I recoil into myself. He's too smooth. Too polished. Too practiced. He knows exactly what to say to make a girl's insides go mushy, and her brain stop working. "You don't need to keep that up. I already gave it up."

"You think I don't mean it?" He turns me, pulling me back to his chest so I can see our reflections in the dark storefront window.

"Experience has taught me that most, if not all, of the things you say are bullshit. You don't have to lie to me, Shade. I don't need rainbows and flowers."

"What do you need?" He runs his rough fingers over my face, watching me closely in the window.

"Just be honest."

He doesn't say anything, but the shadows move around us, sliding into the vent on the door to the store we're in front of. Inky black fog curls like fingers around a lacey robe hanging on a headless mannequin.

Giggling, I turn, pressing my chest to his. "Are you stealing that?"

"Yes."

The silky fabric is pulled through the vent and dropped into his hand.

He sets it around my shoulders.

"No one has ever stolen anything for me before."

He kisses my temple, a sweet, soft gesture that takes me by surprise. The next shop has watches and jewelry displayed behind the thick glass.

"Wait here." Adrenaline courses through me. I haven't done anything like this in years.

Stepping into the doorway, I pull a bobby pin from my hair and jam it into the lock. Behind me, he lets out a quiet laugh.

I'm out of practice. The tumblers won't catch. This is taking longer than it should. I don't have darkness that can creep in and do the job for me.

"Sorry! I'm rusty." I peek over my shoulder.

Finally, the lock clicks.

Once I'm inside, I'm sure I've tripped a silent alarm. I need to be fast. I've always been good at sensing a trap, like a sixth sense for chaos.

I run through the store, searching the glass display cases. My fingers skim over the counter, brushing past watches, tie pins, and rings, until I find them.

Looking over them as carefully as time will allow, I grab the perfect one.

When I step out into his waiting arms, I place a set of cufflinks in his hand.

"Balloon animals?" He studies them. A small smile tugging at his lips.

"I thought they fit the theme. They're very on brand for you."

"Thank you, darling." He holds them in his palm, looking down at the little, silly novelty. "They're my new favorite."

Liar. No way in hell. I watch as he starts to undo the cufflinks on his shirt, calm as ever.

"You don't have to wear them now!" My heart starts racing faster than I want to admit.

"I want to."

Sure, he does.

I stare too long at the easy confidence, the little smirk pulling at his mouth. He's a very good liar, and I hate how much I like it. I hate how the lie tastes sweeter coming from him–like honey with a razor hidden inside.

Something about him makes me want to call his bluff and let it cut me.

CHAPTER NINE

broken pieces

THE BUZZ on the train is palpable and... olfactible.

"Wow." I wave my hand over my face. "It smells like–"

"Sex?"

"I was going to say 'like dead things having sex', but yeah, that works." I scrunch my nose, trying to get the smell out.

He grabs me, pressing his nose into my neck. "You smell like me." His voice does that growly, raspy, sexy thing.

"Oh, yeah?"

He hums, running his hands over my body. "I like it. Anyone who gets close to you knows exactly who you belong to."

I think he is going to fuck me to death. Undoing the buttons on my dress, I let it slip down my shoulders, pooling on the floor around my feet.

His low rumble behind me makes me want to kick my feet.

I said he was going to fuck me to death–I never said I didn't want it. In fact, I'm provoking him every chance I get.

"Sasi." His voice is a warning. I'm pushing him.

Good.

Running my hands over my ass, I give it a squeeze before stepping into the bathtub. "Where are we going now?"

"Seattle."

He's still across the room, but his shadows swirl around me, touching my skin.

"Oh, I love Seattle!" I lean into his touch, letting the slight chill of his darkness cool down my skin.

"I have a friend there that I would like to introduce you to if you're up for it."

Consider my interest piqued. "If I'm up for it?"

"He's a bit unusual."

"What is he?" I've learned quickly that it's likely a what and not a who.

"A dragon."

"What?" Excitement courses through me.

"Are you turned on by that?" He laughs, tightening his grip around my wrists.

"Is he a real dragon or a lizard?" I need to set my expectations here.

"Oh, please don't call him a lizard. He will be very offended." His eyes glint with mischief.

"What else is real? Unicorns? Bigfoot? The Jersey Devil?" I sink into the warm water.

"All your human creatures of myth are real in some form or another. Most are not what you believe them to be." He leans into his high-backed chair, stretching his legs out in front of him. I feel his eyes on my skin, touching me the same way his darkness is.

"Really?" I rest my chin on the side of the tub to stare at him.

"Unicorns are vicious beasts, not loving fairy creatures."

"Now I really want to see one."

"Of course you do."

The shadows dip down into the water and slide over my wet skin.

"Tell me the secrets of the universe." I open my legs to give him room.

"The secrets of the universe?" He hums an amused smile on his lips.

"Yeah, you know. Magic, spiritually, give me the answers."

"Everything just is, love. It's not a secret. We're here. Human life is fleeting, a blink in the expanse of time. There are greater forces than you, but there are also lesser."

"Are there greater forces than you?" I gasp slightly as he washes the tender, overworked skin between my legs.

"I have equal matches."

Interesting. That didn't exactly answer the question.

"How many other human women have you done this with?"

"This?"

"Don't be that guy. You know what I'm asking." My eyes roll into the back of my head with an exaggerated flair.

"A few. But they were different."

God. Even a dark, magical sex god is a fuckboy at heart.

"Not like me, huh?"

He chuckles, a low, deep, rumbling sound that makes my pussy clench.

"Listen! I'm beaten to shit! Stop being handsome and let me take this bath." I shoo his shadowy darkness away with my hands. "I need to relax my muscles."

"Sore, darling?" He coils around my legs like a snake, inching closer to my tender, swollen pussy.

"Yes, very."

"Can I help you with that?"

"Unlikely!" I swat at him again.

He growls but releases me. "Rest up then. Tsilly lives a decent trek from Seattle."

Closing my eyes, I'm acutely aware of his eyes on me.

"Stop staring."

"It's hard not to. You're so lovely."

"Shut up." I snap. "Don't try to sweet talk me with your magic tongue and smooth talk."

"That's not smooth talk, Sasi. You are a beautiful woman. Lush dark hair. Full lips. The kind of curves men have started wars for. Stunning."

"I know this." I dip my head under the water.

"A fucking goddess." His voice dips down–lower, raspier. "Your confidence is…"

Peeking one eye open, I look across the room at his chair. He's got his cock in his hand, slowly, almost lazily stroking himself.

"God damnit, Shade!" I sit up. "Maybe just sixty-nine." I pout. I can't say 'no' to that thing. It's delicious.

He's across the room and in the tub in one second flat.

I shriek as he lifts me up, spinning and flipping me so that I'm above his body.

"Shade! What the fuck?"

Face to face with his cock, I press my tongue firmly against it–little kitten licks–to tease him.

He lets out a stuttered breath and pushes his hips up to meet me.

Ah, fuck it. I plant my knees on his shoulders, spreading my legs slightly to give him better access.

"Don't fucking drop me." I lean into his shadows, letting them support me as I take him into my mouth.

"I wouldn't dream of it." He spreads me open and dives in.

My new necklace dangles in my face as I suction my lips around his piercing and swirl my tongue.

"Wicked little thing." He grunts, bucking his hips up to meet my face.

What's pleasure without a little pain? I grin to myself as I take a deep breath, ready to swallow him.

I start a slow rhythm, matching the strokes of his tongue. He licks, then I do. He flicks his tongue. Then I do. Our own kinky follow the leader.

Slowly, he picks up the pace, and I follow suit. Eventually, I can't keep up. He's not playing fair; he has darkness helping him. I just have my aching jaw.

Fuck, he's got a big dick. This is more of a blow career than a job. I'm really putting in work here.

"Just like that, darling. Your throat feels amazing." He grunts.

Relaxing my throat, I hum to speed things up.

Our little game of back-and-forth ends with a long, drawn-out orgasm from both of us. He gushes down my throat, choking me. But he makes up for it by licking me until I'm drowning in the waves that topple over on top of me.

I'm twisted and turned, dropped gently back into the water on my ass.

Dizzy and disoriented, I wipe my lips and sink down into the now slightly cold water.

"You're a demon."

"I assure you, I'm not." His tongue swipes over his lower lip. "Rest. We'll be in Seattle soon."

Climbing out of the tub, I drop into the bed, wet and naked. I'm too exhausted to care.

The bed dips under his weight as he climbs in with me.

"Where is your favorite place?" I roll over, tucking my body into his side.

"In the spirit realm, there is a place, a sphere, that is so dark it feels endless, like there is no light left anywhere. I like to go there, to release my darkness and draw in more. It's powerful and beautiful."

"Will you take me?" I trace the dips and plains in his stomach with the tips of my fingers.

"One day." He presses his lips to my forehead and keeps them there, letting out a satiated sigh.

My mind is a dark abyss. It's not frightening, there's just nothing there. I know I'm asleep. I feel myself falling. It's peaceful. The nagging urge to self-sabotage, to misbehave, to act out inappropriately is silent. I think it's him. He's quieting my brain.

I love this for me.

A tall, handsome, dark magic daddy with an immaculate cock who relishes eating me out? That alone is a dream come true. But he also lets me be myself.

Again, I have to wonder–is this some kind of drug-induced coma dream that my subconscious is creating for myself because it seems too good to be true?

The train lurches, gliding to a short stop that pulls me from sleep.

He groans slightly, rubbing his hand on my bare thigh. "Ready?"

"Do we have to go?"

"Yes." He rolls, pulling me along with him.

"This dragon better be worth it."

"I have something for you before we go."

He hands me another dress. This one is silk and lace–emerald green. The skirt is silky and cool while the bodice is tight, with ribbed boning that makes me look like a classy escort.

"Oh! I love this!" I slide into it.

"You look good enough to eat." He runs his fingers through my hair, tugging slightly.

"Maybe later." I wink and spin out of his grip. "I need two minutes in the bathroom. A dress like this deserves styled hair."

"I prefer your hair loose and wild."

"Sex hair." I hum, smoothing it into a low ponytail.

By the time I'm finished, he's dressed. A black three-piece suit that looks like it was made for him–it probably was.

"God damn." I watch him slide his feet into his shoes.

He smirks, fully aware of how handsome he is.

We walk through the train, our hands all over each other. Everyone seems much less sex-drunk. The air is oppressively full of it, a thick, hot layer–a mist–covering everything. It's hard to breathe.

He lifts me gently, helping me down from the train. The air is slightly cold, but it's refreshing. Taking a deep breath, I feel myself coming out of the fog.

"There." He points to a little blue sports car parked across the street.

"What is that?" I gasp, stepping toward it.

He places the keys in my hand. "Our ride to Lake Chelan."

"And I'm driving?" I squeal. "I don't know where we're going."

"I can direct you." He opens his arm, gesturing for me to go ahead.

"Do you have any powers that will help me avoid getting a ticket? I can't sit behind the wheel of this thing and drive the speed limit."

"I'll handle it." He opens the driver's side door for me to slip inside. Such a gentleman.

He barely has time to close his door before I peel out.

Shifting gears, I pull the car onto the main road, letting the engine roar.

"So," I press my foot to the pedal, gaining speed to hurry through a changing light. "I want a little straight talk. We have a while."

"What do you want to know?" He doesn't shy away. There is no flicker in his eyes—the telltale signs of a man about to be caught up in his own lies.

"I know I seem very easygoing, but I don't share." My eyes move up his chest. "We just met, I get it. But I can't have you throwing other women…or men, in my face. If you want to do that, I get it, but I absolutely cannot see it."

"What happens if you happen upon it?"

"Well, for your sake and the sake of the other person, I hope there's nothing sharp lying around when I find you." My eye twitches.

Dark shadows— hands—take the steering wheel from me. His actual hand grips my chin. "I can tell you now, if I ever catch anyone inside of you, I will rip them limb from limb and bathe you in their blood. I will make it as slow and as painful as possible. Then, I'll fuck you next to their dismembered corpse to remind you who the fuck you belong to." His fingers dig into my skin, biting painfully.

"Good. As long as we're on the same page." I reach over and run my fingers up the length of his erection. I knew he'd be hard because I'm soaked.

"Communication is key." He sits back, his large frame stuffed into the small cab.

Taking the wheel, I can't help but smile as I merge onto the highway.

It's still early enough that the road is mostly empty.

"Let's see how she does." I press my foot down on the gas pedal, hard. The engine hums as I weave through the sparse traffic.

"Were you taught to drive by street racers?" He's so collected.

Unrattleable. Unscareable. Perfect.

"No, I just like to drive." And this car is a dream.

"It's very attractive."

I shift gears, taking us faster as we leave Seattle behind us.

"Do you drink coffee?" I blurt out the question the second it enters my mind.

"No." He smiles. "Do you?"

"Yes." I pull off the exit we're passing.

"Are we stopping?"

"Yes, we are. If you're going to keep fucking me all night long, you better start producing a cup a few times a day."

"I'll remember that." His shadows creep up my thigh, squeezing gently.

"What do you like?"

"Night. Storms. Moonlight. Cold."

"I'm sensing a theme here. What kind of human essence do you like the most? Do they have a taste? Is each one different?"

After a moment, when he doesn't respond, I look over at him. He's got a strange look on his face. Confusion maybe. Or shock.

He lurches forward unexpectedly, grabbing my neck and yanking me forward. Our mouths meet forcefully. "You are..." He growls against my lips, groaning before slipping his tongue into my mouth. There is a hunger—a desperation in this kiss. He isn't just kissing me, he's speaking. I can feel it in my chest. I understand it. "You don't know how long I've searched for you. You will never escape me, Sasi. If you ever try, I will search this realm and every other. You belong to me."

"And you belong to me, right?" I bite his lower lip.

"You can have all the broken pieces."

"Good."

CHAPTER TEN
voyeuristic dragons

AFTER FOUR AND a half fucking hours, we finally make it to the lake.

This… is not what I was expecting at all.

It's beautiful. Stunning really. Lush trees and crystal blue water, but there are families here. Lots of them. People out enjoying water sports, boating, fishing, and other marine activities. Their noises, the loud, boisterous laughs, and screams of excited children waft through the air.

I don't see how we're going to hang out with a dragon with virtually zero privacy.

Shade looks so out of place. Not that I really blend in this dress, but he's wearing oxfords.

He leads me down a trail, an easy hike away from the water.

"I'm not going to lie to you. I'm starting to feel slightly deceived."

"Why?" He laughs. All sexy and deep.

"Well, for one, it's daytime. I guess I just assumed dragons were nocturnal. And there are a bunch of people around. How's he going to come out with people here?" This place is much more open than I was expecting.

"We're going to his cave."

"He lives in a cave?" How cliché.

"A secret cave with a lagoon."

I hum. Ok, I'm back on board.

"I will warn you beforehand. He will try to touch you. I will not allow it." His tone is stern, like when he was talking to the orgy group on the train.

A shiver runs up my spine, and my heart pounds in my chest. "If he does, what will you do?"

"I've known Tsilly for centuries. I consider him a friend. If he so much as sniffs your hair, I'll gut him."

"Oh, my god." My pussy clenches.

"You are mine." He grabs me suddenly, his hand firm on the back of my neck. "Mine to touch. And fuck. And devour. Say it."

"I'm yours." I feel so small and fragile in his hands. I hate it. But then, deep down, maybe I don't. Not really. I can tell him the truth. He's already seen me, the real me, and he's still here. And more than that, he's claimed it for himself.

"Good." He sucks my neck, undoubtedly leaving a big, red mark behind. "Come, we're almost at the dock."

"Dock?"

"We have to cross the lake."

"What?" This is quickly becoming more trouble than it's worth.

His head drops back, and he laughs. "She's unimpressed!"

"She is." I cross my arms.

"I'm bringing you to see a dragon, and you're bored?"

"Not bored, exactly. This is just a lot of work." I start to count on my fingers. "A long drive, a hike, a boat trip…"

"What if I have him fly us back to Seattle through the spirit realm?"

"That sounds cool." I keep my expression bored and disinterested.

"Your name suits you, darling."

"It's Shashi. It means moon."

"I am aware." His brow quirks up.

"Really?"

"Yes." He grabs my hand and twirls me. "You are moonlight, you wicked little thing. Darkness and shadow, but you shine. Your inky hair and dark eyes. You were made for the night."

"I think you're just trying to distract me with compliments. I will not be manipulated." I take a small step away from him.

"I doubt very much that you are a woman that anyone could manipulate."

"You'd be surprised." I don't know why I say it out loud. Rule number one to enter the stone-cold, super-guarded bad bitches' club is that we don't do vulnerable. Something about him is different. Maybe it's that he sees me so clearly. It's hard to keep a wall up against X-ray vision.

I've known him for less than a week–everything is still new and exciting, but there is a strange comfort to him. Something old and familiar. It's actually terrifying–scarier than any dragon or sex crazed demon.

"I'd hate to see the fury you rain down on anyone who tries." He wraps his arm gently around my neck.

In the distance, a dock comes into view. Good. I need something to distract me from him.

The man waiting in the only boat looks... like someone who died several years ago.

"Um," my steps stutter against the ground.

"Don't worry about him."

He looks like Frankenstein's monster. But I'll keep my mouth shut about that. I'm a bitch. I'm not rude.

"Hey, Billy." Shade waves as we step onto the dock.

He makes a grunting sound but doesn't speak.

"Billy, this is Sasi, my woman. Sasi, Billy is the best waterman in the Pacific Northwest." He holds his hand out to help me into the boat.

"What is Billy?" I whisper to him.

"An Amalgam."

"So a mix of..."

"Lots of different parts." He places his hand on my thigh and squeezes.

Billy gives a hand signal, and the boat jets off into the water. The motor hums, and a fine mist of water sprays into the air, pushed up from our speed.

Leaving the busy shores behind, we move down the long, thin waterway toward the mountains. Whatever he is, an amalgamation of a good waterman is one. He is quick, but the ride is smooth. And he moves around rocks with ease, like he's memorized their locations.

We reach another dock, this one is mostly broken, the waterlogged wooden planks are splintered and cracked.

Before I even have time to say something snarky, his darkness swirls around me, lifting me up and moving me easily to the shore.

"Well, then."

He lifts his brow but doesn't say anything. Smug bastard. He knows me too well already.

"Tsillan?" He calls into the stillness. His darkness is still around me, hovering over me like a cloak. "I've brought a friend. Be on your best behavior, or I will make you pay for it." There is an edge to his voice now, something dangerous–threatening.

If I were the nervous type, I would be very nervous right now.

"I thought you said this guy was your friend?" I lean into him.

His lips quirk slightly. "Oh, he is. Dragons can be…"

"Umbramancer," a voice rises from the shadows.

My breath stutters in my throat. His voice is… ancient, older than time. It came straight up from the depths of hell–curling like smoke–low and deep, it sent vibrations through the ground and up into my bare feet.

So low and rumbling, it sounds like it came up from the depths of hell.

"Tsilly." Shade's voice is so distinctly opposite. Still low and rumbling, but where Tsilly's is hot, his is cool.

"My old friend." The ground rumbles, and the trees sway.

He steps out into the dusky light.

"Whoa, holy shit!" I clap my hand over my mouth.

Their laughter mixes together around me.

He's massive. A fusion of a snake and an alligator with enormous leathery wings. His body glides over the ground, coming closer.

"And who is this?" His molten eyes land on me and never leave.

"My Sasi." Shade smiles. "Isn't she lovely?"

"The loveliest." He turns his head slightly, his tongue running over rows of razor-sharp teeth. "It's been a long time since I've been in the presence of a human. She's so calm." He hums. "Aren't you afraid?" He slithers closer.

"I'm thrilled." I don't take my eyes off of him–don't blink. Fear and anticipation clash inside of me, coursing through my veins.

"Thrilled?" He laughs again. "I can feel your heart beating. The excitement in your veins. Fascinating." His voice dips impossibly lower. "I bet she tastes delicious."

"I can attest to that." Shade smiles. "But she is not for you to taste."

He rolls, coiling his lower body. "A lick?"

"Not a single one." The easy smile is still there, but his voice has an edge of seriousness now.

"Can I watch?" His head tilts again.

My stomach clenches. Turning to Shade, I watch him, waiting for his answer.

"Shall we, darling? Tsilly loves a show." He licks his lips.

I've been known to be something of an exhibitionist, but a dragon...

"We can't let the opportunity pass us by." My skin is buzzing. Actual tingling static pulses through every part of my body.

"She's tantalized!" Tsilly laughs.

"You may watch." Shade turns to him again. "But she is mine. Do not touch her. Not a hair on her head."

"I'll behave." He slithers back into the trees.

He lifts me, carrying me after him into the darkness. With each step, we're further into the wilderness.

"So you only brought me here to show off, then?" I ghost my lips over his cheek.

"I won't lie to you, darling. I need to ask him a favor. Allowing him to watch you, so beautiful wrapped around me, will sweeten the deal and make him more amenable to my request."

"Just tell me next time." I lean back to look at his face.

"I apologize. I–"

I wave my hand. "It's fine. Just be upfront with me."

He stops walking, threading his hand through my hair. His lips find mine, and the world tilts on its axis.

"Forgive me, Sasi."

"I do." I'm already panting from just one kiss. "Just don't do it again."

"I won't." He nips at my jawline.

"So, what do you need? How much of a show do we need to put on here?"

"The best show of your life, baby."

"I got you."

A glowing light catches my attention. The mouth of his cave is illuminated with flickering yellow light, a fire.

There are piles of bones strewn around the ground. One has a distinctly human-looking ribcage in it.

"Yikes." I quickly look away from it.

"You will be leaving here thoroughly fucked, but completely intact." He kisses my forehead.

The inside of the cave is more unpleasant than the outside. It might be because we're in an enclosed space, but the smell is a mixture between sewage and a rotting corpse. By the looks of this place, that very well could be the source of the stench.

If the smell is bothering Shade, he doesn't let it show. He hums beside me, slow and quiet at first, then louder as he starts to use his darkness to cast shadows on the wall.

A circus tent with twinkling lights, clowns, and a Ferris wheel.

"Da da da da, da da da-dada da…" his voice gets louder. There is something menacing about it. That sweet little melody feels almost threatening.

"Lady and gentleman." He pulls a hat out of nowhere and places it on his head with a flourish and a bow. “Do I have a show for you this evening?”

My palms sweat and my heart races.

“We are going to titillate. To enchant. To make you feel the magic.” Ever the charismatic performer, he steps toward me.

Shadows wrap around me, tugging my dress up to my hips. My arms are jerked back and held, tied behind me. My ankles are forced apart, wide.

As soon as he gets a look between my legs, Tsilly lets out a sound that rattles my bones.

“Can you smell it?” Shade taunts. “She’s delicious, isn’t she? Delicate and sweet and dripping just for me.”

“Let me have a taste, Umbramancer. Just a lick. I’ll be gentle, I promise.” He begs.

“All mine.” A tendril of darkness morphs into a hand and sweeps through my wet pussy.

My spine stiffens, and I gasp.

“My needy girl doesn’t like to be teased. Isn’t that right, love?” He plunges the darkness into me as the hands around my ankles tighten, immobilizing me completely.

“Shade.” I grit my teeth.

“I want you dripping on the floor before I put my cock inside you. Come for me, darling.” I feel him moving inside of me, curling and twisting.

Throwing my head back, I let every loud moan and whimper out. They bounce off the walls in the cave. If he wants a show, he’s fucking getting one.

I can’t escape it. I’m bound and suspended–held hostage to the pleasure. My body tries to move, to fight it, to ride it, to escape it. But I can’t.

“Shade!” My voice comes out sharp—pained.

“Open your mouth.” He growls.

I obey because I can’t do anything else. He slips a few of his fingers into my mouth, rubbing them over my tongue.

My body shifts, his darkness tipping me so that my head is back and angled down.

"I'm going to fuck that pretty throat."

Holy hell.

With my head upside down right in front of his crotch, he yanks his pants open. It falls out in all of its thick, veiny, swollen glory.

"Open wide, baby." He groans as he slides it into the back of my throat without a single moment of adjustment time.

My gag reflex kicks in immediately.

I've never felt more helpless in my life. I'm at his mercy, and he's showing me none. I'm so turned on I feel my empty, desperate pussy clenching, pulsating around nothing.

Tsilly isn't letting me forget that he's here watching. His loud, rumbling breaths and groans fill the cave.

He pounds into me, pushing further—deeper—with each snap of his hips.

Holding my head steady, he uses me, brutally assaulting my throat.

"Please, Umbramancer!" Tsilly moans. "Look at the floor! Just let me taste it! I'll lick it up from there." He begs.

"Drip for me, baby. Show him how much you love my cock in your throat." His voice is tight. He ignores Tsilly completely.

When I moan, my throat constricts around him. He jerks forward, finally slowing.

The darkness flips me, yanking me up so that I'm straddling him.

I'm dizzy and disoriented until I catch sight of his face.

"Ride me. Use me." He leans back against his own magic. The darkness in his eyes snaps me back from the almost drunken delirium I feel.

Planting my feet, I drop down onto his cock.

I'm going to ride him like a champion racehorse. He's not going to know what hit him.

Gripping his jacket in my fists, I hold on tight. "Ready?" I wink. He asked for a show. I'm giving him one.

He's got his cock in his hands. It's ghostly white and strange, curled in shape. Interesting. He hums, a wicked smile twisting his lips up, and he watches me stare. I can't look away. I don't even know if I like it or not. It's just so unusual.

Moving my hips in slow, tight circles, I pick up speed gradually until I'm grinding fast.

His hands bite into my thighs, and his grip only gets tighter as my movements get quicker.

I bounce and grind, alternating between fast and slow.

Watching his face, I move into a place of determined euphoria. My body aches, the soreness of overworked muscles, but I can't stop. Not until I take him all the way up.

He's so handsome. Sexual, dark, powerful.

I'm still on his dick, and my mind starts to wander to the next time.

The vein in his neck pulsates, his jaw clenches; he's close.

Grinning down at him, I change up the rhythm of my bounce. It's time to pull out the big guns.

I drop down so that I'm fully seated on him and quickly straighten my leg, sliding it over his body as I spin.

"Sasi!" He groans.

Seated in reverse cowgirl, I look up and give Tsilly a wink as I start to ride again. Supporting myself on his thighs, I roll my hips.

His fingers dig into my ass.

Watching his feet, I wait for them to tell me he's close. When his ankle twitches. I jump off, letting him fall out completely.

He lets out a loud moan, full of frustration.

"Fuck!" His voice is hoarse as he shouts.

Tsilly makes a sound, something between a roar and a laugh. "Hold him on the edge. Don't give in so easily, sweet creature."

"Oh, I don't plan to." I flash him a smile. This is a show, after all. I feel deviant. Monstrous.

"Sasi." Shade growls.

"Are you close, baby?" I sink back down.

Again and again, I ride him right to the edge, then deny him. Three times. Four. Five. Six... I'm not sure how long I plan to torture him, but it's too exciting to stop.

I am power. Woman. Devil.

When I spin around again, the look on his face–pain, pleasure, need–it feeds the torturer inside me.

Resting my knees tight against his hips, I hold eye contact as I start again–slow and steady.

His hands come up, yanking the bodice of my dress down.

Tsilly hums, appreciating the view. "Piercings? How lovely."

"P-Please." He finally pants, and I come on the spot.

"Holy...fuck!" The world blurs around me, a mixture of both of their noises.

I'm overstimulated and sensitive, and he looks deranged. A look of determination takes over his face, like putting on a mask.

He wraps his darkness around me, pinning me down. His hips come up, thrusting hard.

He's taking it now. I'm not in charge anymore.

"Shade." I choke, his cock pushing the air out of my lungs with every hit. I feel the piercing on the tip of his cock so deep it aches.

"Fuck!" He finally roars, his hoarse voice echoing in the cave.

His hips grind desperately as he twitches, emptying himself inside of me.

Collapsing forward, I close my eyes and let him wrap his arms around me.

Tsilly claps, a standing ovation.

I feel myself clinging to consciousness by a very thin thread. Shade shifts beneath me, his hands keeping me steady against him. "Go outside and catch your breath, darling." He kisses my hair. His voice sounds as tired as I feel. Good.

"Tsilly, it's been a pleasure." I bow slightly.

"Come back anytime." He grins. It's only now that I can see that there is cum all over the floor in front of him. Either he came several times, or dragons release a volume unlike anything I've ever seen.

Pulling my dress up, I step out into the cool night air.

Careful not to step on any of the bones, I walk the well-worn path from his cave to the trees. The slight chill seeps into my hot skin.

Staring up at the sky, I wait. It takes several minutes for him to come outside. When he finally does step out, he's got a little vile in his hand. It looks like lava inside, red and glowing.

"I owe you, my wicked little thing."

CHAPTER ELEVEN
wear and tear

IT'S TOO QUIET.

Sitting up, I pull the sheet over my naked body. "Shade?"

Silence.

The train hums quietly, carrying us toward Michigan. Outside of the windows, dark, cloudy skies spread out all around for miles.

After Tsilly flew us back to the carnival, I fell into a coma-like sleep that was only disturbed by Shade's tongue between my legs when he came to bed hours later.

But now he's gone.

Where is my sex-fiend?

Taking his shirt off the back of the armchair, I slip it on and tie up my wild hair. It smells like him—smoky and warm.

Creeping on my tiptoes, I slide the door open. The next car is empty. An old-fashioned little parlor car with high-backed seats and a little fireplace. A chandelier with little candles flickers above me.

As my bare feet sink into the plush carpet, a breeze—a chill—brushes the back of my neck.

The flames in the fireplace jump higher.

I spin around, but nothing's there.

Passing through, I peek into the next car.

It looks empty too, but when I slide the door open, I hear giggling. Then a shuffle.

"Shh! You're going to get us caught!" "Well, you're standing on my toes!"

Very loud whispers come from somewhere.

"Hello?"

Two heads pop out from behind the long velvet curtains, their faces pale and stretched with too-wide smiles. The woman closest to me has hair piled high in coiled, rope-like braids, but they move, shifting and writhing slightly, like they're alive.

"Oh! The human!" She lunges forward with unnatural speed, her fingers brushing my wrist. They're cold.

The cushions on the sofa move, falling onto the floor as a man unfolds himself from beneath them.

"The human?" He blinks slowly, as if waking from a deep slumber, then his painted face brightens. "Oh! The lovely dear! I've been hoping to see you! I'm Hamish, one of the clowns."

"Nice to meet you. I'm Sasi."

"Want to play hide and seek with us?" The woman tugs my hand, and her grip is deceptively strong. "We're hiding from Hyde and Hawthorn. If they find us, we have to—"

Before she can finish, the door bursts open.

"We found you!"

The other clowns spill into the room. Their clothing is a mismatch of harlequin patterns and moth-eaten lace.

"Well, shit," she sighs, and her shoulders slump.

One of the newcomers tilts his head, too far to one side, as if his neck isn't restricted by bones. A slow, wicked grin spreads across his face. "Down on your knees, dearest. Fair is fair."

The air shifts in the room—the energy.

Hamish is already on his knees. His wide, painted smile looks bigger now.

The woman with the moving hair drops down beside him, gracefully.

"Are you playing, love?" The biggest clown turns to me, his round belly almost touching me.

"Maybe next time." I side-step toward the door.

In the next car, there are several sleeping animals lying piled together on large pillows on the floor.

Running on my toes, I slide open the opposite door and slip through it.

"Oh! Hello!" A purring voice draws my attention to the corner.

I walk into the candlelit room.

Standing behind an easel, a tall, slender man is painting.

"It's as if the fates sent you as a gift!" He steps around, grabbing my wrist. "Would you pose for me? This skin? This hair? Those dark eyes? You're a vision!"

"Pose for you?" I move to look at his canvas.

"Oh, wow."

What he has painted now is an orange, a blood orange, cut down the middle. A hand is there, spreading open the fleshy citrus, two fingers thrusting into it.

"That's interesting." I can appreciate the talent. The detail, the shading, he's very talented.

"Aren't fruits just so sensual?" He hums, looking at it thoughtfully. "But you. You ooze it, it's practically dripping out of you. Raw, powerful sexuality."

It probably is...

"While I appreciate the compliment, I'm trying to find Shade. Or, well, Umbramancer."

"A quick sketch? I could finish it in ten minutes!" He moves the canvas aside, already grabbing another before I can refuse.

"Fine." I move across the room to a chair. "How should I pose?"

"Could you undo the top button and give me innocence? Think demure. Think wilting wallflower. Think untouched."

He is very dramatic.

"So, what's your name?"

"I'm Rafael." He looks over the top of the canvas. "I've been hoping to meet you. They said you were delicious and you're even better than they described."

"All of you sure know how to stroke a girl's ego around here." I laugh.

His brows furrow in concentration as he quickly sketches my form on the canvas. I know I'm supposed to be giving him my best 'virgin good girl' but I make sure to pop my ass out just enough to give him something good to draw.

"How are you enjoying our enchanted life?" He smiles.

"It's been enlightening."

"The Umbramancer is smitten."

"Oh, please."

"No, he is. I've been a part of this traveling group of misfit toys for a very long time. I've never seen him like this."

"Are you human, Rafael?"

"I am." His eyes twinkle.

"How long have you been with them? If you don't mind my asking." I sit forward.

He hums, looking up at the ceiling. "I'd say about forty years."

"Wow." I squint to get a better look at him. "You don't look old enough."

He winks. "This life keeps you young."

True to his word, in under ten minutes, he spins the canvas around.

"Wow. That's really good!" I can't believe how much he was able to do in such a short amount of time.

"I am flattered. When I finish it, I will deliver it to our dear Umbramancer." He bows.

"I'm happy I met you." I slide the door open and move into the next car.

That was nice, but I'm ready to find Shade.

The next car makes me stop—my body freezes on the spot. "Whoa, what the fuck?" My mouth drops open. I want to look away, but I physically can't.

A particleboard wall has been set up in the center of the room. It's painted with an archaic Greek-style mural. There are holes cut out of it. Eight of them. Like an amusement park stand-in photo wall that you stick your head through. Except the holes aren't for heads.

Eight long, hard cocks are sticking through holes in the board.

And eight people are eagerly waiting on their knees on the other side to suck them.

It's a carnival glory-hole.

They don't even notice me. The room is humid, and it smells like sweat. It's so loud. Screaming, moaning, speaking in tongues.

I'm not sure how long I stand and watch them. It's captivating in a way. "Fuck." I shake my head, dusting off the trance. I have to find Shade!

Opening the next door, I suck in a breath of cool, fresh air.

"Excuse me." I hurry through the car toward the other door. The abnormally large woman in here is cooking meth or something. I can't get sucked into another thing.

"Oh! Wait!" She gasps. "I'm making an elixir of enhancement! If you would donate, I would be eternally grateful."

"Enhancement of what?"

"The only thing that needs enhancing! Love, passion, pleasure!" She raises her hands with a flourish. The tips of her fingers hit the ceiling.

"What do you mean by a donation?"

"The more people that give, the stronger the elixir. If I could take just a small clipping of hair, that would be perfect!" She looks so hopeful.

"Ah, what the hell. Go for it." I pull my hair down from the bun, keeping it all contained.

She snips a tiny piece from the end. "Thank you so much!"

When she throws it in the bubbling pink liquid in her pot, a little puff of red smoke plumes into the air. The sweet smell of spun sugar fills the car.

"This is going to be my strongest batch yet!" She claps her hands together.

"Good luck!" I wave and continue on my journey.

Each car reveals a menagerie of sleeping animals, contortionists, reptiles, and even a man conducting a symphony of tiny pixie musicians. But no Shade.

I'm pulled into a weed tasting. One puff and I feel like my head has lifted from my shoulders and is floating away in the clouds.

Just when I start to wonder if he's even here, I step into a car, and we're face to face.

"My darling." He sits up from the chaise he's reclining on.

"Shade!" I can't help but gasp at the sight of him. He looks awful.

Incredibly handsome and better in every way than any other person I've ever seen, but awful. His skin, usually glowing with the darkness that swirls beneath, looks pale and clammy.

"What's wrong? Are you sick?" I rush to him. My feet move on their own, racing forward before my mind can think better of it. I don't normally care when people are sick or hurt–it doesn't stir anything in me, but seeing him like this is jarring.

He doesn't look as… regal. The grandeur is tainted—weak.

"I'll be alright. I'm sorry I worried you. I should have left a note for you. I didn't think I would be gone this long." He presses his hand to my cheek, running his thumb over my lips. "You look wonderful wearing my shirt."

I scowl. "You look terrible. What happened?" His usual confidence doesn't fool me—not when he looks like this. I'm not going to take his placations. Something isn't right.

He exhales, slow and measured. "I'll be fine, Sasi. It looks much worse than it is."

I don't like this. Not one bit.

Sitting on the lounge with him, I stare down at my hands. I don't want to have to cry, but I will if it makes him talk.

Testing the waters with a little sniffle, I wait.

His hand comes up to my face, cupping my chin. He swipes his thumb through the single fallen tear on my cheek.

A smile tugs at his lips. "You didn't really think that would work on me, did you?"

"It was worth a shot." I shrug and lean into his touch.

His chuckle is dark, edged with pain. I can see it on his face.

"Manipulative little thing." He kisses me—hard. The kind of kiss that isn't just a kiss but a claim. A demand. A promise of something more.

Every single kiss is like magic, pulling me in—pulling me under.

Breathless and warm, I pull back. "You thought that would work?"

He grins, all arrogance and amusement. "It was worth a shot."

I press my palm against his chest, feeling the steady beat beneath my fingers. "What's going on, really?" I'm going to push until he gives me an answer. A real one.

He sighs. "Just wear and tear, love. I assure you, I'll be fine."

"You look like you're in pain." I run my fingertips over his bare chest. "You're not dying on me, are you, old man?"

His eyes darken, but not with pain. Something else entirely. "Distract me." He leans back, exhaustion showing in his expression.

I arch a brow. "With what? My feminine wiles?"

"With anything. Tell me something about yourself."

I stiffen. Uh oh. Dangerous territory.

He already knows things—more than he should. But how much? Was it all laid bare when he looked inside me, or did he only catch glimpses, fractured and incomplete? This part—the open, vulnerable part—is usually where things start to fall apart.

I opt for misdirection. A little honesty wrapped in charm.

"I have a Rolex collection worth more than half a million dollars."

"Rolex?"

"Expensive watches."

"And how did you procure such a collection?"

"I stole them."

His amusement seems to grow here. "All at once?"

"One at a time." I drag my nails lightly down his abdomen, feeling the way his muscles twitch under my touch. "I have thirty-eight of them. I've been taking them since I was nine."

"Nine?" He laughs.

"Even as a child, I knew what I wanted."

"And what is that?"

"Thrills and money." I smile sweetly.

His hand tightens on my thigh, fingers pressing in a way that makes heat coil low in my stomach. "I can offer you thrills. I haven't much use for money."

I hum, tilting my head. "No. You just take what you want."

He leans in, his voice low against my skin. "I do." His grip tightens. "Everything I want."

And right now, I know exactly what that is.

CHAPTER TWELVE

fearless, lovely thing

"I'VE NEVER BEEN TO MICHIGAN." I stare out the windows as the train pulls to a stop.

"I'll take you to Lake Superior. You'll love it."

"Got any friends there?" I quirk my brow up at him.

"As a matter of fact, I do."

"Shocking."

"Here." He hands me another dress. Blood red velvet with lacy sleeves. It looks like it belongs in some old-world fantasy.

"Where are you getting these dresses?"

"I had them brought in for you. I like to see you in beautiful things. Your skin deserves it."

"They're beautiful." Sliding the dress on, I spin around for him to tie the corset strings on the back.

"Thalora has good taste. And you wear them so well." He runs his fingers over my shoulder, touching me as much as possible as he tightens the fabric around my skin.

"You don't have to do all this," my voice is softer than I mean for it to be.

He tightens the last string, then leans in. "I know. But I want to."

And for a second, I almost believe him.

His hands rub my tense shoulders. "You don't like that." He hums, not asking.

"No. I don't like romance. Sweet gestures or thoughtful gifts–I don't trust them." I stop short of telling him too much.

"I've never met a woman that doesn't want to be wooed–to be swept off her feet."

"Yes, you have. You've met me." I crane my neck to look at him.

"Why?"

"Because at the end of the day, it's all bullshit. The sweet nothings you whisper are just that–nothing. The thoughtful gestures are just so you can appear the way you think you need to in order to get laid, and I'll fuck you, anyway. You don't have to lie your way into my pants."

"How are you so sure that I'm lying?" He spins me so that I'm standing in front of the mirror. His hands run down the bodice of my dress. "You're a stunning woman, Sasi. Everything about you is beguiling. Your eyes are endless, your skin," he kisses my shoulder, moving in toward my neck. "Your pretty mouth. Your attitude." He smiles against my neck.

"I just want truth, Shade. Everything else is bullshit." I lean my head back against his chest.

"All of that is true."

"I know." I chuckle. "I'm gorgeous. You don't have to shower me with compliments. Just tell me something real."

"You want guarantees." He smiles.

"Yes."

"I will show you the world. The one that you know and the one that lives beyond it, the darkness, the magic. I will worship at the altar between your legs every day. I will satisfy you in every way. I will cover your skin in silk and lace. I am old enough to know that there is no guarantee of time. But I can promise that while we are together, I will be wholly devoted to you." The rumble in his voice makes my heart beat faster.

"For now, I'll take it." I spin around, pressing our chests together. "But I still have questions."

"If you said you didn't, I wouldn't believe you." He wraps me in his arms.

He looks better today. When we woke up this morning, the color had come back to his face. He even fucked me in the bathtub.

But I can't help but to search his face, quietly, secretly–looking for signs that he's just hiding it better.

I'm not sure what scares me more, his mystery illness or the fact that it's so concerning to me.

He's the first person who I would truly mourn. If anyone else in my life simply dropped dead, it wouldn't affect me, not really. There might be some inconvenience, a fleeting moment of sadness regarding some future event that won't happen now that they are no longer–but it would be brief. I would move on.

If Shade were to evaporate into his darkness, I would feel it. It would ache in my chest.

"Come, my darling." He takes my hand.

Outside, the carnival is set up, sprawling over a concrete fairground. All glitter and chaos—painted lights spinning in the early dusk, the scent of spun sugar and fried food hangs thick in the air. The light breeze carries music and laughter.

"Are we putting on a show tonight, Ringmaster?" A woman dressed in a dazzling leotard calls out to him.

"If I'm back in time." He calls over his shoulder, not even sparing her a glance.

I arch a brow, mocking sternness. "Are you neglecting your duties?"

"Maybe a bit," he says with a sly grin.

"Shade!"

He shrugs, the way only he can—half boyish mischief, half sovereign disregard for anything that isn't this moment. "I can't help myself. Showing you all the things the world has to offer is more important."

With him, everything feels like a page torn from a dream. The ordinary stretches into magic. The air smells sweeter, the sky wider, bluer, closer. I feel like I stepped out of the static gray of my life and into a Technicolor dream.

I don't know what's waiting for us at Lake Superior, but I want it. I want to chase it with him.

We walk hand in hand, leaving everyone behind.

"Can we hitchhike?" I turn to watch a car speed past us on the road.

"I ordered a car."

"But I've always wanted to hitchhike. I'm reckless, not stupid. It's too dangerous, but with you…"

He stares at me for a moment before holding his hand out, waving down a semi-truck. "I promised you thrills." The gravel crunches beneath the huge tires as he pulls to the side of the road.

"Where ya' headed?" The driver yells from the high-up cab of his truck.

"Lake Superior."

"Jump in. I'll give you a lift."

Shade lifts me up, helping me into the slightly musty-smelling compartment.

"Names' Dave." He holds his hand out. "Where are you two coming from?" He looks at our clothes.

"We're with the carnival." I smile. "I'm Anjelica, and this is my husband Raul."

Shade takes his hand, giving him a firm shake. As soon as their skin makes contact, I can see him siphoning his energy. It's like staring at heat rising from the asphalt, a ripple in the air.

Dave shudders and grips the steering wheel. "How long are you in town?"

"Oh, just for the night." I watch his eyes move down from my face to my chest. "You should stop by. It'll change your life."

Shade brings his arm around my waist, squeezing. "My lovely wife is correct. It is enchanting."

"I'm supposed to be on my way out of town, but I might be able to spare a few minutes." He looks dazed, a lazy smile tugging at his lips.

"Wonderful." Shade's low, raspy voice sends a chill of excitement up my spine. "We hope to see you."

He pulls the truck to a stop in a gravel parking lot. "There she is." His eyes wander out over the blue water.

"Thank you for the ride." I bat my lashes.

"I'll always stop for a pretty lady like you." His eyes are glued to my chest.

"The rest of her is pretty, too," Shade growls. He grabs me, hauling me out of the truck. "Come on. We don't need to stay there while he makes googly eyes at you."

I can't hold in my laughter. "He wasn't making googly eyes. He was all fucked up from you, taking his essence."

"Well, Anjelica, he's lucky I didn't pluck his eyes out."

"So, you only like your friends to look at me? Not mine? That seems unfair."

He barks out a laugh, throwing his head back, the golden light of sunset catching on his face. "He's your friend now?"

"Sure." I shrug. "This is beautiful." I look out at the water.

"This is only half of it. We have to wait until it gets dark."

"Naturally." I follow him to the end of a long, wooden dock.

Lake Superior looks less like a lake and more like the ocean. It stretches so far across the horizon that I can't see the other side—just endless blue, capped with white waves crashing against the shoreline.

"I've never seen a lake with waves before."

"They call it the graveyard of the Great Lakes. The storms roll in so quickly and with such ferocity that many boats have gone asunder." He wraps his arms around me.

"Are you on the Michigan Board of Tourism?"

He tightens his chokehold on my neck for a second.

The water is so blue–so crystal clear I can see all the way down to the rocks at the bottom. "I wonder how deep that is."

"It's deeper than it looks. Would you like another fact?"

"Oh, please, do share."

"It's the third-largest freshwater lake in the world."

I snort. "How do you know this?"

"I know a little of this and a bit of that." I feel him shrug behind me.

We fall into a comfortable quiet as the sun sinks completely beneath the horizon.

"Ready?"

"Yes."

He steps down off the end of the dock. But he doesn't fall into the water. "Step down. I've got you."

Peeking over the end of the dock, I hold his hand tight and step down. His darkness is stretched across the surface of the icy cold water, creating a surface for us to walk on.

"Well, shit." I cling to him.

"Let's go see some friends of mine." He's light and casual, but there is something about his expression that makes my spine tense.

"What are they?"

"Spirits." His eyes shine in the moonlight.

"And that's different from a ghost?"

"Yes." He doesn't elaborate, just leads me further from the shore.

After a few minutes, we're so far away that I can't see the shoreline in the distance anymore.

The moon reflects off the black water, illuminating it just enough for me to see my own feet in the dark.

"I wonder how far above the ground we are now." I wonder out loud.

"Far." He pulls me into him.

Mist begins to rise off the water, not fog, but something else. It shimmers, coiling like tendrils in the air.

Very quickly, it starts to take shape, legs, arms, faces.

They glide along the surface of the water, coming toward us, surrounding us.

One of them turns toward me. The face has no mouth or eyes, but I can feel it watching me.

It's not ominous. There is a strange warmth to it.

"They don't speak," he whispers softly. "Not the way we do."

"They're incredible."

"I knew you would think so, my fearless, lovely thing."

They're unsettling but beautiful, like stardust on the water.

"Come here." He takes me in his arms, lifting me so that my feet are on top of his. He moves, dancing to a song that I can't hear, with steps that I don't know, but he never lets me falter. He holds me tightly, gliding across the water.

All around us, the spirits pair up, dancing with us. They spin, twinkling in the moonlight, leaving me awestruck and breathless.

It's like watching rain dance.

"Shade…" I swallow, considering how to ask this without seeming insecure. "You could have someone like you. A being that belongs in the spirit realm that can do what you do. You have to hold me, bring me, slow down for me. Why–"

"You are perfect, Sasi. You're exactly what I'm looking for." He runs his hand down my neck, stopping on my chest–his hand over my heart. It beats hard and fast. "I want you."

CHAPTER THIRTEEN

red light

OPENING MY EYES, I'm immediately aware of the slight ache in my stomach. The tight, painful ball of crampy muscle. It's still dark, probably just after midnight. The world is still and quiet outside.

"Aw man, fuck." I grumble, rolling over. My hand instinctively moves down to press against the ache in my stomach.

He shifts in his sleep, reaching out for me. His hand lands on my waist, pulling me toward him. Even in sleep, we gravitate toward each other.

I need to get up and assess the damage, but I can already feel it. Shit.

His eyes snap open, wild and hungry. "You're on your period." Something about the unnatural glow in his eyes, the excitement, it seems like he might have been waiting for this.

"Um, yeah." I start to sit up, but he tightens his grip, holding me against his hard body.

He looks like a predator–more like the night we met. "I can help you feel better."

"Oh, yeah?" I try to keep it casual, but the second I meet his eyes, I know I've lost control of the situation.

He's feral.

I can't contain this.

His pupils are blown wide, his chest rising and falling like he's been running, like he hasn't had a hit in days. "You're on your period," he says again, lower this time—reverent. "Fuck, I knew it. I felt it."

I blink slowly. "Ok, that's weird."

But he's already pushing himself up, caging me in with his arms on either side of my body. "Do you have any idea what that does to me?"

I don't have time to answer. He's sucking my neck, leaving dark marks, I'm sure.

"I woke up hard as a rock. It's not just want—it's need." He leans in, his nose brushing my jaw, inhaling like he's starving. "The scent of it? You all swollen and sensitive and raw? It's fucking perfect."

I open my mouth to speak, but his hand slides down my stomach, slipping between my legs. He groans loudly, the muscles in his chest twitching.

"Please," he whispers, full of desperation now. "Let me fuck you like this. Let me taste you. Let me worship between your legs."

My body reacts before my brain does—hips tilting toward him, thighs parting.

He notices, and his mouth curls into something dark and wicked. "You smell like heaven, and I want every part of it."

He moves quickly, dropping down to his knees and dragging me with him.

For several seconds, that feel eternal, he just stares. I haven't had a chance to investigate yet, but I can only assume there is a mess down there.

His fingers sweep through it, collecting it.

He hums, sucking his fingers into his mouth. His neck rolls, muscles twitching beneath his skin–he looks like he's barely contained by his skin.

Two fingers press into me, slow and deep, curling inside, making my body jolt.

Looking down, I watch his face. He's mesmerized.

"Keep these open wide." He spreads my legs, dark shadows

swirling around them to keep them in place. "I'm going to devour you, and I want you to watch." His voice trembles.

He slips his finger out, leaving me for a second with no touch—no friction.

"I need you to tell me when it's too much. I won't be able to tell. I'm too worked up." He gulps a shaky breath and leans in. "Woman." He groans, swiping his nose through the mess.

When he finally starts, it's like an assault on my senses.

Watching him, so completely manic, makes me feel high. An instantaneous, intense euphoria.

Listening to the rough, desperate sounds he's making makes me drunk on the power. Part of me wants to make him stop, to push him away, to make him beg. Just because I can.

I wonder how far I could go. How much I could push him before he snaps.

I let him make me come—grinding against his face, using his tongue.

But then…

"Stop!" I grit through my teeth.

He immediately releases me, his eyes jerking up to find mine.

Pressing the bottom of my foot to his shoulder, I lean up and push him back at the same time.

His eyes go dark—he knows me so well already.

"How bad do you want it?"

"Sasi." He wipes his bloody mouth. "Don't toy with me right now."

"Why not?" I slide my foot down his chest.

"Because I can't…" his words morph into a moan when I run my toes gently over his cock. "Do you want me to beg you?"

"Yes." I bite into my lip. "I want you to beg, then, when I'm satisfied, I want back shots all night long."

"Fuck, Sasi." He hangs his head. "I–"

"Let me see some of that darkness." I'll run if I have to. "I'll give you what you want, but you have to earn it."

He lunges forward, yanking me off the bed, catching me before I hit the ground. With inhuman speed, he climbs over my body, pressing me into the ground with his weight. "Give it to me."

"No." I lift my head, catching his lower lip in my teeth.

"I'm going to destroy you, Sasi. Keep teasing me. I need it. Your blood…" his voice is unrecognizable. Every breath is ragged- it's primal—its urges and instinct with no restraint.

"You're going to destroy me?" I cock my head to the side and give him my most innocent smile.

"I could pin you down and take you. You wouldn't be able to stop me." He wraps his hand around his cock.

"Ah, ah. Don't touch. You don't have permission for that." I inch forward, spreading my legs wider, letting him get a good look at all of it.

There's blood all over his face, his neck, his chest. He looks like a wild animal.

"You absolutely could pin me down and take whatever you wanted. I wouldn't even be able to fight back, but you won't do that, will you?" I taunt him, sweeping my fingers through the bloody, wet skin between my legs.

"No." He whispers hoarsely.

"Why do you want it so badly?"

"The blood." He clenches his fist, moving his hand to hold his cock again, but he stops himself. Good boy.

"You like it?"

"I love it." He chokes.

"You like the taste?"

"The taste, the smell, the way it feels on my skin. I want to mix my cum with it." He slicks his lip, staring down at it.

"If you want to have your kink, I want to have mine." I dip two fingers inside.

"Anything."

"You're so powerful, so dark, and full of magic." I gasp, my body tensing as I move my fingers slowly. "But I've got you on your knees."

"Yes, darling."

Suddenly, the idea of having a period every month for the next forty fucking years doesn't seem all that unappealing. Now that we can play like this.

"I want you to be so worked up and close to the edge that when I finally let you inside, you come while I count down from five." The drawn-out moan that heaves from his chest only adds to this feeling–this power trip.

"I'll do it." He nods desperately.

"Such a big, powerful man on his knees for me." I lift my leg, placing my foot on his shoulder, one leg, then the other. "Eat it, make me come again. You've fucked my throat, now I want to fuck your tongue. I want to ride on it."

In a whirlwind, he snatches me up off the floor, using his extra hands to hold me up. He drops my pussy right down on his face, supporting me while he dives in.

Gluttonous.

Loud.

Sinful.

Starving.

He doesn't just eat–he's sucking my soul out of me, one orgasm at a time.

After each one, he pauses, whimpers, and asks if he can fuck me.

The giddiness I feel denying him makes my toes curl.

There is something about knowing that he could take it if he wanted to—but watching him hold back.

"Sasi," he pants after the fifth round. "I can't take another."

"Put me down." I'm just as eager as him–maybe not just as eager, but I want his cock so badly. I need to be filled to the brim.

"I'm not going to last five seconds." His voice is gruff, strained with desperation.

I have to look at him, to take in the product of my torture. Torture indeed. He's drenched in blood, sweat, and tears. His hair is disheveled, and the calm, cool demeanor that usually oozes from him is nowhere to be seen.

And his cock.

So swollen it hangs, like it's heavy, solid as a rock. It's leaking, a long string of pre-cum hangs from it. This is exactly what I wanted.

Dropping down to my knees, I spread my legs wide, opening up for him.

His breath wavers as the crown touches me. Bracing, I press my palms into the ground as he slams forward.

A strangled cry, pain, and relief mixed together rip through his chest.

"Five."

He slides out and pounds forward.

"Four."

He falters already. Two fucking seconds.

"Sasi." His grip on my ass is too sharp.

"Fill me up," I whisper, and he falls forward, his hands dropping to the ground on either side of mine. His whole body shakes, rough, tortured sounds pouring out of him.

Everyone in this fucking train has to be able to hear this.

It's glorious.

And I did it to him.

For a moment, he's still, breathing through the aftershocks of what just tore through him.

"You said back shots all night?" He growls against my ear, wrapping my hair around his wrist tightly.

"I did."

He hums, sinister and wicked, before thrusting in again. "Let's see if we can bruise those knees, darling."

CHAPTER FOURTEEN

a quad

"YOU'RE AN EVIL WOMAN." He kneads my ass roughly in his hand.

I'm too tired to speak. I grumble something incoherently without bothering to open my eyes.

"Sleep." He rolls, tucking my body into his. "We're off to the North East."

I start to respond, but I'm asleep before the words make it from my brain to my mouth.

He swirls around in my dreams. I can't escape him. I'm not necessarily trying to, but it feels strange.

It's like I've been possessed. He has infiltrated my organs, weaving his way into everything. It feels dangerous–like he could remove himself at any time, leaving big, gaping wounds behind.

The world is black and white as he holds me close to him, dancing in the dark. There's nothing around us but the twinkle of stars. He is as handsome as ever in an ornate Victorian jacket and top hat. My gothic-style dress ruffles at the waist. We're the only beings anywhere–the only life in the universe.

As he spins me, stardust wraps around us.

That feeling creeps in again. The power of being immortal. I feel eternal—limitless. I can do anything, go anywhere. I'm free of the limitations and constraints of a human body.

He brings my soul with him into the beyond.

The necklace feels heavy around my neck. The pendant radiates—magic.

My heart beats fast and hard, thumping in my chest. This is a dream–a series of magical sensations that my mind is conjuring up while I sleep. But he could make this real for me, I just know it.

He can make anything real.

We float in the abyss, swallowed by a starry night, moving with ease–a dance we both know the steps to.

"Love me." He pulls me in closer. "I will be yours, your prisoner, your slave, yours to command and own. Just love me."

"Do you love me?"

"With every beat of your heart."

"Shouldn't it be with your heart?"

"Yours is more precious."

Gasping, my eyes snap open. We're lying in bed, our faces so close that our noses almost touch.

"Bad dream?" He smiles. There is still blood all over his face. It looks like he ripped into an animal. He's like a wolf, a sly predator that sneaks and hunts.

"No. Not bad."

"We're here." He runs his fingers over my hip, up to my waist, sending goosebumps over my skin.

"Where is here?" I look past him to the window. The darkening sky and streaks of pink and orange could be dusk or dawn.

"Connecticut."

Humming, I watch him climb out of bed, his muscles moving beneath his skin, flexing and rolling, the veins in his forearms drawing my gaze like a magnet.

I'm a fiend.

It's not just want. I crave him. I'm hungry for him.

Sex is power. I can use it to get what I want, and it has the added bonus of occasionally feeling good.

It's different with him. I still feel that sense of power, but I don't want anything from him.

"What's wrong?" He bends down, pressing a kiss to my lips.

"What do you mean?"

"Your face was scrunched up."

"Oh," I laugh it off. Just the physical manifestation of the confusion in my mind. No big deal. "I'm in existential crisis."

"And why is that?" He takes my hand, helping me out of bed. "Let's bathe. While I love you covered in blood and cum, I want to keep the sight for my eyes only."

"Weird. I was thinking the same thing."

I step into the tub. Sitting on one side, he slides in on the other. "So? What is the crisis?"

I sigh. "Well," I scrub my arms. "It's probably just the top-notch dick, but you're making me swoon a little bit."

He laughs, one of his low, sinister chuckles that makes my body clench. "I see. And this is bad?"

"Obviously."

"You're going to have to explain it. Multiple orgasms hardly seem like a problem to me."

"I don't get mushy over men." Even shadow magic men with a wonder-tongue. "It's not my style. Aloof and barely interested is more my vibe. Men don't make me all...fluttery." I cringe.

"If it makes you feel any better, I'm not really a man."

"Basically." I rub the soft, floral-smelling soap against my legs, scrubbing the dried blood away.

"How can I help?"

"I don't know. Maybe do a bad job fucking me every once in a while."

He laughs, taking my foot and placing it on his shoulder. "I'm sorry, darling, but it looks like you're just going to have to remain in crisis. I like feeling you cumming all over my cock, or my fingers—gushing on my tongue." He hums, kissing my ankle. "Far too much."

Closing my eyes, I ignore the way my stomach flutters. Damn him.

"Well, maybe you could stop being so attractive. When we get out of here, don't style your hair. I'm sure you will be less swoon-worthy with air-dried hair."

"I will try it." He sets my foot down and stands, holding his hand out to me. Of course, he turns on the handheld water spout and rinses my body because he can't help himself.

Once we're really clean, he goes to the closet and pulls out a dress. Emerald green and skin tight with a thigh-high slit that stops just before it becomes indecent.

"I love it!" I touch the silky fabric.

"I knew you would." He zips the back, running his finger up my spine as he does.

"Are you putting on a show tonight?"

"I'm afraid I must. Duty calls. I've neglected them for too long." His warm lips leave a trail of featherlight kisses over my shoulder. "But I'll show you something new after."

"Can I sit in the crowd and watch you?"

"Of course."

By the time my hair is styled, he's dressed.

Unbelievable! "Shade!" I gasp. "Your hair!"

It's disheveled and clearly not styled, just an air-dried, natural look, but he looks amazing. A slight wave runs through the strands, with one falling down over his forehead.

"Sorry." He smiles, not looking even remotely apologetic.

"Let's go." I pout, spinning around so that I don't have to look at him.

"You look incredible." He snakes his arm around my waist, pulling me into him as I try to make my escape.

"Yeah, yeah. You, too."

The carnival opens up before us, the sights, sounds, and smells becoming familiar now.

"Would you like another corn dog?" I don't have to look at him to know that he's smirking.

"No. I'll look around for another phallic-shaped food."

"Like what? How many could there be?"

"A chocolate-covered banana? A churro?"

"If those do not satisfy, I am always ready to feed you the real thing."

"Oh, I'm sure you are." I roll my eyes. "I'll see you in there?" We stop outside the tent.

"I'll be looking for you."

Something about the softness of his tone makes my heart feel strange. I don't like it.

Squaring my shoulders and pushing the feeling down into the depths where it can be forgotten, I march through the growing crowds in search of food.

All around me, people are excited. It's buzzing in the air. They're happy and free, enjoying a night of carnival magic. It's making me slightly nauseous.

I find myself pushing through the throngs of people out the front entrance.

The sticky-sweet smell of cotton candy fades into the background, and I can breathe.

With the sounds of merriment and twinkling lights behind me, I walk through the parking lot, casually checking for unlocked doors as I go.

The first unlocked door is a Lincoln Navigator. A rich suburban mom's car. Lovely.

Climbing inside, I open the center console first. Gucci sunglasses.

"Don't mind if I do!"

Sliding them onto my face, I dig around for anything else that tickles my fancy. A newspaper in the front seat catches my attention. First, because who reads physical newspapers anymore? Second, because of the headline on the national news section.

Four Found Slain Near Michigan's Upper Peninsula in Chilling Discovery

We just left Michigan's Upper Peninsula.

Taking the paper, I skim over the article. Three women and one man were found on the shore of Lake Superior. They don't appear to have any connection other than being found together. No cause of death could be determined. The coroner's office is ruling it suspicious based on the complete lack of evidence.

Hopping out of the car, I move on, checking a few more doors with no success.

I'll have to ask Shade about that. It seems too coincidental. Maybe someone was a bit overly hungry.

Across the street from the parking lot, there are a few scattered houses, then a whole lot of nothing. Groaning, I stare up at the sky. I just want to escape for a second.

He's too intoxicating.

Turning back, I amble back, taking my sweet time. Once surrounded by the hordes, I just wander, aimless and leisurely.

The time passes in a blur of people watching and contemplation.

Before I know it, it's late, and the crowds are starting to dissipate. I feel him before I see him.

"Sasi, darling." He parts the lingering people to get to me. If he's upset, he doesn't show it. "You never came."

"I lost track of time."

"Contemplating your crisis?"

"Yes."

"And? Did you come to any conclusions on the matter?"

"No." I shrug.

"Are you coming with me to Maine?"

"Yes."

"Good."

"Did you find any phallic foods that satiated your cravings?" His lips turn slightly upward.

"I had a churro, but I wouldn't say I'm satiated."

"I will remedy that."

He wraps his arm around my shoulder, and we walk through the litter-covered fairgrounds. The evidence of everyone's fun is scattered across the ground, debris left behind from the night they were unwittingly feasted upon.

"Nice glasses."

"Oh, yeah. I forgot about those." I pull them from the top of my head. "Can I ask you a question?"

"Of course."

"I saw a newspaper article about the Upper Peninsula of Michigan. Some bodies were found on the shoreline of Lake Superior. Was that–"

"It was." He doesn't even need me to finish the question. "They all know the rules. No human is supposed to die, but sometimes they get overeager and take too much."

"The report said that the coroner can't find a cause of death."

"They won't find anything other than their hearts simply stopped beating."

He stops walking, turning me to face him.

"How do you feel about that?"

"What do you mean?" I'm caught off guard by the question.

"Are you upset, or are you sad, or are you angry? Disgusted?"

"No. I suppose their families are all of those things. But I didn't know those people."

He smiles, a wide one that twinkles in his dark eyes. "My wicked little darling."

"It's not wicked. Only people directly affected by their deaths really care about it. Anyone who acts like they're truly distraught is putting on a show. They think they're supposed to cry and mourn, but they aren't, not for total strangers. They will go on living tomorrow and forget all about them."

"So, still not a limit, then?"

"No."

He starts to walk again when a scream ripples through the air. A woman, raw fear and panic, laced in her cry for help.

Grabbing a glass bottle from the ground, I crack the end against the ground, breaking it into shards.

"What are you doing?" He's still smiling.

"Going to see what that is." I step into the tent. "But I'm not going to get myself killed for being a Good Samaritan. Fuck that."

"Remind me to get you a better weapon." He laughs, but I'm too focused on investigating.

Inside, the tent is dark except for a lone spotlight shining down in the center.

"Whoa, what the fuck?" I step forward, but he grabs my arm.

"Just watch."

A woman is on the ground, her dress torn and her lip bloody as she tries to fight them off.

Three men circle her like filthy animals around their prey.

Shade brings up a smoke screen, a wall of darkness.

"Hey! Don't do that! She won't even know that we're here!" I try to walk through it, but I can't push through the resistance. "Shade! What the fuck?"

One of the men grabs her by the ankle, sliding her across the ground. She screams, begging him to stop–to let her go.

"Get down there and make those pigs stop!" I clench my teeth. It wouldn't even take any effort.

"Just watch, Sasi." He reaches for me, but I pull away.

"Shade, I'm serious–"

She gasps, whimpering as he rolls her onto his lap and pulls her down onto his cock. One of the other men is ready and waiting, lining himself up to push into her ass.

"Hey! Get off of her!" I scream, but it's muted, muffled by this fucking fog dome he has surrounding us.

Turning, I narrow my eyes at him. He's watching me, not them, with a small smile on his face.

"Move the darkness," I growl.

She cries out, begging them to stop again. Her voice is strained and getting weaker.

They're pounding into her from both sides while the third man watches.

"Shade." He has five fucking seconds.

"Sasi–"

I push past him, but he grabs my arm, pulling me back. Without thinking, I press the broken end of the bottle up to his neck.

His eyes twinkle as I press until a drop of dark blood rolls down beneath his collar.

A moment passes between us, a few seconds that feel much longer. We're daring each other. He wants me to slit his throat, and the longer he stares at me like that, the more I want to do it. It's a dare. A challenge.

"Let me go. If you won't stop this. I will." I grit my teeth.

"My wicked little thing." He pulls my hand back, bringing the bottle to his lips to lick the blood. His eyes flickering.

"I'm fucking serious, Shade–"

"It's a performance, Sasi." His lips twitch. "She is a willing participant. Look." He moves the darkness, and there are several other groups around the perimeter of the tent, watching them.

Someone shouts out something, and the woman moans loudly, her eyes rolling back.

"They do this sometimes. They are a quad. This is completely consensual."

"Oh." The anger quickly leaves my body. "Well, why didn't you say so?"

"It seems you're not entirely amoral." He smiles, pulling me into his chest, lifting me off my feet.

"I'm not into a woman being raped. Men take our power all the time. Because they think they're entitled to it. I won't stand by that."

He hums, kissing my cheek as the group comes to a loud orgasm in the distance.

"We've found your limit, then." His lips trail down my jawline.

"Huh," I drop my head back, giving him access to my neck. "I guess I do have one."

"Good to know." He lifts me, his hard cock pressed into my stomach.

I run the tip of my finger over the cut on his neck. It's already healed. Pressing a gentle kiss to it, he groans, and it vibrates against my mouth. His blood doesn't taste like iron. I can't quite place it. It's something else.

Something older.
"I wish you would have told me. I would have liked it then..."

CHAPTER FIFTEEN

omission counts, mother fucker!

THE WATER SLOSHES SOFTLY, rocking from side to side as the train hums. I've been awake for over an hour and seen hide nor hair of him.

It's probably nothing. Or, he might be sprawled out on a chaise lounge in pain again.

With each second that passes, I feel more sure that it is likely the worst-case scenario. My stomach is in a tight knot that no amount of soaking in warm water seems to loosen.

Forcing my eyes closed, I try to relax in the soft, floral-scented water. Lavender is supposed to be relaxing, right? Why the fuck isn't it working? With each breath, the smell gets more nauseating. I hate lavender. Why did I think this would work?

My mind keeps going back to how weak he looked last time. I hate the way it makes my chest feel. It's almost painful. Like a pinch right beneath my ribs that aches with each breath.

This motherfucker. How has he done this to me? I hate how much I care, but I can't seem to stop myself. How did he wiggle under my skin? Slipping beneath the surface of the water, I close my eyes and blow the air out of my mouth.

"Fuck it." I jump out of the water and dig around for something to put on. I'm sure everyone would be more than fine with me going naked, but I don't have time to deal with that right now.

Where does he get the dresses from? It's like he plucks them out of the air.

In the armoire, there are only his clothes.

Taking one of his shirts again, I slip it on and secure a few of the buttons. This time, I'm going to walk around the sides instead of through each car. As enlightening as it was, it was very time-consuming. Today, I don't feel like being dragged into their shenanigans. I just want to find him.

I'm just a person. I doubt I can solve supernatural problems, and I'm not so egotistical to assume that I can, but I have to wonder when the last time he fed was. I haven't seen him do it.

The air is freezing as I walk the thin metal ledge around the side of the train.

Inside the first car, there is a group working with clay, making nude busts with live models. Clearly, walking along the outside, no matter how freezing the wind, was a good idea.

Car after car, it's more of the same. These fucking weirdos get up to the strangest shit. Potions, paintings, and pornography. When you have forever, there is no hobby too odd or out there to explore. Good for them, I guess.

Stepping into the car where I found him last time, I huff. It's empty. Maybe this is a good sign. Maybe he's completely fine.

Sliding the door open, I stop, catching Thalora's voice, sharp and angry. I can't quite make out what she's saying from here. I think they're in the next car.

Instinctively coming up to my tiptoes, I creep across the car like a cat burglar.

"Stop it, Thalora." Shade's voice is a low warning.

"No! You–"

"If I ask too soon, it will put her off." He growls. "She's smart. I can't–"

She cuts him off with a loud, angry laugh. "Are you sure that's all it is? You seem pretty fucking cozy, Umbramancer!"

"Thalora, you don't understand. You can't."

"Why? What is so hard to understand? You like her. Just admit it. Normally, you would have asked already."

"You can't possibly know what I would do. I've never found anyone like her!" His voice gets louder at the end. I can feel his fury from here. "Don't fucking question me, Thalora! This is not your concern. I know what I'm doing. When the time is right, I will ask her. Do not bring this up to me again, or I will get angry. I promise you, if I get angry, you will not like the consequences."

My own rage is growing by the second. The chances that they are talking about someone else are slim to none. Obviously, he has been withholding something from me. Something that others know about.

That cock-sucking, mother-fucking liar!

Storming through the train car, I slide the door open so hard it slams against the wall and closes in front of me again.

As I pass through each car, everyone stops doing whatever it is that they're doing, but I assume the look on my face keeps them from approaching me. This time, I walk through, and no one even attempts to stop me.

Back in his room, I pace the floor, my mind rolling over on itself.

What is he hiding from me?

Looking around his room, I start to toss things: cushions, blankets, the contents of his closet. There isn't anything here. I don't even know what I'm looking for, but I can only assume I'll know it when I see it, whatever it is.

On his bookshelf, I pull down each book. Most of them aren't in English. They look ancient, most of them religious in nature–all of them incredibly creepy.

One book has a woman on the cover. Her pale, naked body is flayed open, from sternum to navel. Stopping, I flip it open.

The Exhumation of Spirits.

Interesting.

Sitting on the floor, I flip through the pages, reading the passages between the very graphic, detailed illustrations. It would seem that exercising a demon is not so tricky as it would appear. The process is fairly straightforward.

The door slides open, and I don't look up. "What are you doing, darling?"

"Just some light reading." The page in front of me has a man tied to a tree with a demon crawling out of his unhinged jaw.

"On exhuming spirits?" He sounds incredulous.

"Yeah."

"What happened in here? It looks like you were searching for something." He picks up one of his shirts from the floor.

"Maybe I was."

"Would you like to tell me what you were looking for?"

"What are you hiding from me, Umbramancer?" I slam the book closed.

"Umbramancer?" His brows come up, but there is amusement in his tone that pisses me off.

"Yeah. Are you lying to me? And just so you're aware, I already know that you are, so you should respond with that knowledge in mind."

He sighs and sits down on the edge of the bed. A sigh is never a good sign.

"Come here."

"No." I shake my head. "I would like to keep a bit of distance between us."

"Alright." He rubs his hand over the back of his neck.

"And don't try anything with your darkness, either. Keep it away from me."

"I won't try anything." He sighs again.

For a moment, he's quiet. With each second, my anger grows.

"Are you trying to think of a lie?" I narrow my eyes and stare at his stupid, handsome face.

"No."

"Then spit it out."

"I'm being hunted." He crosses his arms. "We are. All of us."

I cross my arms and wait.

"They are a group of supernaturals that want to eradicate darkness completely. They misunderstand us as their enemies."

"Misunderstand?"

"They think of us as enemies. That isn't how we see them. While we don't want to live the way they do, we aren't incensed by their existence. Dark and light balance each other. Neither can survive without the other. We aren't enemies, merely the other side of the same coin."

"What does this have to do with me? I heard you and Thalora. She's pressuring you to ask me to do something. What is it?" I take a breath, trying to stay calm.

He's hesitating.

"Shade."

"I need something."

Again, I wait.

"A weapon."

Ok. This piques my interest. "And you need me? Why?"

"Because the location of said weapon is the only place, here or in the human realm, that I cannot go."

Ok, now I'm really interested. "What is the weapon used for?"

"It is called Umbralius. It is a living being. It is a shadow blade."

"A knife?"

"Yes, to your understanding. But he is much more than that. He is an extension of me, of my darkness. With Umbralius, I would be able to defend myself against someone attempting to harm me using light as a weapon." He looks so fucking genuine.

"Why didn't you just tell me this? Have I given you the impression that if you asked got a favor, I wouldn't help you?" I'm offended, honestly.

"No!" He stands, taking a step toward me, but I hold my hand up, stopping him. He nods and sits again. "You haven't. But I hate to ask. I didn't want you to think that was the only reason I—"

"It's not?" I quirk my brow. This might be the crux of the entire issue. How believable his answer is will be the linchpin of my response. Answer wisely, motherfucker.

"Absolutely not. I did not seek you out that night because I thought you could get him for me. Of course, the conversation came up when it became clear that you would be joining us, and you were receptive to our existence."

I hum.

"Sasi." He slips down from the bed onto the floor, not touching me, but closer.

"It just seems very coincidental. We find each other, and you sweep me into this fairytale, all the while, you need a big favor that apparently only I can do for you?" I suck my teeth. "Very fishy, Umbramancer."

"I know how it looks." He reaches into the pile of books and pulls out a very old one. The leather-bound spine is cracked and breaking. Quickly flipping through the pages, he sets it down, open, in front of me.

A shiny black sword with engravings down the length of the blade is illustrated on the page. The text isn't in English.

"What does it say?"

"Umbralius, the dark maker." He looks at the picture like he's looking at his newborn baby.

"Where is it?"

"Greenland."

My mind is working double time. I hate myself right now. The fact that I'm even considering it, and I'm not demanding the train be stopped so I can get off, is so out of character it's frightening. I've cut men off for far less.

I don't want everything that has happened up to this point to have just been bullshit.

"What happens if I refuse?"

"Then I don't get him."

"That simple?"

"I can't force you, darling. If you don't want to, you don't have to. I hate to even ask. It seems wrong to send you into a place I can't go to do something that I can't do for myself."

"Is it dangerous?"

"No." He answers too quickly.

"I have questions."

"I thought you might." He smiles.

"If it's yours, why don't you have it with you?"

"It was stolen from me. It cannot be destroyed. My darkness lives within it. The only way it can be broken is if it is used to kill me. But in my possession, it is more powerful, as am I." He just has all the answers, doesn't he?

"I'll get it for you." I roll my eyes.

"What?" He laughs.

"I said, I'll get it for you," I mumble.

"Really? Just like that?"

"Yeah. Whatever." I stand up, putting more space between us again. "You are going to have to do some serious groveling, and by groveling, I do mean on your knees, eating my pussy."

"Oh, darling, if that is my punishment for bad behavior, I may begin to upset you more often." He licks his lips slowly, hungry, predatory.

"I don't like a fucking liar, Shade."

"I never lied." He steps toward me, his darkness swirling around him like tentacles about to grab me.

"Omission counts, motherfucker!"

CHAPTER SIXTEEN

fuck me into compliance

STRETCHING MY SORE MUSCLES, I unwrap my legs from around his head. I guess we fell asleep like that.

He slides over, sprawling across the bed. His hand comes up to his chin as he moves his jaw around.

"Sore?"

He hums and sits up, running his hand up the length of my leg. "Nothing I can't handle."

"Are we going straight to Greenland?"

"No, we have a date in New Jersey first." He drops down again, lazily pressing his face into my stomach.

"Do we have to go?" I run my fingers through his hair.

"No." He looks up. "Do you have other things in mind?"

"Yeah, sleep, you fiend! Keep that thing away from me!"

"That isn't what you were screaming last night." He licks his lips.

"I want to go to a restaurant." I roll out from beneath him, putting space between us.

"A restaurant?"

"Yes, I want everything. The works. Bacon, eggs, French toast with strawberries and whipped cream." I tug at his hand. "Let's go out."

"Let me get you a dress."

"Actually, can I pick?"

"Of course." Outside of the bedroom, in the sitting room, he opens an ancient-looking wardrobe, revealing at least fifty stunning dresses.

They're all darker colors, black or jewel tones. Lace, silk, velvet.

Running my fingers over them, I stop on a sheer black robe with velvet floral patterns.

Slipping it on, I secure it with a black leather belt.

"Fuck." He grumbles behind me. "We should go before I take you to bed and keep you there for the rest of the day."

Digging through the closet, I find a few lingerie pieces. High-waisted black panties with a garter belt and stockings.

"Perfect."

Bringing my foot up to rest on his leg, I tug the stocking up and secure the clips.

"You know I'm in a weakened state, darling. Are you trying to kill me?"

Placing the other foot on his leg, I start to pull the stocking up, but he stops me, pressing a trail of kisses up my thigh. His fingers gently clip the stocking in place, lingering too long.

"Feed me before I starve." I pull away from his grasp.

He hums, low and rumbling. "Then you can feed me."

Insatiable…

"When was the last time you ate?" I let him wrap his arms around me as we walk through the train. He stops, opening a cabinet and pulling out a large stack of cash.

"Last night."

"You know what I mean." I roll my eyes.

"Last night, darling."

Stopping, I spin around. "Wait. When you eat me out, are you taking my essence?"

"Not in the same capacity, but yes, essentially. Your release can sustain me for a very long time." The rumble in his voice almost makes my muscles clench. Almost.

"Holy shit." I don't know if I should be annoyed or turned on. "Why didn't you tell me?"

His head tilts to one side, a thoughtful expression on his face. "I haven't ever told anyone. Does that bother you?"

"I would have given it to you. It just seems shiesty that you haven't mentioned it."

"Shiesty?"

"Yeah, you know. Shady and dishonest."

Strike two. I step slightly out of his way as we cross the street. Not far, but just enough for him to notice it.

"I—"

"I don't like your high-handed secretive behavior."

He opens the door to a small diner, holding it for me.

"Are there more secret things? Do you always eat via oral sex?"

"No. But I can, and with you, I enjoy it very much. I have done it before, but never exclusively." He looks at the hostess, who is clearly swooning. "Two, please."

"Right this way." She leads us through the small dining room toward a booth for two.

"Thank you." He smiles at her, and her cheeks flush red.

Sliding into my seat, I flip through the menu.

"Sasi." He reaches across the table for my hand. "I know this will sound like lip service to you, but I don't usually–" He pauses, tilting his head while he considers his words. "I don't usually bring women with me. I have had my fair share of fun, but I am on a learning curve here. I have not had to disclose my preferences, activities, or history before, nor would it have occurred to me to do so."

"Hmm."

"What's that?" His lips twitch.

"Nothing." I look over the menu.

"That wasn't nothing."

"You're angry."

"No." I shake my head. "Not angry."

His darkness creeps across the table, slipping over the sides.

"Shade." I quirk my brow at him. "Do you think that the answer to every squabble can be found in sex?"

"Yes, I do." He licks his lips.

Parting my legs slightly, I make room for him to slide between my thighs.

"You can't just fuck me into compliance." I bite into my cheek as he presses–the perfect pressure only he seems to be able to achieve–into my clit.

"I can try, though, can't I?"

He works in little circles, the kind that makes me crazy.

"Have you had a chance to look over the menu?" Someone's grandma comes to the table, a pink apron tied around her waist.

"I'll take the French toast breakfast. Strawberries and whipped cream on the side. Bacon, crispy. Eggs over easy." My voice stays perfectly even though he's making my heart rate rise.

"And for you?" She turns to him.

"I've got everything I need." He smiles.

"I'll have that right out for you." She looks suspiciously at both of us before turning and walking away.

"I think she suspects us."

"Maybe she wants to watch." He presses harder, moving faster.

My breath catches. "Maybe."

"She's not the only one." He presses into me.

"Really? Who?"

Letting my eyes wander around the dining room, I catch a man sitting across the room, tucked into the corner. He's staring right at us.

Smirking, I look him in the eye. His mouth falls open as he takes panting breaths.

"So, we do have an audience." I gesture in his direction.

"Can you feel his darkness, love? He's been looking at you since we sat down."

"Has he?"

"Yes." His eyes never leave mine. He pins me down with his gaze. "Give in to me."

Leaning back in my seat, I let the feeling take over.

"Surrender yourself to me, Sasi. Give me your heart. Your head. Your soul."

I fight it, pushing back against the urge to give him everything he wants. "It's not fair to ask me now." I grit my teeth.

His smile spreads, growing larger. "I know. I never said I would play fair."

The server comes, setting my plate on the table in front of me. Pressing my nails into my palm, I try not to moan.

"Enjoy."

"Thank you." I press my feet into the ground. The feeling moves from between my legs, spreading outward. It tightens in my belly, ripples up my spine, and burns in my muscles.

Our captive audience shifts in his seat, watching us.

"Let him see you. Show him how lovely you are when you come." He whispers across the table.

If anyone else happened to look over, he would look completely serene, not suspicious at all. The darkness beneath the table is doing all the dirty work for him.

I want to push him away, but it's so fucking good.

My shoulders press into the booth.

"Give it to me, darling. Right here in front of everyone. Make a mess all over your seat." His voice is low, coaxing.

"S-Shade!" It's almost impossible to stay quiet.

A tendril moves over my plate, dipping into the whipped cream.

"Open your mouth." His darkened eyes watch me.

I part my lips, waiting.

"Good girl." He rewards my obedience with sweet cream on my tongue.

The circles get tighter with perfect pressure.

"God!" I grit my teeth. "Shade."

"Tell me about it, darling."

"It feels so—"

My spine arches forward, pushing off the seatback. I can't finish my sentence because my brain is melting, and there aren't any words left.

It starts almost quietly, a tingle on my skin, a whisper. Heat builds in my stomach, getting higher and spreading further with each pulsating beat between my legs. Then it erupts, burning so hot it leaves scorched earth behind. My body is a casualty of carnage left after the wreck.

"This is all about you. I get nothing but the agonizing ache of watching you." His voice is low, full of that low strain that makes my pulse spike.

My hands grip the edge of the table, holding on for dear life as he drags it out of me. Pulling it with force.

I've never come so much in my life. Every day, repeatedly, but it's never enough. I'm still left longing for the next one.

Without a care in the world, I moan, my body trembling under his careful attention.

My senses are slow to return to me, but when they do, I find the man on his feet, pressed into the corner. He's slack-jawed and sweaty.

Good.

Taking a big bite of my waffle, I lick the whipped cream from my lips.

"You're a wicked little tease." Shade groans.

"Hard?"

"As a rock." He grunts.

Humming to myself, I take another bite. "Good."

Maybe it's the post orgasmic afterglow, but these are the best fucking waffles I've ever had.

I sit, feeling overly relaxed, and finish the entire plate.

"I should bring you to breakfast more often." He seems to enjoy watching me eat. To be fair, I enjoy watching him eat, also.

"When do we leave for Greenland?"

"Tonight after the carnival."

I nod. "At some point, you're going to have to explain what I have to do."

"I will." He holds his hand out to me.

Sliding out of the booth, I walk, wrapped in his arm, through the restaurant. Turning my attention to the man in the corner, I wink as we step out in the morning sunshine.

I like being away from the carnival with him. The playing field feels more even. I know it's an illusion. He's manipulating everything, but I'll take the illusion.

"Here." He brings his other arm around, opening his hand in front of me. Lying in his palm is a watch.

"Shade!" I gasp. "Where did you get this?"

It's a Rolex.

"I picked it up for you. Is it good enough for your collection?"

"Yes!" I turn it over. "There's an inscription on the back."

TYJ

I run my fingers over the etched letters.

"Thank you. I love it."

CHAPTER SEVENTEEN

orgy. for sure.

"HUH," my head tilts as we reach the ground. "The name is misleading, don't you think? I thought Greenland would be greener."

A faint smile ghosts his lips. "It's going to be cold at night, but the days will be nice. I got you this." He pulls out a plush, white fur coat. There are also boots lined with the same thick fur.

"Oh, my god! This is luxurious!" I slip into it. "I feel like Cruella de Vil!" I sway slightly, running my fingers through the soft hair.

His brow furrows. That reference didn't land. But he doesn't say anything.

The train sits at the base of a mountain. There is a road in the distance leading up, but otherwise, it's deserted. He's right, it's not cold. But it looks cold. The air has that kind of super clear crispness that is usually icy.

"I'll walk with you as long as I'm able." He wraps his arm around my shoulder.

"They're human?"

"Yes. But they're enlightened. They live here in the mountains, one with nature and the spirit realm. They can't enter it, but they can sense it, communicate with it."

"Interesting."

As we walk across the field of swaying yellow grass, I look back, something tugging at me. Thalora is standing at the end of the train, watching us.

"Did you ever have a relationship with Thalora?" I watch his eyes, waiting for a tick.

"No."

"Never? Not a single time?" That's hard to believe.

"No."

"Why?" She's stunning, and clearly she wants him. It practically pours out of her eyes every time she looks at him.

"Because she is an integral part of our system. She is a magic manipulator. Without her, there would be cracks, and people with a less shrewd eye than you would be able to see them. She loves me, and I do not feel the same. If I fuck her, it would ruin everything." His thumb skims over the vein in my neck.

"That's very responsible of you."

He smiles, his sharp teeth pressing into his lower lip. "No one has ever accused me of that."

Our shoes crunch against the gravel as we reach the base of the mountain. It looks bigger.

"I can't go further than this." He stops, spinning me so that he can place his hands on my shoulders.

"What happens if you try?"

A mischievous smirk plays on his lips. "Would you like to see?"

"Yes." I straighten.

With the flair of an entertainer, he steps forward, walking, but his body doesn't move. It looks like something out of a cartoon. His feet are walking, but he isn't going anywhere.

"That is so weird."

"I would go with you if I could." He kisses my hair. His lips linger a moment too long.

Something about the look on his face makes me believe him.

"See you soon."

"I'll be waiting, love."

Turning, I walk onto the path with ease. I meet no resistance whatsoever. Looking back over my shoulder, I give him a small wave, and something tightens in my chest.

Yuck. Who is this love-struck teenager? What in the no-you-hang-up-first is this nonsense? Someone slap me.

The mountain road stretched ahead, quiet and winding, and for the first time in what feels like forever, I'm alone.

The air is sharp and clean as I amble up the path. I feel different—free and light. Without Shade beside me, there is no heat, no restless itch. That strange magnetic pull that makes me want to cling to him is gone.

I never realized how much space he takes up until right now. Not just physically, but inside of me.

Now, each breath is easy, and my mind is all mine. I think he crept in more than I want to admit.

The quiet isn't filled with the weight of his gaze or the awareness of how my body reacted to his voice, his nearness.

I feel more myself, not a thing being slowly unraveled.

Turning around, I look back, but the forest obscures my view of anything beyond a few feet.

A sound in the distance pulls my attention. It's a low, rumbling bellowing, like a horn.

A bend in the path blocks my view forward. I'm in a blind spot. I can't see ahead or behind.

Creeping forward, I hug the tree line and search for signs of the highly evolved creatures I'm supposed to find up here.

The trail starts to flatten out. I follow it around the curve to where it opens into a kind of valley.

Nestled in the dip of the mountain is a perfect little village—like something off a postcard or out of a dream someone else is having. Little alpine cottages with ivy-covered walls and hand-painted shutters sit in perfect rows. It looks like Candy Land.

Wildflowers bloom everywhere. Except for the walking path, they cover the ground.

A waterfall flows gently over the ridge into a glacial stream.

There are a few people walking around, laughing and smiling at each other.

Someone sees me and waves. A big, enthusiastic wave that children usually give to someone they're excited to see.

Everyone's smiles seem to grow.

Creepy.

A woman breaks off from the others and heads straight for me. Barefoot, blonde, glowing like a sunbeam. Her smile is stuck in place, eyes bright.

"Aluu!" She reaches for my hand, but I yank it back.

"Hi."

"You must be tired," she says in this slow, sticky-sweet voice. "Come. We'll get you something warm to drink."

Every instinct I have screams no. I want to run away from her. Didn't anyone teach these people not to talk to strangers?

"Um, I was just passing through on a hike. I didn't know people lived up here." I lie, remembering my mission. I don't want to arouse suspicions.

"Welcome!" Another woman successfully grabs my hand this time.

I yelp and pull away. She snuck up on me.

"We are having a festival today. You are welcome to join us, stranger." A man opens his arms.

"Thank you." I try not to cringe.

Immediately, I scan the area, hoping they have the stupid sword sitting out like a decoration. I want to get out of here in less than five minutes.

These people, with their screwed-on smiles, are freaking me out.

He said it was in the mountains. Inside. That doesn't seem as easy as it did before.

"What kind of festival?" I follow them into the center of the village.

"Tonight is the midnight sun!" One of them turns her bright eyes to me. "It happens once every twenty years. It's incredibly lucky that you arrived today."

"Yeah, lucky." I bite back a groan. This better be a coincidence. It seems highly unlikely that I show up here now. If he did this on purpose, I'm going to stab him with that fucking sword he asked me to steal.

"We have twenty-four hours of sunlight. A blessing from the sky." One of them looks up dreamily.

"Cool." I give her a stiff thumbs up. I've wandered into a cult. Great.

"We will break bread together. Then the ceremony begins." She smiles with all her teeth. "You came at the perfect moment."

Right.

In the center of the village, an enormous banquet table has been set up. Apparently, we're late. There are at least fifty people already seated, waiting.

This is awkward.

"What's your name, friend?" A sunny blond man asks me as I slide into a seat.

"Sasi."

"What a great name!" His head bobbles around. "That's fantastic."

"Thanks." I outwardly cringe, unable to hide it any longer. "So, the mountain—any good trails? I heard there's a system of caverns? I'm kind of a big hiker." I try to steer the conversation.

"Oh, there are trails," one of them says vaguely, waving her hand. "But tonight, everything leads to the ritual."

I try again. "I'm really interested in old caves. History stuff, you know? Just want to get a peek inside."

Another soft laugh. "There will be time. The Midnight Sun comes first."

I open my mouth to ask again, but soft music starts. It's low but not eerie. It's kind of pretty, actually.

"My dearest friends! Let us share this meal together beneath the sky." A man with a long white beard stands. Everyone joins hands.

I feel like the Grinch at Who Christmas.

"We have been eternally blessed to experience the Midnight Sun. Love one another. Absorb the light!"

The people on both sides of me squeeze my hands, then release me.

A quiet chaos erupts around the table. Everyone passes plates and bowls, pitchers of a lavender colored liquid.

Food is served on the plate in front of me, and I realize how hungry I actually am.

I dig in, eating the vegetarian-style meal.

"This is delicious."

"We grew everything ourselves!"

"What is the ritual?"

His face splits into a huge smile. "It comes in two parts. We'll break bread together, then bathe in the lake," he says cheerfully. "The lumee fish will make your skin glow."

I blink. "Come again?"

"They light the water," he explains. "It's tradition. You'll feel reborn." He smiles like it's a compliment.

Right.

"And then?" I'm not sure I want to know.

"We dance beneath the midnight sun."

Dance?

Around the table, I'm catching snippets of other conversations. They keep talking about the ritual. The more I listen, the more it sounds like a mix of folk myth, bonfire party, and a drunken orgy. Not the worst thing in the world. I've been to weirder. But the reverent tone they use makes it all feel strange. Not sinister, just off.

They're all kind. Genuinely so. Too kind. Touching shoulders, passing plates, laughing easily. I don't trust it. I don't trust anything that doesn't want something.

Are they nice or super weird? To me, it's one and the same.

I make it a point to have food in my mouth at all times. Generally, that helps me avoid small talk, but these people won't take the hint.

"Where are you from?" "What do you do?" "What is your spirit frequency?" It never ends.

The people here are from everywhere. Russia, Australia, Taiwan, Peru, Norway. They all ended up here somehow.

By the time we finish the bounty on the table, my social battery is at an all-time low.

"Time to bathe!" The man to my left seems particularly excited about this. Perv.

"Great!" I get up, hanging my coat on the back of my chair.

Following the lead of the rest of the group, I strip off my clothes, letting them fall wherever they land.

By the time we reach the smooth stones at the edge of the water, everyone is naked.

The turquoise water looks deep; the rocks and fallen trees on the bottom are probably much farther away than they look.

Little flecks of light flash around, darting through the water, thousands of them.

"Those are the lumee fish." Someone taps my arm. "They don't hurt you. They just renew."

Well, fuck it. I step into the water, and the shock of it punches a gasp from my lungs. The glacial water wraps around my ankles. It's freezing, but not the sharp, biting cold I was expecting.

I go in farther; the chill climbing my legs, my spine. Each breath tightens, but I don't stop. Diving in, I force myself to adjust quickly.

For a moment, I feel weightless, suspended in a void of blue ice and muffled sound.

All around me, bodies are swimming, circling, floating. When I break the surface, I hear the music again. It's loader now. I can't understand the language, but it feels like water.

The fish tickle my skin, touching me everywhere. It doesn't hurt, but the sensation of featherlight touches all over my body at once is overwhelming.

I swim out into the middle of the lake, floating on my back. With my eyes closed, the sun warms my skin, glowing behind my eyelids.

Shade comes to mind. A strange tug pulls in my chest.

I think I miss him. I'll never admit that to him, though.

I would do things to him that would make every person here blush.

Pulling myself upright, I tread in the center of the lake, looking for a sign. There must be trails or a cave. Though I'm a bit wary of caves now. I'm not trying to be eaten.

The sky is still bright; the sun shining directly above us, but there are signs that it is later than it seems. There is a quiet that falls over everything, a peaceful, dusky feeling.

There are a few places that look like they could be trails leading into the mountain. There is a place behind the waterfall that looks promising. And a few narrow trails through the flowers that lead into the dense forest.

"What do you think?" A man's voice cuts into my plotting.

"Oh, it's nice." I give him a thumbs up. I don't think I've ever given more than one awkward thumbs up in a single day.

"Ready for the next part?" His smile tells me everything I need to know about the next part. Orgy. For sure.

I've never witnessed a cult orgy before. Game on.

"Let's do it."

CHAPTER EIGHTEEN
the mother

THEY HAND me a cup of a luminous blue liquid. It's iridescent. It moves and shimmers like it has a life of its own.

Swirling it around my glass, I sniff it. Fruity and sweet.

"What is this?"

"It's time to dance." Someone, somewhere, gives me an answer–not to the question I asked, but an answer still.

"Is dance code for ritual sacrifice or something?" Why are they being so cloak-and-dagger about this?

Laughter surrounds me. "No. This drink is made from the berries of the Mother."

"Um, what?" I blink.

"The Mother. It's a tree that grows out of the mountain. She only gives a single harvest of berries each year. We press them into the drink. It's full of nutrients. It is a gift."

"So, no one is going to die tonight or anything?" I feel the need for further clarification.

"Of course not!" The man from dinner looks horrified that I could even think of such a thing.

They are giving strong cult energy. I had to ask.

The same man from earlier stands on a table in front of the

group. "Tonight, we bask in the light of the midnight sun! We drink the fruit of the Mother, and we love one another." He holds up his glass.

Everyone follows suit.

"Down the hatch," I guess. I gulp it down quickly, worried it will be gross, but it's amazing. The juice dances on my tongue. The taste is indescribable. Sweet and fruity, fresh and tangy. I could drink this exclusively for the rest of my life. I feel awake. Alive. Rejuvenated. "Wow! That was–"

The world around me slows down. Everything is somehow in and out of focus.

"Wow, that was quick." I clear my throat. "I am–"

"Feeling the effects?" The man beside me laughs, taking my hands in his. "Dance with me, Sasi!"

We sway together as everyone around us starts to move. Some alone, others in groups of couples, everyone dances. Naked and fucked out of their minds on Mother juice.

Closing my eyes, I spin. Maybe it's assisted by the juice, but I feel confident. My feet barely touch the ground. I'm floating.

Everyone looks beautiful. The warmth of the sun shines down on us, golden and soft.

These nice freaks are growing on me.

Time and space drift away. The sun never falters, and the light is steady as we move together in a giant group. Slow-moving bodies, spinning, grinding, holding on tight. We glisten. We shine.

I feel like a diamond.

It *might* be the drink. But I feel better than I've ever felt. A sense of clarity washes over me. Mental, physical, emotional, metaphysical. I feel everything. I know everything.

I am everything. And everything is me.

"Wow," I whisper, looking at my hands. "We really are just a formation of cells, floating on a giant rock."

"You get it!" A woman spins past me, touching my face as she does, then she disappears into the mass of rolling bodies.

"We are everything and nothing. We are the only thing that

matters, but we're a blip in time and space. Your heart–" He places his hand on my chest. "It's a miracle."

"Yours too." I float away.

"You should stay with us forever! Your dark spirit is beautiful." Someone grabs me, twirling me like a ballerina.

"Forever?" I lean into her, pressing a kiss to her neck.

"Live with us under the sun. The mountain provides! We are one organism. One heart. We belong together."

For a second, the thought lingers in my mind before Shade quickly moves in, covering it in darkness. Shade.

"Oh, I can't." I shake my head. "I have a man at…home."

A big, strong, dark shadow man.

"We are all one. He is here in all of us." She smiles. "You will feel his presence here. Love never dies. You will still be with him here with us!"

Yeah, no.

"Girl, you don't understand. The dick is immaculate. I'm not giving that up." I snap out of the fog.

All around me, people are still moving. The romance is gone. I don't see a bunch of earth angels. I see a group of sweaty, uncoordinated people humping.

The magic is still clinging to me, but I move along the outside of the group. I shimmy here and there so they don't notice.

Once I'm safely away from them, I wonder how many hours have passed. At least a few.

I need to bottle that juice. I would be a millionaire in a week.

Creeping through the village, a beat plays in my head. It's a pop-rock jam that makes me dance again.

I'm supposed to be sneaking, but I can't help but hum.

I search everywhere, looking for anything that looks like the picture of the sword or a place where one would be hidden.

Eventually, my mind starts to drift again. I know what I'm supposed to be doing, but I'm naked and strutting around while singing the words so loudly I'm sure everyone can hear me.

Dancing as I walk, I start to look inside the houses. They're so bare.

I could never live here. I want things. Material goods. Luxury and excess.

Then, I see it. A tree growing directly out of the mountain. It's beautiful. A willow with pink and purple plumes. It looks like a bursting firework.

"You must be the Mother." I curtsey.

The long strands hang all the way down to the ground like a canopy. Stepping inside, I breathe in the soft smell.

If I were going to hide something, this would not be the place. It's so obvious. It's the first place any decent thief would look.

"Ah-ha." I smile triumphantly to myself. A cave. I found it. Dizzy off of mother berries, I found it.

A hole, I guess. It's too small to be a cave.

Whatever it is, it looks like what I've been looking for. I wish he had more information about this. I'm looking for a needle in a haystack.

Crawling inside, I make my way up the tunnel. It slowly opens up, eventually becoming large enough that I can stand. The ground is sharp and rocky, and with each step, I'm getting colder.

I have a fur coat out there. This is bullshit.

Using the song as a distraction, I sing loudly, my voice echoing through the cave. A dim blue light glows in the distance. It ripples as I get closer, like water.

The tunnel opens into a cavernous place, like the entire mountain has been carved out and is hollow.

The light is just bright enough to barely see. Using my hands to supplement my poor vision, I move forward.

That fucking song is stuck in my head now, so I sing it while I creep around.

My mouth opens wide, my voice echoing off the walls. Stopping, I belt out the chorus like I'm giving a concert. The cheerful lyrics pour out of me. For a moment, I lose myself.

Stopping mid-verse, I blush. I'm supposed to be quietly searching.

I can feel myself unraveling, but I can't stop it.

"In the mountain," I whisper. "The blade is in the mountain." I press forward until I come to a lagoon. It's so still and blue, at first, it doesn't look like water. It's like they've painted it on the floor.

Touching it with my toe, a thin bit of ice cracks, sending a ripple moving across the glass surface. The water is freezing. Not just cold like the water outside, the surface is frozen.

Right in the center of the pool, something catches my eye.

"Mother fucker." I look up at the ceiling. It's in the middle of the lake. "Umbralius, come!" I tap my thighs like I'm calling to a dog.

It's not that I thought that would work, but I had to try.

I pause for a moment, contemplating my next move. Does he really deserve this? I could back out of here and tell him I didn't find anything. No dick in the world is worth this shit.

"Fuck!" I shout, my frustration bouncing off the walls.

He owes me. He is going to need to grovel and do unspeakable things to me to make up for this.

"Unbelievable." I step into the water, and my skin prickles. This is so much worse than the water earlier. It's painfully cold. It takes everything to make myself keep going—every ounce of willpower I can muster. Cursing under my breath, I push forward.

Humming the song again, I distract myself from the painful sting that's growing by the second.

The water reaches my waist, and my legs are starting to feel numb. My muscles are stiff and slow. I want to hurry, but my body won't move.

Standing over the sword, I attempt to use my foot to grab it and pull it up. It's so heavy. I can't get the handle between my toes at all.

"Fuck you, Shade. Seriously." I take a deep breath and slip below the surface.

A gasp punches out of my lungs as I come up.

"Holy shit, that's cold." I drag the sword behind me. "Cold. Cold. Cold. Fuck you too, Umbralius!"

My heart pounds against my ribs with so much force it's painful. I can't seem to catch my breath.

By the time I reach the shore, I'm struggling to hold the blade. It's like my hands are too stiff to grip it.

The air chafes my skin as I try to drag myself and the sword back to the tunnel. It's as big as my leg. There is no way I'm going to be able to hide this thing under my coat.

Each step is a battle. I'm shaking so hard I can hardly stay upright.

"Come on, Sasi!" I pep-talk myself. "You can do this."

I'm normally a realist. I don't lie to myself about the harsh reality I'm facing.

It must be the juice. I'm too optimistic. It's still there, not as strong, but definitely altering my mind.

The tunnel starts to shrink around me, and warm air flows in through the mouth of the cave. I can see the sunlight.

When I crawl into the pink and purple canopy of willow vines, I collapse on the warm grass. Lying there, I let the feeling come back to my limbs.

I got it. I did it!

I have no clue where I'm going to hide it or how I'm going to smuggle it out of here, but I found it.

I stand slowly, pulling the sword behind me. Peeking out of the vines, I check that the coast is clear before running into the open. My adrenaline spikes as I rush toward the rows of houses. I'll hide it behind the last house. After I get my things, it will be waiting for me to bring it down to Shade.

In the space between each tiny cottage, I see them, still naked, still dancing. They're passing another round of the juice through the crowd.

I should just leave now while they're distracted.

But I'm not walking down the mountain without my shoes. I have to sneak back in for them.

Placing the sword beneath the leaves of a dense bush, I wander back to the group casually.

"Sasi!" A glass is placed in my hand. "You're just in time! Where were you? I was looking everywhere!"

"What?" I gulp down the sweet nectar. "I've been here the whole time."

CHAPTER NINETEEN
wreck me

JUST WHEN I was starting to feel like myself again, they drag me back in.

Not that it took much convincing. This shit is amazing.

Licking my lips, I spin around and grind against the closest body.

The effects hit me just as hard and fast, but they're different this time. "Was that the same juice?" I hear my words slurring.

"Mostly."

A giggle wiggles in my throat. "What do you mean, mostly?"

"The second round has a little extra punch." He smiles a big, wide, horny smile.

"For the orgy?"

He hums, wrapping his arms around my waist. "It's not an orgy. It's a ceremony of love. Join us, Sasi. Let us love you."

Something that has never happened to me before happens right here, in the arms of this beautiful sunshine man. I feel a tug in my chest.

What the fuck is that?

Panic courses through me, and my heart rate spikes.

What is this feeling? Unease watches over me, and I feel too warm. For a second, I think I might just throw up on him, and I feel relieved.

But that's not what this is. I'm not sick. It's something else. Oh god, no. Anything but this!

I gasp and stumble away. My chest feels like it's in a knot. A rock is stuck between my ribs, and each breath hurts.

"Holy shit, what the fuck?" I fall out of the group.

Is this guilt?

Grabbing a woman by the shoulders, I shake her slightly.

"What is happening to me? What is this?" Tears burn in my eyes. "I think someone poisoned me!"

"Take a breath." She places her palm on my chest. "In. And out. Very good. No one poisoned you. What are you feeling?"

"I don't know! It's awful! I feel like I'm betraying Shade. The likelihood that he would actually give a single fuck about this is probably low, but I can't shake this terrible feeling that it will hurt him somehow." I shake her again. "What is that?"

"It sounds like you feel guilty." Her voice is gentle as she gives me a soft smile. How could she smile at a thing like that? This is the worst thing that has ever happened to me.

"Guilty?" I've never felt that before. "Oh god. I hate this."

Staggering away from her, I stumble through the dining area to my seat. Fuck the dress, but I'm not leaving my new coat behind.

The world feels like it's rolling. It's slow, but each step feels unsteady. This is unlike any high I've ever experienced. It's all mixed up, too fast and too slow. I feel my body so acutely. My hair follicles and my blood. The things I don't normally notice are vivid and more intense. I'm open and exposed.

Crawling along the bushes, I search for the blade.

It would have been helpful to remember which bush I set it under.

"There you are!" I drag him out from the shrubs and make my way back down the mountain.

There is a sense of urgency humming beneath my skin, but every leaf and rock distracts me from the task at hand.

I belong here. The mountains are speaking to me, welcoming me.

I feel one with the earth.

I am a goddess—a divinely gifted woman with power in my mind, in my body, and between my legs.

The sweet, syrupy taste of the juice still lingers on my tongue. It's like it coated my mouth and took root, spreading through my skull, burrowing into my brain.

My steps become more forceful. My feet hit the ground with purpose.

He's waiting for me.

When I see him, I'm going to share what I've learned. I'm going to teach it to him.

Umbralius drags behind me, the only thing keeping my feet on the ground. I might float away if it weren't for his weight.

My hips sway while I walk. I notice my body, the tingle in my skin.

The breeze hits me, whispering sacred secrets to my body in a language I don't know but somehow understand.

I'm swollen and wet and everything aches so good.

The mountain wants me. The sky sighs my name. The Earth is eager to watch.

Each step is bringing me closer.

My feet move like a dance, sliding over the ground in a pattern of quick steps and kicks. The song comes back into my head, and I shimmy down the trail.

Running my free hand over my body, I touch my skin, relishing in how soft it is.

I picture Shade. His big body. His face. His cock.

He's so tasty.

When I see him, I have so many ideas of ways he can repay me for this hardship. The more I think about it, the harder it gets to walk.

With each step, the feeling grows. It's beyond desire. This deep, needy, restless energy has seeped into my brain. My hand touching my stomach is too much. I'm sensitive everywhere.

A bend in the path looks familiar suddenly.

I should be coming into the last straight. The tree line is breaking, growing more sparse. I'll be able to see the train in the distance in a minute. My body comes alive at the thought. I walk faster, my arm forgetting the soreness of dragging this sword.

The path curves beneath my feet, and I see him. He's waiting for me, just beyond the barrier.

He's already standing, pacing, really, watching me.

By the time I break through the barrier, I'm running.

He grabs me, pushing his hands beneath my coat to slide it off. It falls to the ground with Umbralius.

In one sweeping motion, we're on the ground, my back against the dirt and soft grass.

"My wicked little thing." He presses his face into my neck and breathes.

"Fuck me, Shade." I'll beg on my knees if I have to. I want him to rip me open. I need it. I'd bleed myself dry for him, crawl through glass, climb a fucking mountain, and steal. "Put all of your weight on me."

He pulls back, a small smile on his lips. Fucking gorgeous and cruel. "Your pupils are dilated. What did you do up there?"

"I drank from the mother. And I swam with lumee fish while they took little bites of me." I writhe beneath him, shifting my hips so that my pussy can rub against his cock, so he can feel how wet it is.

"Lucky lumee fish." He leans in, sucking my skin sharply, drawing blood to the surface with his lips. "You smell delicious–like sin and honey. I could eat you alive."

"I am delicious." I wrap my legs around his waist, tight, locking my ankles together. "Taste it. Fuck it. Wreck me. Do whatever you want, just make me come."

He groans and yanks my legs up with bruising force, bringing my ankles to his shoulders. "You want me to ruin you?" He snarls. "You asked for this."

He snaps his hips forward, tearing into me so hard and deep it punches a scream from my chest. No warning, no mercy.

This is exactly what I needed. Raw and punishing. The stretch is so deep and brutal, I see stars. I clench, my body fighting against it, rebelling. I want it, but it's too much. Basic survival instinct tries to force him out.

He pulls moans out of me like a magician with silk scarves. They're never-ending. I can't stop them or hold them back.

He fucks me like our lives depend on it.

"Say that you need me."

"I need you!" I scream.

"Say that you're mine!" He grits his teeth.

"I'm yours!"

His grip on my hips tightens as he slams into me. It's ravenous and relentless. He's trying to fuck my soul.

"I missed you." He growls. "I missed this tight little cunt. My perfect Sasi."

The world tilts, the sky above us, and the dirt below, I don't know which way is up. My mind and my body disconnect. I'm floating, weightless, above us. I watch him, the muscles beneath his sweat-slicked skin–the way his hair falls forward, the darkness that is spreading out like fog around us.

My mind goes blank, a clean slate for anything to be written.

"I worship you." He holds my head tenderly. "My salvation is between your legs."

"Never stop," I whisper, my voice cracking from emotion and exhaustion.

"Never." He promises. The truth feels different than a lie. I can almost smell it.

This is real.

The mountain bends to watch us. The birds sit still in the trees, listening.

Tighter and tighter, the knot in my stomach is being wound dangerously taut. My muscles shake violently, rippling outward, sending shockwaves through the ground.

The sky cracks, lightning blazing above us. Thunder rumbles, a stampede racing toward us.

When I come, it's vicious. A bloodthirsty beast that crawls like tar from beneath my ribs. It spread over my skin, then his, consuming both of us. He fills me with cum, then starts again. And again. And again.

This is divine. It's satanic. It's manifested by fate. He belongs to me, and I belong to him.

For the first time in my life, I know I have met my match. Forever or for a season, he is the only one. This is our wedding ceremony, and these are our vows. Before this realm and the next, we give ourselves over to each other.

He is a mirror that reflects me. He is the voice in my head. The air in my lungs.

"Be mine forever." I hold his face in my hands.

"You're the heartbeat in my chest, Sasi." His eyes blaze with the kind of fire that can only be true.

We fuck for hours or days. There is no end. My skin is bruised, raw, and chaffed. He never stops, not until the frenzy in my blood finally wears away.

When my eyes finally close, I can't speak. I can hardly breathe.

He lifts my dirty body from the ground, holding me like a precious thing against his chest.

"Sleep." I feel his lips on my temple.

CHAPTER TWENTY
blink twice

"SHADE?" I blink my eyes open in the dark and feel around for him in the bed.

"I'm here."

The pain in his voice makes me jolt upright. I was still partially asleep, but now I'm wide awake.

"What is it? What's wrong?" I slip out of the warm bed, goose-bumps spreading over my skin as I find him slumped over in a chair by the fireplace. Kneeling beside him, I take his face in my hands. His skin is so cold.

"I'm fine, love." He smiles, his sharp teeth are stained red.

"Whoa!" I force him back. "Is your mouth bleeding? Oh, my god! What the fuck?"

"No." He brushes it off.

"Shade, what the fuck is happening?" I don't know what to do. It looks like he's dying. "What do I do? I don't know what to do!" My heart feels like it's beating too fast.

"Sasi, I'm alright." He attempts to cover a cough by acting like he's clearing his throat.

"Do I need to get someone? Who can help?" I start to jump up, but he grabs my arm.

"Don't go. Just sit with me. Warm me up." He shivers.

"I'm not just going to fucking sit here while you die!" I can hear the fear in my voice–it's sharp and loud.

"I'm not dying."

"It looks like you are." Something creeps up my spine, a tight, awful feeling that I don't recognize. It twists, leaving behind an ache. "Tell me how to help, or I'm going to get Thalora."

When he doesn't say anything, I rush to the door. As soon as I touch the handle, a thought pops into my head.

"Eat from me!"

"No." He shakes his head. "I don't want to–"

"I'm not fucking asking!" I march toward him.

I push his chest harder than I actually meant to and climb into his lap.

"Take it."

I'm straddling him, and he's not hard. This is serious.

He looks up at me, and for a moment, I feel a wave of warmth wash over me. The look in his eyes is so different from what I'm used to. It's not lust, it's softer.

And it's freaking me the fuck out.

But I also like it. A little bit.

"Shade, I don't want you to die." It takes everything for me to get the words out. "Fuck, I need to see a therapist." I laugh nervously. It really shouldn't be painful to tell another person you don't want them to die. But I've never cared before.

"I'll only take a little bit. It's different taking like this. Drinking your lust isn't the same as taking your essence. That's part of your soul." He tucks my hair behind my ear.

"Does it hurt?"

"No. You'll feel…" he pauses. "Euphoric."

"That doesn't sound bad." I've probably done worse things to feel euphoric.

He brushes my hair over to one shoulder with one hand while the other gently holds my neck.

He leans in and kisses me so softly it feels like our first kiss. He's never been this gentle. "I'll be careful." He promises before kissing a trail down my jaw to my neck.

He alternates between kissing and scraping his pointed teeth against my pulse point. His hands roam over my body, under the loose, silky material of my nightgown.

"God, Shade. If you're not going to fuck me, you better stop doing that! Just take it!" I whimper, struggling to keep myself from grinding down on his lap.

"You're sure, love?" He whispers.

"Yes! I offered. I want to. Just take it."

He hums and kisses me again, but this time, I feel it. Not just the feeling of his lips, but more. It's like standing in the sun. Warmth spreads through me, and my eyes snap shut. Liquid and golden light pool in my chest, then spreads through my limbs.

It's almost like having blood drawn or riding in an elevator. There is a buzz, a slight dizziness.

A low hum vibrates in my ear, and a subtle pressure builds behind my eyes.

Time slips into nothingness. It doesn't exist. His darkness surrounds us, enveloping us like fog.

When I open my eyes, I'm in a theater, sitting in the crowd. My fingers brush over the red velvet seats. It's cold and dark. The air smells dusty–like old wood and dried flowers. The edges of my vision are blurred and hazy. This is a dream.

The room feels alive. Like the walls are breathing.

The stage is hidden behind long, black curtains.

Somehow, I just know there is something behind them that I want to see. It has my undivided attention, whatever it is. There is an invisible pull, keeping my attention there.

Anticipation ripples through the audience. Everyone is as excited as I am.

Music plays in the background, a quiet, slow melody that whispers over the hum of the crowd. It's familiar, but I can't place it.

The lights dim, and a ripple rolls through the now silent audience. I find myself sitting forward, on the edge of my seat.

A drum beat starts. A single note playing in rapid succession. Then another is added. Then another.

The curtain rolls away, opening up to reveal a stream of colorful lights beaming down from the ceiling to the floor. Purples, blues, reds.

My head tilts to one side as I squint, trying to see more.

The drum beats stop suddenly, and the theater is left in complete silence.

Seconds tick by, everyone is holding their breath. Then there he is.

It's as if he came up from the floorboards.

He looks strong, larger than life, beautiful. Instead of his usual black outfit, he's wearing red, a magician's ensemble complete with top hat. But the golden mandible mask is there, glinting in the light.

"Ladies and gentlemen, children of shadow, monsters and heathens, gather close if you dare! And prepare to be amazed." His voice booms through the theater, spreading over the crowd like a breeze. "Tonight, your hearts will be unfettered, your minds will be ensnared, your bodies will be bewitched. I have conjured marvels not meant for human eyes to behold! I have illusions to perplex the wisest among you. Amusements to haunt your dreams and magic, real, true magic, that defies all reason and cannot be explained." He bows, tipping his hat in his gloved hand.

We make eye contact, and he winks.

Sitting back against my seat, I watch him do magic tricks. Most are run-of-the-mill, card tricks, doves in his hat, sleight of hand, and misdirection. He's charming and charismatic, he has all eyes on him. They can't look away.

But then he brings out a mirror.

He stands before it, moving slowly, his reflection mirroring his movements.

But then it moves on its own. It's just a simple smile on the face of the reflection that Shade doesn't have on his. A shocked gasp moves through the crowd.

Then it happens again. The reflection winks.

Then it blows the crowd a kiss.

The audience is disarmed. We grow used to the reflection's antics. But slowly, the features change. It's his eyes first. They're bigger. And blue.

He morphs into a snake. A big, white boa with hypnotic eyes.

Shade isn't moving at all anymore. In fact, he seems mesmerized by the snake.

Tendrils of smoke reach out from inside the mirror, curling across the floor. The snake follows, slowly slithering out onto the stage.

He winds around Shade's ankles, wrapping his body tightly, coiling up, up, up. The snake turns, looking out at the stunned audience with a smile on his face, then he winks and, as fast as lightning, swallows Shade whole.

I gasp, clutching my chest.

I don't move, I can't. My heart hammers against my ribs, and shallow, quick breaths heave from my chest.

The snake moves slowly across the empty stage, flicking its tail end toward the mirror, breaking the glass and sending it all over the floor. It slithers to the end of the stage and moves slowly, making eye contact with each of us in the front row.

I can still see him. He's different. He's a snake. Those aren't his eyes. It's not his face, but there's something there, an essence, an aura.

When he looks at me, it confirms it.

I sit forward, holding eye contact as it hovers half off stage in front of me.

It's a game of chicken. A challenge. First to blink loses.

Biting into my lip, I slide out of my seat and step toward him.

Reaching out slowly, carefully, I place my hand on his head, resting my hand on his cold skin.

As soon as we touch, the snake disappears, and Shade falls from the sky, landing on his feet in the center of the stage.

"It looks like we have a volunteer." Even with the mask, I know he's smiling. The smile isn't for the audience. It's for me. "Come, darling, be my assistant."

Rolling my eyes, I walk up the stairs on the side of the stage.

"Come on, let's give our lovely assistant a round of applause." He starts to clap, and the crowd follows, cheering loudly as I curtsy.

He grabs my waist, spinning my body into his before leading me around the stage in a fast-paced dance. The steps are graceful, and we move like we've practiced the choreography together forever. The steps are in our bones. Our bodies are fluid, indistinguishable from one another. We're one.

"My wicked thing." He spins me to the center of the stage where a black rose is floating in the center of the stage.

He plucks it out of the air and hands it to me.

A thorn pricks the skin of my palm, drawing a droplet of blood to the surface. Before I can react, he takes my hand and licks the blood, spinning me around again.

I bring the rose up to smell it. It's smoky. Not like a flower at all, but a fire.

I start to feel dizzy, like the room is swaying around me. The lights pulse, and the music is muffled.

My body drops, my knees buckling, but I don't hit the ground. Shade has me in his arms.

"This, ladies and gentlemen, is called the kiss of death." He presses his lips to mine. "My lovely has fallen victim to the curse of the dead rose. But I can bring her back!"

The audience gasps. I hear everything, but I can't see or move.

I'm locked here inside my body, his to use as he pleases. Goosebumps roll over my skin. Being completely vulnerable and at his disposal is exciting. It's like being bound without the physical restraints.

He sets me down on a table, arranging my body just the way he wants it.

"Shall I save her?" He calls to the crowd.

The whoop and yell, excited to watch the magic of true love's kiss. But if I know Shade, it will be more than that.

And, as usual, he doesn't disappoint.

He walks beside the table, letting his hand trail over my body, from my feet, up to my head.

"Would you like to show them what a good girl you are? Do you want them to see how good you can make me feel?" He whispers down, caressing my chin.

Yep. I blink twice, and he smiles.

"I thought you might."

He pulls me across the table, bringing me up so that my head dangles over the edge.

"And now, lovers and friends, watch how our love brings her back!" He unzips his pants and his cock springs free.

He rubs the piercing on the crown of his cock against my lips. My body reacts, desperate to move, but I can't, not at all. Using his hands, he manipulates my head, positioning it perfectly so that he can slide right down my throat.

He keeps one hand on my face, holding me gently while he rocks his hips. There isn't a warmup, no easing into it. He fucks my throat.

I can't see him in this position; only his legs are visible, but I can hear him. And he's enjoying himself.

A violent stream of expletives pours out of him. He uses my mouth like it's his own personal fuck toy.

The audience is captivated. I can feel them holding their breath collectively. I ache everywhere, but I can't move to relieve it. The craving grows by the second. If I could, I would beg him to touch me.

His thrusts are getting sloppier, faltering from their brutal rhythm.

When he comes, he leans forward, placing his hand flat on my throat.

As soon as he pulls out a string of cum and drool connecting my mouth to the crown of his cock, I can feel my limbs. Sitting up, I wipe the tears from my eyes and look out at the crowd.

It's not a theater.

It's the tent.

The dreamlike haze is gone. This isn't a dream at all.

His arm wraps around my chest, holding me close to him. "Welcome back, love."

"I should say the same to you. You look like you're feeling better." I wipe my mouth with the scrap of fabric I'm wearing.

"I would like to thank you for what you did."

"You don't have to thank me."

"I do. Let's get ready. I made plans for us."

"Well, I can't argue with that."

CHAPTER TWENTY-ONE
black manhattan

I FEEL LIKE JESSICA RABBIT.

Dark makeup, big hair, the sexiest fucking dress I've ever seen.

My heels click against the ground as we walk down the dark streets. I have no idea where we're headed. He just told me to dress to impress.

I met the challenge.

"You never told me about Greenland." He rubs his thumb over my neck as he slides his hand beneath my hair.

"It was interesting." I hardly remember it. It's as if the memories have been locked behind a veil of smoke. "Definitely strange."

"How so?"

"I remember the people were friendly. Overly friendly. There was a feast. And we swam naked. I might have performed a song at some point." That part is especially fuzzy.

"Did you?" He lets out a laugh that vibrates through my chest.

"I distinctly remember singing."

He leads me down a dark, empty alley. The signs on the buildings aren't in English or in any other language I recognize.

"Where are you taking me? I'm not dressed for a dogfight." I step over a ripped-open bag of garbage.

"Well, I'm glad I decided against that, then. We're here." He opens a black door at the end of the building.

Where exactly is 'here'?

Behind the door is a staircase. But it already looks like a different world from the outside entrance.

Sconces with pillar candles hang on the brick walls, illuminating the ground as we climb.

Six stories up, we reach another black door.

He opens it, stepping aside for me to walk in first.

"What is this?" I chuckle. A bar opens up in front of us. "How on earth did you find this place?"

It's not the place you just stumble into. You have to know it. It's got an accent, a secretive vibe that makes an excited chill run down my spine.

"Umbramancer." The bartender calls to him as he slips my coat from my shoulders and folds it over his arm.

"Long time no see." He gestures for me to take a seat at the bar.

"I heard you were in town. I hoped you'd stop by."

The more he talks, the more I'm sure he's not human. Curious.

"And who is this?" He sets his sights on me.

"Mine." Shade places his hand on my shoulder. "And she's thirsty. Make her something dark and sweet."

"On it." He bows slightly and gets to work.

"Come, let's take a table." He leads me to a quiet corner where we can see everything, but we're slightly hidden.

The bar is dimly lit but obviously well-kept. Everything looks like it belongs in the grand study of some wealthy old man's estate.

The music is slow and melancholic, a low, haunting rhythm that suits the room just right.

"You look good." I don't mean to be so freely complimentary, but he really does. His skin is bright, his shoulders look bigger, and his hair is thicker. My contribution to his body is clearly working wonders.

"Are you checking me out right now, love?" He teases, but I recognize the genuine flattery in his voice.

"Maybe." I shrug.

"For the lady." The bartender seems to float out from beneath the table. "A Black Manhattan."

"Thank you."

He's already across the room before I even finish. At least he doesn't linger around.

Shade opens his mouth to speak, but another man is standing at our table.

"Can I interest you in a cigar?" He opens a wooden case, offering it to him. He takes two and shoos him away.

"Cigar?"

"Please." I take a sip of the drink. "This is good." I hold it out, offering him a sip.

"I'll taste it on your tongue later."

"Even better."

He clips my cigar and lights it before passing it across the table.

I draw the smoke into my mouth, spicy and woodsy. I hold it there, savoring it before blowing it out.

"You look like you've done that before." His lips twitch into a lopsided grin that makes me want to crawl across this table.

"Maybe a few times." I pull another drag. "This is a good one."

"They only serve the finer things here."

"Where are we?"

"Istanbul."

Sipping my drink slowly, I let the taste linger as I look around the room. There are at least a few humans here, slung on the arms of different kinds of beasts, draped in luxury brands.

In the other corner, a very tall, slender man is sitting with four stunning women.

He's feeding one of them grapes from a vine. Literally. They look like a work of art.

He's not particularly handsome, not in the traditional sense, not like Shade, but there is a sort of magnetic draw to him. There is a hum around him. He has an energy.

"Vampire." Shade whispers across the table.

"No kidding." I hum, puffing my cigar. "Tell me something interesting."

His eyes move over my face, slow and confident. "What do you want to know?"

"Anything. Impress me."

He chuckles, leaning forward with a hint of a smile on his lips. "I have a feeling that's a difficult task."

"Not for you."

"I knew King Henry the Eighth."

"Really? What was he like?"

"Awful. Petulant and whiny. Spoiled. He had no redeeming qualities." The disdain in his face is clear. "You know that good behavior, manners, lawfulness, none of that really matters to me. But he went beyond that."

"Did you know any of his wives?"

"Anne Boleyn." He nods. "She was not a monstrous beast. Just a woman being used by a pawn."

"She wasn't a manipulative seductress?" The image is shattered in my mind.

"No, not at all. She was clever, don't get me wrong." There is a hint of mischief in his eyes.

"Pity. I looked at her as somewhat of a role model."

He chokes on a laugh. "You would have mopped the floor with her, trust me. She was no match for your wiles."

Sliding the pointed toe of my boot up his calf, I look around nonchalantly. "What about that guy?" I tip my chin. "Who is he?"

His fingers wrap around my ankle tightly. "A moth man." The playful look on his face spurs me on. I bring my other foot up, resting the pointed heel of my boot right between his legs.

"He looks a little bit like a moth." I tilt my head. "As much as a person could, anyway." A memory suddenly pops into my head, and my spine straightens. "Hey! When I was a little girl, we had a neighbor, a really old woman. I would watch her from my window at night because she would turn into a fox or a coyote or something. No one ever believed me. But I know what I saw. Whenever we would see each other, she would look at me so strangely, like she might hurt me, but she never did."

"Sounds like a shapeshifter." He tightens his grip on my ankle.

"I knew it!" I take a vindicated sip of my drink.

"You are endlessly fascinating."

"Me?" I laugh to cover the heat creeping up my cheeks.

"It seems you've always been able to see us." His lips twitch, but it's the look in his eyes that catches me off guard. Softness. I feel seen again.

"I guess so." I clear my throat. It's nerve-wracking to be looked at with so much reverence.

His smile tilts as he leans in. The air shifts, gravity changing around us. His face isn't playful anymore. His eyes burn. They worship. "My pretty wicked thing."

CHAPTER TWENTY-TWO

just a chat

I SHOULD BE in a post sex coma but I can't shut my brain off.

It could be my own self deprecating need to sabotage any good things that come my way, but my spidey senses are tingling.

The date was fucking perfect.

We just sat together for hours, talking and sipping cocktails. He didn't try to impress me. There wasn't any big, overdone gesture or fake attempts at charm.

He was a gentleman. He held my coat, opened doors, lit my cigar…

It wasn't until we got back to the train that he was so disrespectful I came multiple times. He fucked me so hard; I blacked out, and when I came to, he was still at it.

Without a doubt, it was the best date of my life.

Then why can't I sleep?

Rolling over, I stare at his face.

What the fuck do I do?

My chest feels tight. I might be having a heart attack. I don't stare tenderly at people while they sleep, or memorize the shape of their faces, or the way their chests move with each breath. But with him, I know it all. I've committed every detail to memory–stored it away in a special place so that I'll never forget it.

I want him. And not just because of the sex. The sex is a religious experience, but it's more than that. It's this. The quiet steady. The warmth. I'm comfortable in a way that I can't really understand. He sees me.

I like falling asleep beside him, wrapped around him. I like waking up beside him even more. It's fucking terrifying.

What is this? I don't fucking attach.

I'm feeling very attached. Swoony. Pathetic.

We've moved beyond casual, surface level bullshit into something deep and tangled. He's under my skin. And I want to crawl into his chest and live there.

Could it really be this easy? Just a woman and a shadow, traveling the world together, weaving in and out of the realms–live, laugh, loving? I'm sick to my stomach.

It's less horrifying than getting married to an accountant or something. It's not domesticated bliss.

But it's still too committed.

Maybe we could forge our own thing. Something that I can make work in my fucked up brain.

Morticia Addams did it…

I reach out, my hand trembling like I'm reaching for an alligator, and I brush the tips of my fingers over his chest.

Do I love him? This foreign feeling lodged in my throat feels more like I'm asphyxiating. It's a strange blend of food poisoning and the sensation of falling and being unable to stop it.

Sitting up, I drag myself away. I need space to gain clarity.

Grabbing the sheer robe from the chair, I slip it on and let it billow around me as I walk out into the sitting car.

Someone on this train will have something to smoke. A cigarette, a joint, at this point, I don't care.

As I make my way through the cars, I wonder what my life would look like if I walked away. I could get off at the next stop and never look back.

But what is waiting for me? What kind of life would I go back to?

A shitty apartment that I can't afford without a roommate. No job.

No relationships worth salvaging. The monotonous task of living–working a dead-end job just to pay to be alive.

It's so ordinary it makes my chest hurt.

I want magic. And carnage. I want riches beyond what a simple human mind can dream of. Wealth that is more than just money or gold. Not just material things, but enchantment and supernatural wonder. I deserve that.

I don't just want to exist. I deserve more.

I want money, power, and glory.

Delusions of grandeur.

"Holy shit." The thought stops me dead. The last thing I ever expected was the words of a therapist to pop into my head.

She said I had delusions of grandeur. I laughed it off; it rolled off my shoulders. But now…

Is it delusional? Why do I think I deserve a life of glitter and gold? What makes me so special?

I've chased it for so long, looking for something bigger and better. I flit from thing to thing, always waiting for something more magical to come along.

All this time, I never stopped to consider if I'm the problem. I just assumed it was everyone else.

I teeter on my toes, wondering if I should just go back to bed.

I catch my reflection in the long window.

On instinct, my hands move up, over my stomach and chest to my neck where Shade has left a scattered trail of hickeys on my skin.

I'm a goddess. I've seen and done things that would scar a lesser woman. There is power thrumming beneath my skin.

I'm not delusional. I'm just too big for them to understand.

Everything I've been searching for is in front of me. All I have to do is reach out and grab it.

Magic. Mayhem. Possibility.

Rolling my shoulders back, I walk through the cars, passing the chaos by, unfazed.

"Sasi," Thalora calls after me. When I turn, I find her behind me, outside.

Stepping back out, I follow her up a small ladder onto the roof of the car. I assume she does this often because there is a setup of large pillows spread out.

We sit, lounging on the cushions.

"Smoke?" She holds out a silver metal case.

"You read my mind." I take one of the neatly rolled joints and hold it between my lips so she can light it.

Inhaling the smoke into my mouth, I let it sit before taking a breath into my lungs.

"You're stunning." She stares at me in a way that makes me feel confident, not uncomfortable. Her eyes move down from my face to my body beneath the sheer robe.

The familiar ease of an absolutely top-shelf plant spreads through my limbs.

"So are you." I offer her the joint.

She hums, taking a drag and blowing it into the cold, black air.

"I've been meaning to talk to you." I lean back on my hands, closing my eyes as if the sun were on my face.

"Really?" Her tone is light, but there is a sharpness beneath it. "What about?"

"I've met everyone. Had a few interesting conversations. But we've never had the chance to chat." I don't mention that I've seen her watching me, sizing me up from a distance. We both know that she does it.

"He told me you were a curious one." She smiles, stamping out the lit end of the joint and placing it back in the tin. "Said you like to poke around."

"That's a very interesting necklace." I ignore her attempt to steer the conversation to him. We don't have to talk about him. "What is it?"

"Oh, this old thing?" She holds up the little vial of swirling liquid. "This is unicorn blood. Useful to have in a tight spot."

"I'm sure."

"You call him Shade?" She circles us back to him immediately.

"I do."

“It suits him.”

“I thought so.” I peek one eye open, staring at her. What is her angle here?

“You know, he collected this group of misfits, brought us all together. He protects us.” I recognize the reverence in her voice now. She worships him. “We’ve been rejected and thrown out, but he watches out for us.” She looks like she might cry.

I understand how she feels. He plucked me out of the crowd, too. “He–”

“He’s getting weaker, Sasi. You must see it. Even in the short time that you’ve been here.” She reaches out, grabbing my hand desperately.

“I’ve noticed.”

Her voice trembles. “His power is dwindling. He keeps all of this going. We are here, alive, because he gives us all that he has! Everything here runs because of him.”

I wait, letting the words hang in the space between us for a moment.

“Are you asking me to do something, Thalora? Speak plainly, please. If there is something that you want from me, just say it.”

She sniffles, but her lips tug up into a smile. “You’re as clever as he said you were.”

“Seems the two of you have spent a lot of time talking about me.” I keep my expression and voice flat. She’s skirting around something.

“You brought Umbralius down from the mountain.” Her eyes light up with hope.

“Right.” I’m suspicious of the direction she’s taking this conversation. Something feels off. If Shade wanted me to do something, I hope he would ask. I thought we were done with this sneaky shit.

This private conversation makes me think that whatever she wants me to do is something that he doesn’t want me to do.

I’m not one for obliging the whims of a man, but I trust him over her at this point.

“Do you think you could—”

Whatever she's about to say, Shade's low growl stops her.

He appears on the ladder, and the look on his face makes me cower back. Holy shit, he's pissed.

"What the fuck are you doing, Thalora?" He grits through clenched teeth.

"Nothing! I was just going to—"

"You were just going directly against what I clearly told you already! What happens between us is between us. It's none of your fucking business." He grabs her arm, not roughly, but tight enough to pull her toward him. "Your job is not to whisper in her ear. If I ever find you attempting to go behind my back again, you will be removed from this train." His darkness is coiling around him like a snake about to strike. It slithers in the air, growing larger and more imposing by the second.

"You need help! We all see it!" Tears spill over her long lashes. "If you won't do what needs to be done, then I will! I'm not going to sit idly by and watch you deteriorate, Umbramancer!"

She loves him. It's pouring out of her. But it's not met with warmth from him.

He's angry.

"She is not the answer. Leave her alone." The whites of his eyes are disappearing. Black spreads like ink until there is nothing there but darkness.

There is something about his word choice here. It's like they have had a conversation before this one, something I'm not privy to. She thinks I can help, and he is shutting it down.

But why?

"She–"

"Enough!" His voice booms like a clap of thunder. The train lurches to a halt. "I will allow you the courtesy of gathering your belongings. Go. Now. You have five minutes to get the fuck off my train."

The shocked gasp that ripples through the air is the first clue that we're not alone here. Everyone is listening from the car below.

"Umbramancer! Please!" She reaches for him with her free hand, but he backs away, releasing his grip on her arm.

"Go, Thalora. I won't repeat myself."

CHAPTER TWENTY-THREE

birdfeeder

HIS BARE SHOULDERS move up and down, his chest heaving with each breath. There is raw fury in his eyes.

"If any one of you wants to join her," his voice shakes the ground as he yells to everyone listening. "Be my fucking guest! If you choose to stay, know that this conversation is closed as of right now. If anyone tries to do anything behind my back, with my fucking woman, you will pay for it with your home! If you don't think it's possible to mind your own fucking business, get out now!"

Silence.

His fucking woman.

Am I his fucking woman?

No one speaks, but no one leaves either. Thalora is on her own.

"Come to bed, Sasi." He holds his hand out to me.

"Yeah, absolutely not. You're not getting out of this that easily." I laugh at the audacity of him. "We're having a conversation about this."

The second the words leave my mouth, his darkness grabs me, flipping me around so that I'm bent, ass up, like I'm being carried over a shoulder.

"How dare you!" I scream as he walks past the crowd of beasts gathered to watch. He ignores me completely.

I thrash, but it's useless. With each movement, the grip gets tighter.

"Put me down!"

When we reach our car, he pins me against the door. "Don't ever let anyone try to talk you into hurting yourself to help me." His lips graze mine. "Don't even entertain it, Sasi."

"What? She didn't actually get that far. I don't know what she wanted me to do."

He lets out a low, rumbling sound from his chest.

"What was she going to ask me to do?" I run my fingers through his sleep-disheveled hair.

"I don't even want the idea in your head, Sasi." He pulls back.

He doesn't think it's going to be that easy, does he? There is no way I'm just going to drop it and leave it alone.

I watch him walk out of the bedroom and drop into one of the armchairs in the sitting room. His muscles are tense as he stares angrily at the embers of the dying fire in the hearth.

Letting my hips sway while I walk, I make my way across the room, my robe sweeping the ground. I glide with deliberate grace, pausing in the doorway.

His anger is palpable. Because she disobeyed him? Or because of what she was going to ask me to do?

I pull at the tie, letting it fall open as I reach him.

"Hey," I wrap my arms around his neck. "Don't keep me in the dark." I let my voice dip down into that raspy place that he always responds to. Slow and steady, I've got to draw him onto the hook.

His shoulders stiffen. "Sasi." His voice is a warning.

I slide onto his lap, my thighs locking on either side of his legs.

"Shade," I warn back. Running the tips of my fingernails down his chest, I watch his eyes dilate.

I'm going to get the truth out of him, eventually.

His breath hitches in his throat. "You're not playing fair."

"That's usually my line." I press a soft kiss to his jaw. "She mentioned that you talk about me." I let my lips barely graze his. "What do you say?"

He groans slightly, "That you're very distracting."

"Am I?" I smile.

He hums, his chest tensing.

"What did I say about lying to me, Shade?" I nibble at his earlobe.

"I'm not lying to you. I just don't want to tell you this." He pants.

"Once, not that long ago, you told me you would never deny me anything. Tell me the truth." I grind my hips down. "I don't like climbing fucking mountains, Shade. I climbed a real one for you. Now don't make me climb mental ones to get honesty from you."

"Your blood." He hesitates.

When I lock eyes with him, I can see something unfamiliar. It's not fear…

"My blood what?" I coax him, reaching down between us to pull his hard cock out of his pants.

He grunts when I squeeze him too tight…accidentally.

"Your blood could give me power, but I don't want to take it. It's a slippery slope." He lets out a huff of frustration when I rub him through my soaking wet pussy, but don't actually take him in. The piercing rubs against my clit, and my body shudders.

"Keep going." I sound more forceful than I'm feeling.

"It can be easy to take too much. I don't want to risk it."

"Risk me?" I brush my thumb over his lips.

"I don't want to risk you." He takes my face in his hands.

"She mentioned Umbralius." I sink down, taking him in one quick motion. The rippling stretch is immediate. It knocks the air out of me like a punch in the stomach.

"Fuck!" He groans, his head falling back. "She was very fucking chatty, apparently." He grits his teeth.

"Very."

"Using Umbralius to draw your blood would strengthen both of us. His magic is tied to mine, so if I used him to cut you and then I took the blood, it would make both of us stronger."

I roll my hips. "So, you don't actually have to kill me?"

"No!" His eyes jerk up to mine.

"Were you going to ask me?"

"No." He thrusts up to meet my hips.

"Why not?" My voice sounds breathier–strained.

"Because I won't risk it. It's dangerous, and I don't want to hurt you." The honesty on his face looks different now. I can feel it in my chest. He doesn't want to hurt me.

"What if I offer it to you?" I bounce slightly, building up a faster-paced rhythm.

His eyes flicker, like bolts of lightning flashing in them. "Would you do that? For me?"

"For you, I might."

It's terrifying that I really mean that. For him, I really would. It's not even a hard choice.

"Sasi." The look of vulnerability on his face makes something tug in my chest.

I can't explain it. I'm not sure if I like it. But it's here, and I can't ignore it.

"If you asked me to, I would do it," I whisper, the words catching in my throat.

"I can't ask that of you." He rolls his hips, hitting a place so deep it makes my body spasm.

"Holy shit, Shade! What the fuck is this?" I'm on the verge of panic. I think I might be dying. It feels so good. I can't think straight, but it's too much.

Nothing in the world could have prepared me for this. I've touched myself before. I've been touched. But this is something else.

I thought I felt the depths of where this could go—how deep it could truly get, but I had no idea. This is cavernous and unending.

"No." I shake my head, my voice trembling.

"Don't run away from it. Feel it. Stay here with me." He begs, his voice shaking as much as mine. "Look at me."

"I—" Tears prick in my eyes, burning like acid as they slide down my face. "Fuck. I don't like this."

"Let it happen. Open." He moves his hand down to my neck, holding it with just enough pressure on my throat to calm me—to ground me here with him.

This feels like grief and magic at the same time. Like something that's going to ruin my life.

He builds faster and harder until I sob, the pleasure mixed with this deep, connected feeling bursting open inside of me. It's all raw nerves and existential dread.

There isn't anywhere to hide from it. He can see it all.

"Sasi!" He groans, pressing his lips to mine in a useless kiss. Our mouths fumble together, messy and wet.

He wraps around me, pinning my arms to my sides as he holds me tight against him. I bury my face in his neck and scream through an orgasm so hard, I'm afraid it's going to kill me.

He shudders, pushing as deep as he can before sobbing into my shoulder. It's a garbled mix of my name and a moan.

Our bodies slump together, too exhausted to move.

I'm lifted. Without opening my eyes, I let my limp body go, surrendering to whatever he's about to do.

His darkness holds me up, propping me on my back with my legs spread wide.

Forcing my eyes open, I watch him. His eyes are intensely focused on me.

"You're dripping." He drops out of the chair onto his knees in front of me. "I'm going to slurp it out of you, then bird feed it to you."

"Oh, holy fuck." I'm wide awake again. Any thoughts I had of sleep are long gone.

"We can't waste it." He gets to work, sucking the mixture of our mess into his mouth. His fingers rub against my clit, making my body jerk.

Loud, unabashed moans pour out of him, and his fingers bite into my thighs where he's holding me open.

"God! I'm about to—"

Tendrils of darkness reach for me, spreading over my skin, touching me everywhere. The coil tightens harder and harder until the cord breaks. The snap is violent.

I gush into his mouth and scream into the air.

He comes up, bringing his mouth to mine.

His pupils are blown out as he watches me open my mouth, ready to take it.

He drops it into my mouth, a little at a time.

My body writhes against the dark restraints.

"Mine. Forever." He comes up, wrapping his hand in my hair, tugging my head back at the same time that he slams into me again.

"Yes!" I hear myself agreeing. His. Forever.

CHAPTER TWENTY-FOUR

a woman scorned

"I'M GOING TO EXPLORE." I come up on my toes and press a quick kiss to his cheek. When I try to turn away, he grabs me. And sucks my soul out through my mouth. He doesn't just kiss me, he's marking his territory.

It's not just affection, it's possession. A slow, wet, deliberate claim. Like he's marking me as his territory before I go.

I'm not going to be able to walk straight after this.

"What was that for?" I wipe my lips.

"Just a reminder of what's waiting here for you when you come back." He grins, boyish–adorable–but there is something serious beneath it. Something primal.

"Scared I'm going to fall in love out there?"

"The castle district is pretty magical." He digs his fingers into my waist.

"Then I might have to take a Hungarian lover and leave you behind." I pull away, but he doesn't let go that easily.

He opens the wardrobe and pulls out a sheer black scarf. "It's windy out." He drapes it over my head, wrapping it around my neck. "You look lovely."

"So do you. Break a leg." I wink before sliding my glasses onto my face and stepping out the door.

He groans loudly as the door slides closed behind me.

He wasn't kidding about this city being magical. I've never seen anything so incredible. The parliament building is a masterpiece of architecture and beauty.

My head feels clear again. The effect of Shade-free oxygen.

I feel free, walking through this city on my own.

With light, unhurried steps, I weave through the crowds. There is a softness to being alone.

I can't tell if it's better or just different.

I need space and perspective. He clouds up everything and makes it hard to see through the haze. One thing I won't do is take his word for it. Something is off. I know he's still hiding something from me. And at this point, I can't help but feel that it's important. If it wasn't, he would just tell me.

The sounds of the carnival start to fade into the background, the tightly packed crowd growing more sparse and leisurely. People are just exploring now.

I feel like a shadow as I move through the crowds. I've never been here, but I'm not like the rest of them—loud, obvious tourists with fanny packs and walking shoes paired with dresses.

I blend. I'm a ghost floating through.

I pick a few pockets, snag a few watches.

Nothing major.

"You're good." A voice from behind me stops me in my tracks. "None of them even suspected."

"Hello, Thalora." I spin around. She doesn't look destitute.

She looks fabulous.

Her hair is a wild mane of curls streaked with red. A post-breakup hairstyle change, I assume. Her dress fades from yellow to black like a sunset.

"You look great." I walk beside her. "I love the fire thing you have going on."

"Oh, you know. A woman scorned and all that. I'm a bit theatrical. I like the symbolism."

"Well, it's working for you." I offer her one of the watches. It's not a Rolex, I don't really want it.

"Thanks." She clasps it around her wrist.

"What is he not telling me?" I cut right to the chase.

Her head falls back, and she laughs. "You're a lot smarter than he gives you credit for. You're not some naïve little creature, are you?"

"No, I'm not. But I am missing pieces of the puzzle." I wait for her to start explaining, but after several steps, she hasn't said anything. "Care to help a girl out?"

She sighs, running her ring-clad fingers through her hair. "Not really."

"Not much of a girl's girl, are you?"

"No." She shakes her head. "I'm a 'me' girl."

"Same." I shrug. No hard feelings.

"He's going to regret sending me away. He can't treat me like this. I've stood by his side for centuries." There is a brokenness in her voice that almost makes me feel bad for her. "Years slipped by. I'm his helper. Anything he wants, I get it for him."

Girl, you've made yourself way too available…

"And now he has you, and he casts me aside! He's acting like my contributions were meaningless!" Anger rises with each word.

"Thalora," I shrug. I don't even know what to say. She's emotional, and I don't really know how to deal with that. "You're stunning. Your body is absolutely out of this world. You can dance and sing. You're the total package. You don't have to worry about the constraints of mortality or the law. Why are you pining after a man who doesn't want you? Go get someone else."

She opens her mouth, then snaps it shut. Her wide eyes meet mine for a moment before a low laugh rumbles in her chest. "Holy shit."

It's like she's only just realizing all of this now.

"He threw me away like trash." She rolls her shoulders back. "I'll make him sorry. Then, you're right. I'm too good to sit around waiting for him to see all that I bring to the table."

"Wait…" I feel the need to backtrack here. I'm all for exacting your revenge, but I don't want her to hurt Shade. Toe to toe, I'm not sure I can take her. She has the element of not being human on her side.

"Tell Umbramancer that I'll be seeing you in Morocco." She grins, a wolfish smile that shows too many teeth.

"Shit." I sigh as she traipses into the crowd, her head high. I might have hyped her up too much.

I walk along the Danube, lost in my own thoughts. I have no idea where I'm going, but my feet follow a path, walking as if they know where to go.

I find myself outside the Gellert Thermal Bath.

Something is drawing me in. An instinct? A malevolent force?

It's closed. The doors are shut, and there is no one around. But there is a light inside, beckoning me in.

I step inside the unlocked door, breathing in the mineral-rich, humid air. Intricate mosaics adorn the walls. And skylights let the dewy glow of the moon in. It illuminates the steam curling out of the water like fingers.

Further inside, I pass several marble statues. There isn't anything particularly remarkable about them, but I do check that their eyes aren't following me around.

I'm not alone. I can feel someone else here with me.

"Hello?" I slip my sandal off, dipping my toes into the pool.

"Hello, precious." A voice like stone rolls through the room. Hard and cold, it sends a ripple through the water.

Immediately. Instantly. I know I fucked up.

"Oh, man. This was a mistake." I step back from the water. "I'll just be going."

"No, I don't think so." A slimy black tentacle slithers out of the water over the tiled edge of the pool.

It wraps around my ankle and holds tight.

"Fuck." I take a slow breath. I need a plan.

"Join us." Another voice rolls out of the dark.

"No, thanks."

A slick laugh fills the room, a wet gurgling cackle that makes my skin crawl.

"You followed our call, walked right through the door. We can't just let you leave." The water ripples again, and a murky figure steps out of the shadows on the far end of the pool.

I try to step back, but the tentacled arm wraps tighter.

"I'm Levian. We're so pleased to have you here." A grotesque mixture between a man, a squid, and a nightmare steps into the dim moonlight. "Join us." His voice purrs like a cat. A smile splits his face too wide.

"I—" before I can finish, another figure emerges from the steam. He's tall and thin, really tall, and really thin. He is skin stretched over bone with nothing else to him.

"Come here." His voice is more forceful.

I'm yanked forward hard. My foot skids across the wet tile before slipping out from under me. I go down, hitting the ground first, then the water in rapid succession.

With his grip on my foot, he tugs, and I glide below the surface of the water the length of the bath.

When I break the surface, I gasp, spitting water, gagging, and choking. The steam rises around me, clinging to me like it's a living thing, too.

Spinning around, I'm able to see them both more clearly. I wish I couldn't.

"Listen." I put my hands up. "I'm sure you're both great. But I'm spoken for. You–"

"Spoken for?" The tall one wades toward me. "If you were mine, I wouldn't let such a precious treasure wander around all alone... Unprotected."

My spine stiffens. "Well, I'm not yours, and I do what I want." I fold my arms over my chest. I'm in trouble. From where I'm standing, I see no way out of here.

There is still a tentacle wrapped around my ankle, but even if there wasn't, I'm sure they're faster than me.

"Defiant little thing." A tentacled arm comes up, touching my cheek.

"Stop that." I swat it away. "I don't want to be here with you. Am I free to leave, or are we fighting?"

A gurgling laugh hacks from him. "Straight to the point, huh?"

"I don't like to beat around the bush." I see no world where I beat them, but I won't go down easy. There is a calmness now, like the moment before a storm. Violence is coming.

The tall one has been inching closer, almost imperceptibly, but he could grab me if he reached out his long, spindly arm.

"You smell divine." He sniffs the air in a way that makes my stomach roll.

He's on me so quickly, I don't have time to scream. His large, bony hands wrap around my arms, and his teeth sink into my neck.

The intensity of the pain is unlike anything I've ever experienced. It sears into my skin, then moves deeper—down to the muscle, then down to the bone.

It draws a scream from the deepest, darkest place in me. My necklace tugs, like someone is pulling it into my skin with as much force as they can muster.

But then, it's gone.

His arms aren't holding me anymore, his face isn't tucked into my neck.

There is a sickening whooshing sound, then more wet, gurgling. The tentacle around my ankle releases.

I'm sprayed with warm water. It explodes around me, like it fell from the ceiling.

I blink, my heart racing. Red. The water is red now.

The body of the kraken floats on the surface, ripped to shreds. Something bobs in my peripheral vision–the other body.

Spinning around, I'm met with his heaving chest. "Did he bite you, Sasi?"

"Yeah." I touch the painful, festering, hot wound on my neck.

"Fuck. Come here." He wraps his arms around me, and we're gone, floating–flying.

When I open my eyes again, we're in our train car. He's rushing around, but it's all hazy, slow motion to me.

Someone runs in, the giant woman. She inspects me. Her presence is reassuring, even though I can't hear her.

The pain starts to fade. It's like I'm asleep, but my eyes are open, and I can see everything happening around me.

Shade's handsome face is dripping blood everywhere, and a deep line creases between his brows. He's talking to me, but I can't hear him.

He takes Umbralius, sliding him across his chest. The wound opens, but blood doesn't come out of it. From the cut, darkness spills out, like black rays of sunlight shooting from his chest. A kaleidoscope of dark colors, all black but somehow distinguishably different, like a shadow rainbow.

He spreads the wound and puts his hand inside.

It looks painful. His jaw tightens as he reaches deeper. The tightness in his body, the shudder of his muscles, I can almost feel it.

Sharp. Burning.

But it's next to me, not in me.

He pulls something out of his chest, a little iridescent liquid, the deepest, darkest purple, swirling with magic. It's just a few drops, but he rubs it on the bite mark, and almost immediately, I can hear again, muffled and far away, but it's there.

The sleepy feeling slips away.

"Sasi?" He cups my face in his hands. "Can you hear me?"

"Yes." I watch the wound on his chest slowly close. "What was that?"

"I gave you my blood. I don't have much, but a drop or two should reverse the damage." His eyes dart around my face.

"What damage?"

"That was a ghoul. A bite from him is lethal." His eyes dart around, looking over my face, searching me for something—signs of impending death maybe.

"Oh, shit." I sit up, touching the wound. It's not throbbing anymore, and the heat is gone.

"What the fuck happened?" He wraps his arms around me.

"It's hard to say." I shrug against his chest. "I felt pulled toward them, like something was drawing me in."

His fingers knot into my tangled hair. "Let's get cleaned up."

"So, quick question. Did you materialize out of my necklace?"

He grins. "As long as you're wearing it, I'll be able to get to you."

"You failed to mention that part before."

His eyes darken, "I need to be able to reach my bratty girl, all the time."

I roll my eyes, but it makes my heart flutter around in my chest. "Did that hurt you?" I don't let go of him.

"I'll be alright."

"That didn't answer my question."

"It was excruciating."

"Thank you." I kiss the almost healed cut on his chest.

CHAPTER TWENTY-FIVE

the memory

"I THINK WE SHOULD STAY HERE." I crane my neck to look up at him.

"What do you mean?" His thumb traces circles on my back.

"Let the carnival go to Morocco, and we stay behind, just for a while."

"Why?" The easy, slightly tired softness in his voice is replaced by a sharp edge.

"I ran into Thalora."

His chest tenses beneath my cheek. "Did you?"

"Yes."

"Is she alright?"

"She looked fantastic. But I think emotionally she's struggling." I peel myself away from my warm, comfortable spot to look at his face. "She's hurting right now. She wants you to hurt the same way. I think we should stay here."

"I have never sent the carnival on without me. I need to be here for them. I shield and protect them." He's still leaning back in the tub, his body relaxed, but there is an edge to his voice now.

"Who shields you? Who protects you, Shade?" My voice is harsher than I mean for it to be, but it seems he's dead set on doing exactly what he wants to do with no regard for me.

"Sasi–"

"No," I pull away. "I'm telling you that I think this is a bad idea, and you're blowing me off."

"I'm not blowing you off. I hear you." His darkness grabs me, keeping me from climbing out of the bathtub.

"This isn't fair." I jerk against it completely uselessly. "Let go of me."

"Never." He smiles.

I don't return the gesture.

"Don't be angry with me, Sasi." The darkness brings me toward him so he can take me in his arms.

"Don't disregard my concerns." I keep my eyes down. He can force my body, but he can't make me look at him.

He sighs and releases me. "I'm not disregarding your concerns. I know Thalora. She won't do anything to cause me serious harm."

"That is such a fuckboy thing to say." I climb out of the tub.

He laughs loudly. "Why?"

"It just is. Your narcissism is showing." I wrap myself in a robe, wincing when the material touches the bite on my neck. "You're forgetting that you publicly humiliated her. She's a woman scorned. You threw her out of her home and family."

"Come here, love. Let me take care of you." He stands, water running off his hard body.

"No, thank you."

He sits on the bed beside me. "I hear your concerns, but I don't want to leave them to fend for themselves. Especially without Thalora here. Without supervision, this carnival would turn into a nightmare quickly. We don't need to draw attention from the Light forces."

"So you're just a babysitter."

"Technically." He tugs at my hand. "Come here."

I let him pull me to stand between his legs.

"You're a brat." He runs his hands over my hips.

"I've always been honest about that."

He hums, pressing a soft kiss to the bite mark. I hiss but don't pull back.

"I wish I could bring him back and kill him again." He growls. "Who the fuck does he think he is, touching what's mine?"

"I tried to warn him." I lean into his touch, letting his lips ease the ache in my skin.

"Did you?"

Humming, my eyes flutter closed. "I told him I was spoken for."

The head of his cock presses into my stomach. "Can I bring you somewhere? I want to show you something."

"Right now?" I pout.

"I want you to see it. I promise, I'll fuck you half to death later."

"Promise?" I smile sweetly and let my robe slide down my shoulders.

"You'll have to beg me to stop."

"Fine." I dig around the wardrobe for something that matches my mood. I feel temperamental tonight, and I want it reflected in my clothes.

A little red dress with black beadwork catches my attention. The swirling pattern of the tiny crystal beads looks like Shade's darkness.

We'll be matchy. Gross.

I slip the dress on, running my fingers over the slightly sharp bumps.

Turning, I look at myself in the mirror. "What the fuck?" I gasp, stumbling forward toward the glass. The mark on my neck looks like a zombie bite from a gory horror movie.

The wound itself is much bigger than I thought, with black veins spreading under my skin.

"Am I still dying?"

"No, just that bit of flesh. It will heal." He wraps his arms around me. "Does it still hurt?"

"Yes. But it's manageable."

He kisses it again. Now that I'm aware of how truly disgusting it is, that small gesture feels like a much more grandiose act of love.

"Stop kissing it." I swat him away.

"Why?"

"Because it's rotting!"

He smiles, the sharp points of his teeth pressing into his lower lip. "I don't mind a little rot. Not from you."

"You're such a romantic."

Something shifts in his eyes, a flicker of recognition.

"Just for you." The playfulness is gone now.

Alarm bells and sirens. Flags and signs. Dangerous territory ahead!

"Where are you taking me?" I change the subject.

"Come see." He doesn't push further.

Gathering my hair, I arrange it over my shoulder to cover the monstrosity that will frighten small children and nauseate any adult who sees it.

We walk through the remnants of the carnival.

"It's sort of sad, isn't it?" I look at the litter on the ground.

"The leftovers?" He smiles, wrapping his arm around my waist.

"Yeah. It's like the memory is still here in the air, but the life has gone out of it." I kick a water bottle.

"I always like this part." He hums, his grip tightening slightly.

"The end?"

"No, the quiet."

We move in silence, enjoying the quiet. I didn't know I could like stillness so much.

He leads me through the streets, around corners, and down darkened alleys. Then to a bridge.

"Do you trust me?" His fingers brush over my neck, causing the wound to burn as he places his fingers on it.

"Yes."

"Jump."

"Off the bridge?"

"Yes, feet first, right into the circle of light."

Holding the railing, I lean over and look down at the black water. There is a beam of light inexplicably cutting through the dark.

"Help me up?" I tug at my short skirt.

"Of course." He picks me up, setting my feet on the ledge.

"Are you coming too?"

"Right behind you."

I jump off the ledge, pointing my toes as I aim for the light.

The water engulfs me and then disappears. I'm beneath the surface, but it's like I'm in a bubble. I sink down to the bottom of the river, my feet landing on dry dirt.

Just a moment behind me, he appears in a swirling coil of darkness.

"Where are we?"

"I'm taking you to The Memory."

"The memory of what?" A black circus tent appears in the distance.

"You'll see."

We walk along the bottom of the river, the water above us casting rippling shadows on the ground.

The tent is dusty and abandoned. It doesn't look like anything special.

He unties the flaps, holding one side open for me to walk in.

The inside looks nothing like the outside. The crumbling tent holds magic inside. It's like stepping into a mirror. My reflection is fractured, breaking into pieces and surrounding us.

I see myself, my life, spread out before me.

"That's my tenth birthday." I touch the glass, and it ripples, changing into something else.

I walk deeper in, watching my younger self.

Memory after memory, I look back on my life. Some are good, some are not. Others, I'm not sure actually happened.

Is this my mind?

I'm not afraid. There isn't anything frightening about it.

I watch as I creep away, separating myself from the birthday party happening in the backyard, to creep into the master closet. The day I stole my first watch. I remember the rush of adrenaline and the pride I felt. No one suspected a thing.

"What is this?" He calls from further in.

He's watching me in my childhood bedroom. I'm sitting on my bed, in a frilly pink dress with bows in my hair. The picture of innocence.

But sitting beside me was a creature, a thing so vile and disgusting it looks like it was dug out of a grave after several days of decomposing.

"Oh, that's Henri." I almost forgot about him.

"And what exactly is your connection to Henri?"

"He was my imaginary friend, I guess. I've always been fairly certain he was real. He was a violent little guy, but he was nice to me."

A smile tugs at his lips. "He's very real. He never hurt you?"

"No." I think back on our adventures fondly. "He protected me."

"My wicked little darling. So lovely, even an imp couldn't harm you." He pulls me into his arms, pressing a kiss to my hair.

"An imp?"

"Horrible little beasts." He shudders.

"Well, he was sweet," I shrug.

We walk, my back to his chest, perusing my life.

"Whose funeral was this?" He stops, watching the group of black-clad mourners standing around a hole in the ground.

"I'm not sure. I've only been to a few funerals, though. It might have been my grandmother." I scan the crowd. "Oh, no, there she is." I point her out. "This must be my grandfather."

"You're smiling." He chuckles.

"No, I'm not!" I squint to see my face. "Oh, shit. I am."

"Were you pleased by his death?"

"No, not pleased. I didn't really feel anything. He meant nothing to me. He was from the generation that believed children should not be heard. I probably spoke three words to him in the ten years we had together."

"Then why smile?"

"I remember thinking it was funny." I hum. "Not his death, but the funeral. He was my fathers, father. They hated each other, and everyone knew it. But my dad gave a speech about what a strong man he was and a bunch of other bullshit. It's all so fake and ridiculous."

"Grief is a performance, most of the time." He always seems to know exactly how I feel.

"Why are we only seeing my memories? Don't you have any?" I spin around to hug his waist.

"Are you sure you want to see mine? They are quite dreadful." His handsome face flickers with something I've never seen from him before.

"Shade!" I gasp. "Are you nervous?"

"No." He clears his throat and stands taller, but it's too late.

"Show me." I come up on my toes, grazing his lips with mine. "Let me see everything."

The tent gets dark and cold. There is a weight in the air that wasn't there just a second before.

In the mirrors, there are flickers, fire, and shadow. He's standing before a burning village, people scream, running out of buildings as they collapse. There are bodies in the mud. It's chaos.

His arms are outstretched, darkness flows from his open mouth, his eyes, his nose, his ears. He is raw power.

The darkness sweeps through like a breeze, killing everything it touches. People fall where they stand, their spirits rising from their lifeless bodies to join the dark.

I step closer, watching the mess. "What did it feel like?"

"In my younger years, I didn't have the same control I do now." He steps beside me, his eyes darting over the madness he caused. "It felt like vengeance. It felt good. But it came at a cost. Everything does."

Reaching out, I'm drawn to the mirror.

I touch him, and he shivers. A single finger on his forehead. It's like a glitch. I see into him, past the skin, into his soul. It's dark and lonely. Frost spreads from my finger up my arm and through my whole body. It's the coldest kind of cold, sinking into my bones, freezing my blood.

I press harder.

He gasps behind me.

There is a flicker. Then he starts to peel away. Layer by layer. Taller, like a shadow, endless and reaching.

There are eyes everywhere. Some blink, some stare blankly. They see through my skin.

His skin ripples like water, shiny and black like oil.

I see death and fear, war and greed, the worst of us, reflected in his skin.

My breath stutters in my chest as I study him. I don't want to miss anything.

His darkness moves like tentacles floating around us.

"Is this your real face?" I run my finger down from his forehead to his lips. Rows of razor-sharp teeth glint when he smiles.

"Yes."

CHAPTER TWENTY-SIX

the umbramancer

SPINNING AROUND, I look up at his face. He's watching me so intensely that it makes me shiver.

I step toward him. "Can I see you?"

Darkness coils around my wrists like chains, holding me too tightly.

"You think you can handle it?" His head tilts to one side.

I nod, I know I can.

His eyes go dark, pitch black as he starts to shift. It's slow, not a sudden change. It creeps, morphing him into this thing. The Umbramancer. In the flesh.

A gust of icy wind blows through the tent, his darkness rushes forward, surging like fog rolling on the ocean. It hits me, and I feel it in my lungs–him. He's coursing through me, touching everything he can along the way.

He moves slowly toward me, like a predator about to devour me. I feel so small in front of him.

Excitement rolls over my skin as he finally gets close enough to touch.

"You're not afraid?" His voice is lower, deeper, it's all strength and power. Velvet and thunder.

"No." I shake my head, but my bones tremble.

All the eyes blink at once, a slow, lazy lust that is deceptively calm. I know he's not going to be this calm the whole time.

"Get on your knees."

I kneel down in front of him, panting already.

He walks around me, letting darkness graze my back. My dress falls open, drooping down, exposing my skin.

"There she is." He sweeps over me. "I have never set my eyes on a more perfect creature."

The weight of his eyes, all of them, on me at once makes my breath hitch.

Then it starts. Slow at first.

From inside my body, a swirling, churning pressure builds right between my legs.

Gasping, I lean forward, holding myself up with my hands. I brace, waiting for the impact of whatever this is.

It vibrates. From the inside.

"Oh, holy fuck! What is that?" I moan, the muscles in my stomach and thighs spasming. He's everywhere at once, spread to the farthest reaches of my mind. It's more than physical.

My eyes pinch closed as I breathe against the pleasure so intense it borders on pain.

I have no control. I can't move. I can't stop it.

"Umbramancer!" I scream as tears stream down my face.

Colors I've never seen before burst before my eyes. I'm suspended in a void between heaven and hell, watching as the world bends around me.

A cathedral of glass and bone ripples like water, and the doors burst open. Angels with hollow faces pour out and take to the air. They cry, black tears that hit my skin, each one a tiny tingling zap that makes my body writhe against invisible restraints.

I think I'm screaming.

A garden grows down from the sky, the vines twisting around me, reaching in.

Over and over again, my body gives in to the raw, savage pleasure that he's forcing into me.

I'm clay in his hands. He's breaking me down and rebuilding me.

His voice echoes in my head, soft and soothing. He encourages me.

He's behind me now, physically. My mind is still scattered in the wind, moving in whatever direction he demands.

His hands come down on top of mine, his chest to my back. He engulfs me. Now, physically, mentally, and metaphysically, he is everywhere. There is no part of me that is secret or safe. He has invaded.

He slips between my legs.

It's different.

It's bigger. Harder. Notches rub places that I didn't know existed.

My mouth is moving, words with no meaning spill from my lips, a language that he understands, but I don't.

"You're fucking amazing." A hand here, a tendril of darkness there. He's everywhere. "You just have to take it. Don't fight it. Let me all the way in."

He pushes forward. More. Deeper.

With stars in my eyes, I take a breath and release it slowly. "Take everything." It's the last coherent thing in my brain. Complete surrender.

I'm scared. This is too vulnerable. Too full of trust. Too open.

He groans. It crackles like fire as he wraps around me, holding me up.

"My Sasi. You're the only one."

I open my mouth to respond, but I can't. My voice is lost in the darkness.

"I know, love." He caresses my face. "I know."

Everything is open. It pours out of me. I can't contain it, and I don't want to. I know it's safe in his arms. Even if that scares the absolute shit out of me, I know it's true.

"What do you need, my love?" He asks before the need even occurs in my brain.

"I want to see your face."

"Come here," he lifts me effortlessly, turning me to face him.

Reaching out with trembling hands, I touch him. It's still him. If I look closely, I see it. He's in there.

"She looks into the eyes of the beast and doesn't blink." His voice is different, deep and booming. It echoes, the words coming from somewhere else and landing here. It's seductive and threatening.

I'm helpless in his darkness, held open.

Holding his face, I burn in the heat of his gaze, but I won't look away. I want to feel all of it.

I expect violence, but it's not. It's rough. But he isn't hurting me, not physically. I'm overwhelmed by the rawness–the purity.

This feels like the only true thing in the world. In this realm or any other.

He's showing himself to me and taking all I am in return. It's his essence, the part he hides–the raw, unfiltered, beautiful truth.

I thought we were united before, but the drugs in my system corrupted that. This is a thing apart.

"Reach in." His voice vibrates around me.

Somehow, I know exactly what that means. Without questioning it, I reach my hand forward, pressing it into his chest. It gives. The skin swallows my hand, pulling it inside.

The universe spreads out before me, and we fade away, dissolved into stardust and magic.

The deep bruised purples and electric blues of the galaxy shimmer with stars as his heart beats against my hand.

"You could rip me to shreds. You could crush it–break it." His eyes, all of them, blink among the stars, surrounding me.

"I won't."

"I know."

I can't say the words out loud. But he could, too. His hands aren't in my chest, but he's still holding my heart. If he wanted to, he could tear it apart.

Unlike before, this time, the climb is slow. It builds, brick by brick. A trickle.

My body morphs into his. He holds me. My hand explores and touches, feeling things I shouldn't, but he lets me.

He moves inside of me, in my blood, in the air I breathe.

I think we might be a shooting star. All around us, the atmosphere bursts into brightly colored explosions.

"I've searched the world for you, Sasi. Centuries burned to ash. Time moved with no meaning. I didn't think I would ever find you."

His voice isn't audible. It's inside of me. I hear it like a thought in my brain.

"I had given up hope." The reverence in his voice warms my skin. "I didn't even know I was looking for you. I'm going to bring you everywhere–show you everything."

Higher and higher. My mind frays at the edges.

Everything builds, forcing me into him, holding me open, exposing me. I can't hide anything. It's a tidal wave with nothing to crash against but him.

This is a reckoning. I don't know that I ever really believed in souls until this moment, not as a real, tangible thing anyway. But they're here, right before my eyes–his and mine, mixing, fusing, bound together.

"Don't try to hide it from me," He coaxes. "I want to see it. I want everything about you. The good, the broken, and the brutal. You are perfect in my eyes."

I arch toward him, my bones reaching out.

"Yes." He hums.

My blood boils–it sings, it screams– my lungs seize. I think I might actually be dying, here and now, but I don't want to stop.

"Give it to me." He whispers in the dark.

"Take it!" My voice sounds far away, like it's surrounding us. It's part of the vastness of space.

He doesn't need to be told twice. He takes it all, leaving nothing left.

If this is what death feels like–if this is the end–I welcome it. Euphoria.

He grows. The oil slick skin of his monstrous form, swelling our shadows spread across the ground, growing larger, moving. We're as infinite as the sky. We are the storm. We're a myth that will be whispered in dark corners forever.

He consumes me. And I consume him.

By the end, we're trembling ruins, just fragments of ourselves.

"How?" I whimper.

"Mine forever." He hums.

I think I love him. All the cruel, crooked pieces. They belong to me now.

CHAPTER TWENTY-SEVEN
flying

I'M in a strange place between consciousness and sleep. I know what's going on around me. I can feel and hear, but I can't pull myself out of it. My eyelids are heavy, and my tongue is made of lead.

I know I'm not alone, though. I can feel him beside me. His skin is cool against my back.

I have questions.

Last night, I was too caught up in the moment to ask them. But now I want answers.

He hums, a tired laugh rumbling in his chest as he pulls me into him.

"I knew I wouldn't escape unscathed. What do you want to know?"

"So, you're inside my head?" I try to open my eyes, but they're still too tired.

"Yes. And you're in mine." He sounds peaceful.

"Is that your real form?"

"No," he pauses. "It's difficult to explain. That was my spirit. That is what I look like in the spirit realm. Here, in this realm, I look like this. My body isn't a mask."

"When we got there, were you hiding? Using it as a mask to keep me from seeing what your soul looks like?"

"Yes." He tightens around me. "I don't show people that part of me. It's vulnerable."

"Is it?" That surprises me. "It didn't seem weak."

"I didn't say weak." There is a smile in his voice. "I said vulnerable."

"Thank you for showing me."

"Thank you for not running away."

"You could have run too, you know? You saw my bad parts in the reflection of those memories." I force my body to move, rolling so that I can rest my head on his chest.

"Those are my favorite parts of you. Raw and honest. You never cease to surprise me, Sasi."

I force my eyes open, desperate to look at his face. "You know, you're pretty romantic for a monster."

"A monster?" His head drops back as he laughs.

"Are we in Morocco?" I look out the window at the water. Forcing myself away, I climb out of bed and sit on the edge of the bath. Some distance between us is good.

"Yes."

I hum but don't respond. I made my feelings clear. Whatever happens here is his problem to deal with.

"I want to take you somewhere tonight, right at dusk." He pushes past my obvious irritation, ignoring it the same way he's ignoring my warning.

"Something to show me?" I adjust the water, warming it up for a bath.

"Always."

"What is it this time? The Cave of Wonders?"

"The what?" He looks at me like I'm crazy.

"Aw, that's not an actual place? I was hoping it would be."

Stepping into the bathtub, I sit in the water as it starts to fill. Pouring soap into my hand, I rub it into a lather.

"Stop staring at me." I run the soap over my neck and shoulder, wincing slightly.

"Never." He drops his pants and steps forward. "Let me wash it for you."

"You just want to touch my rotting skin, you freak."

He runs his tongue over his sharp teeth. "I don't deny it."

I slide forward, making space behind me. He slips in, pulling my back flush against his chest. His fingers move up my arm, touching the bite mark carefully.

"It's healing." He hums, leaning in to kiss it.

"Where are you taking me?" I rest my head on his chest. "A den of vipers? A haunted asylum? A shipwreck?"

His chest rumbles beneath me. "Next time. Tonight we venture into the desert."

"And what wonders await?"

"You'll see. Wear something breezy."

Letting my eyes flutter closed, I rest against his body. The warm water and his presence lull me to sleep. I just woke up, but my body feels heavy and weak.

It feels like a single second that I let myself drift, but when I open my eyes again, I'm alone in the dark. The room is quiet. I'm wrapped in a blanket, tucked into bed by myself.

Outside, the carnival is in full-swing. The lights twinkle against the black sky.

There is a sheer red dress hanging on the wardrobe door. Smiling, I pull it on. Breezy.

As I step in front of the mirror to fix my hair, something catches my eye.

It's a mask. A golden mandible with diamonds in the teeth. It's similar to his, but unique in its own way. Smaller. Like it's meant to fit someone else.

Me.

Lifting it to my mouth, I secure it beneath my hair.

Without bothering to find shoes, I rush out of the car to find him.

It doesn't take long for his voice to float toward me in the breeze. I run into the tent, my eyes landing on him immediately. At the top of the tent on a platform.

He tips his hat and winks before jumping, soaring toward the ground. The crowd gasps, everyone in the tent holding their breath together.

He lands in a roll, ending up on his feet in front of me.

His arms wrap around me, his forehead meeting mine. "You look delicious."

"I love the mask."

"It suits you, my wicked darling. Are you ready to go?"

"Yes."

He carries me like a princess through the crowds, the seas parting around us like we're royalty.

The desert feels like a living thing. I feel it breathing beneath my bare feet. The sand has a heartbeat.

"Welcome to the Erg Chebbi." He spins me in the sand. It looks like a sea of melted gold in the moonlight. Endless hills of sand that curve, rising and falling beneath the stars, as far as I can see in every direction.

He leads me deeper, our footsteps erased by the breeze. It's like we are the only people left in the world. Just us.

"Can you hear it?" He whispers, closing his eyes as he listens.

"Hear what?"

"The desert dreaming."

A shiver runs down my spine as I close my eyes. I do hear something. A soft hum. The sand shifts around us, warm against my ankles.

"This is incredible." He spins me, the stars swirling above us.

We slide in the sand; the dune giving way beneath our feet. At the bottom of the hill, I sit, resting my back against the incline we slid from.

"This is nice."

"It feels like we're truly alone, doesn't it?" He leans back beside me.

"A lot of the places you take me are like this. Magical but lonely."

He hums, his jaw clenching.

"Uh oh, did I hit a nerve?" I roll onto my side to face him.

"Before you, I spent most of my time alone. I liked it that way."

"And now?" I pull the mask off, setting it in my lap.

"I still like to be alone, just with you."

"I think you need a refresher on the definition of alone." I stare up at the stars. Shifting my body in the sand, I let myself sink in slightly.

But then the sand moves on its own. I'm perfectly still, but the sand isn't.

It brushes my ankle.

Then higher up my calf.

The touch is firmer now.

The sand is now a tiny hand on a thin arm. It's moving up my leg. Another hand, then another and another move, touching me.

"Whoa, what the fuck?" I brush it away. "I'm sure you're lovely, but I don't want sand in… places."

"Look but don't touch." Shade's stern voice is all it takes to make it, whatever it is, retreat. "It seems no one can help themselves around you." He rolls over on top of me, rubbing himself between my legs.

The darkness curls around us, lifting us from the ground. As we rise in the air, the wind whips around us. My hair blows in every direction, wild and free. My head falls back, a mixture of a laugh and a moan in my throat as he kisses my neck.

Clouds roll in, blocking out the light from the stars.

There is a crack, then a flash of white light. Just as thunder booms all around us, the sky opens up. Warm summer rain soaks through my dress in a second.

His darkness is all over me, moving like hands on my body.

"Only I can touch you." He growls, scraping his teeth over my skin. The possessiveness of his tone makes my stomach clench, and my thighs squeeze together. "Say it."

"Only you can touch me."

"Yes."

We fall, hurtling toward the ground. Like on a rollercoaster, my heart is in my throat as I scream and laugh. Just before we hit the ground, he turns us. It's as if we're gliding over the sand.

The storm builds, raindrops pelting our skin. The world is a blur.

Up and down, upside down and sideways, we fly.

It's magic and chaos. I can't catch my breath.

"Higher?" He smiles against my lips.

"Higher!"

He doesn't hesitate. In five seconds flat, we're so high above the ground it's lost below the clouds.

Laughter pours out of me. I've never felt so truly free.

"I never want to go back down!"

He smoothes my hair back, holding my face in his hands while the darkness wraps around me, holding me up. Something flashes in his eyes. It's deep and endless. Sorrow.

"Shade?" I touch his cheeks.

His eyes pinch closed, and he lets out a sound that aches in my soul. It vibrates in my ribs and crushes my lungs.

"What's the matter? What happened?"

"Do you trust me, Sasi?" His lips tug up into a sad smile.

"Yes."

"Do you want to feel what it's like to fly?" His voice is low, wrapping around my heart and squeezing.

"Yes."

He drops me. My body slips through the air. Gravity takes me. I gasp against the wind and spread my arms wide.

I fall through the clouds. The sand glitters below me, approaching faster and faster.

There isn't even a moment of fear.

The sand is so close now that I can see it shifting in the wind.

Then, impact.

But it's not mine.

My body jerks, and I gasp. He lands hard on his feet, with me in his arms.

His lips are on mine before I have time to take a breath. I don't need it anyway.

"Let's go back to the carnival." He only pulls away enough to speak, then his mouth is back in mine.

I nod, wrapping my arms around his neck.

The sadness from his expression before keeps popping into my head. The picture of his grief and pain still aches.

What is he grieving? What did he lose?

I'm weightless in his arms as he brings me home. The train comes into view in the distance, glowing on the dark horizon.

"Umbramancer!" A voice reaches us. "Thalora is here. She's looking for you!" There is a tightness in it. Fear. It makes me afraid.

"Wait right here." He sets me down. "I'll be back for you. Stay here, Sasi."

He looks like he doesn't believe I will be here when he returns.

"Fine." I cross my arms. Even I'm not sure I believe it.

As he walks away, he keeps looking back over his shoulder.

I sit on a stone wall looking out over the Straight of Gibraltar. A snake slithers across the ground. Stopping at my feet.

"He said he'd be back," I tell it as it coils up beside me to wait.

CHAPTER TWENTY-EIGHT
prince charming

MINUTES PASS, and I feel my irritation growing by the second. My stomach feels hot, and I'm starting to sigh and bounce my knee. What the fuck?

I'm naturally a very impatient person. It's who I am. It's woven into my DNA.

But this is ridiculous. The snake looks at me like it understands–his beady little black eyes meet mine, then he slithers away, leaving me waiting alone. It's like he was mocking me. He didn't have to stay here, but I did. And to punctuate that, he left.

There is a loud bang in the dark, followed quickly by a scream. It cracks through the air like a gunshot.

My spine stiffens, and I look around frantically for the source of the sounds.

Fear burns in my chest as I jump to my feet. Something is wrong. Not in the general sense, I'm in trouble.

A thud from behind me catches my attention.

I twist around. Someone has a ladder against the wall I'm sitting on. There are people crawling up the wall. What is this? What's happening? It feels like a medieval castle siege or something.

I move to run, but someone grabs me tightly.

"Let go!" I thrash wildly, kicking my legs as they lift me off my feet.

"Stop struggling!" A man grunts as I plant my elbow in his ribcage as hard as I can manage.

"Fuck you!" I scream, trying my elbow again.

He throws me over his shoulder and steps onto the ladder. My options are limited here. If I fight him and we fall, I die too.

He curses under his breath, adjusting my weight so that we don't fall to our deaths.

"Let me go, asshole!" I watch the rocks below us get closer. As soon as he reaches the bottom, I'm going to make a break for it.

He picked the wrong one. I'm not going down without a fight.

His feet land on the gravelly beach with a crunch. That's my cue. I kick my legs as hard as I can.

When he doubles over, I roll, falling from his shoulder to the ground.

"Damn it, woman." He growls, hobbling after me.

"Shade!" I scream as loudly as I can. "Shade!"

"Stop struggling!" He shouts, pulling me into an airplane hovering over the water.

"No! Let me go, motherfucker!" I rear my head back into his face. The way his nose crunches is satisfying.

"Fuck!" He roars, dropping me onto the floor. Blood immediately pours from him. Good.

I scramble toward the door, but it's too late. It's closing, and we're lifting above the water.

"Sit down." Another man steps in, giving the other some time to tend to his bloody nose. "We're rescuing you, damn it."

I freeze, spinning around. "Rescuing me? From what?" I glare at them, my chest heaving.

The ground disappears beneath us, and we whizz through the air just a bit too quickly.

"Are you guys human?" I look at them.

They exchange surprised glances but don't answer my question.

Annoyed and out of breath, I sit in one of the seats, staring out the panoramic windshield. It's just darkness, like when the night train travels through the spirit realm.

I think that's where we are.

The lonely spirit highway in the void.

The journey to wherever we are is a short one. We slow between two mountains, dropping down toward the ground over a thick canopy of trees.

"Please don't make this difficult." One of them stands. He's eyeing me warily, like he's afraid of me. "We're going to take you down."

"Yeah, you clearly don't know me. Difficult is my middle name." I smile sweetly.

"Just come here." He snarls, lunging to get me.

I try to yank my arm back, but he grabs hold of me tightly and pulls me up to his chest.

He throws me over his shoulder like a rag doll and jumps out of the side of the plane like a fucking Green Beret.

We land on the ground, and he rushes me into a metal tunnel.

"Get the fuck off!" I ball up my fists and hit his lower back until he's annoyed enough to put me down.

"You are–" He starts to yell, pointing his finger in my face.

"Our guest." A voice rings out, pinging off the metal surrounding us. It's stern and commanding. It makes the man stop immediately.

"Sorry, sir." He drops his finger and rolls his shoulders back.

"I'll take her up from here." He smiles at me.

God damn. He is…

Everything about him is the opposite of Shade. Where he is all dark and broody, this guy is like his light equivalent. Tall, blond, and handsome with pale blue eyes.

"And who might you be?" I bat my lashes.

"I'm Gordon Livingston. The head of the Light forgers."

"A Light forger?" I roll my lips into my mouth to swallow down the laugh that wants to escape. "Really?" I accidentally snort.

"What?" He frowns, obviously offended.

"I don't know. Light forger? That's kind of stupid."

He narrows his eyes. "I'm a paladin in charge of keeping dark forces at bay."

Yeah, he's definitely hot in a goody two-shoes, teacher's pet, Prince Charming kind of way.

"And what exactly do you want with me, Lightforger Gordon?"

"We're rescuing you." He looks shocked.

"From what?"

His pretty mouth falls open as he sputters, unable to form a response.

"You kidnapped me." I cross my arms as we step out of the unbelievable into a huge cave.

"We did not! We were saving you!"

"I didn't need saving."

The cave is set up like an office. Rows of people are running around like a NASA control room, and computers and monitors are everywhere.

"You were—"

"What is this place?" I look at the people scurrying around, rushing between consoles. Everyone seems so busy.

"Our headquarters." He's looking at me like I'm an alien. "What do you mean you didn't need saving? You were—"

"I wasn't being held hostage. I was exactly where I wanted to be."

"You wanted to be with them? They're evil beings. They leave death and tragedy in their wake. We've been following them around the world, waiting for the opportunity to take them down."

"Take them down? Did you hurt anyone? Did you hurt Shade?" Bile rises in my throat. "The Unbramancer! Did you hurt him?"

He doesn't say anything for several seconds. I broke him. He can't make heads or tails of me.

Ordinarily, this would please me. But right now, I want information out of him.

"Did you hurt him?" I almost grab him and shake him. If he doesn't start answering my questions, I'll swing on him. My patience is always very thin, but right now it's nonexistent.

"You're worried about the Umbramancer"

"Of course, I am! He's my—"

"This is worse than I thought. Come with me." He starts to take a step forward, but stops. "I'm going to need you to give me that necklace."

I cover it up, my instinct to protect it.

"It's a key. He'll be able to use it to get to you."

Which is exactly why I want to keep it.

For a moment, we're in a standoff. He has his hand outstretched, palm open, waiting.

And I'm not making any moves to lose my necklace.

"This was a gift."

"You can't have it here."

"Then, I'll be going."

He frowns and stares me down.

"Fine." I unclasp it carefully and place it in his hand.

"Thank you, let's go." He leads me to an elevator that looks like it will take us into the heart of the mountain. The glass tube disappears into the rock and continues on forever.

"I would like to be released." I fold my arms over my chest and tap my toe impatiently.

"Just listen to what I have to say first. I promise, you're going to want to stay after you hear it."

I highly doubt that.

When we step out of the elevator, we're in a metal hallway. It's not the same as the tunnel. It's spacious, just heavily armed. A fortress of steel.

He leads me to a door with two guards in full riot gear standing at attention on either side. He looks at me, then turns his body to shield the keypad as he punches in the code.

Ew. I don't care how hot he is. Gross. I can never unsee that.

I follow him into the room, a huge window looks out over a waterfall that feeds into a crystal blue lake running into the valley between the mountains we landed between.

"I'm going to show you something that is going to upset you. I need you to know that you're safe."

"I was never unsafe." I don't try to hide my eyes rolling.

"You have no idea just how wrong you are." He pulls out a chair. "Please, sit."

CHAPTER TWENTY-NINE

real & true

"I'LL STAND."

He sighs and sits in another seat.

I could have just taken the seat to appease him, but I'm not that kind of girl. He should know that going in.

"The group you have been traveling with is dangerous." He says carefully. He's acting like I don't already know, like he's breaking some news to me that is going to send me into a spiral.

Dangerous? The understatement of the century.

I don't respond.

"I don't know what lies you've been told, but you aren't safe with them." He spins a laptop around, turning the screen in my direction. "This isn't even half of it." He scrolls through several pages that don't mean anything to me. It looks like data: dates, times, locations. A spreadsheet of wrongdoing. "This is a list of crimes–theft, assaults, drug overdoses, mysterious deaths–all occurring in the hours of the carnival's presence."

I'm not impressed with his statistics. Any idiot can add words to a page.

When he doesn't get the reaction he's hoping for, he clicks to a different screen. The picture grabs my attention.

Leaning in, I study the ancient-looking illustration. It looks like something from one of Shade's books. It's old and grainy. But the essence of the image is clear as day.

Shit.

"Do you recognize this?"

"It's Shade." I nod. I would know him anywhere. It's more than just his physical looks; it's his spirit. I recognize it.

"Can you see what he's doing?" He's gentle, coaxing.

"I can't make it out." I lie. It's grainy, but I would recognize him anywhere.

He increases the size. The picture takes up the whole screen. I wish he hadn't done that.

My breath catches. A figure–Shade–is standing over a limp woman. She's sprawled out on the ground beneath the shade of a tree. Her chest is open, not torn but split like it burst from the inside. He's cradling her heart in his hands. It's not symbolic or romantic. It's real. Bleeding and horrifying.

I blink, trying to understand.

"It's real." Gordon's voice is low. "This is from an ancient text. We've run it through every verification process. It hasn't been doctored or altered in any way."

I shake my head. I'm not understanding what this is supposed to mean. So, he cut someone's heart out. What does that mean with regard to me?

Maybe I'm a cold-hearted bitch, but I don't see why I'm supposed to care about this.

"He has been grooming you." He slides a printed copy of the picture across the table.

"No."

"Yes." He nods.

"For what?" I feel the warmth of impatience bloom in my chest.

"Your heart. He needs it."

Narrowing my eyes, I wait for him to continue.

"He needs your heart. Given willingly." He continues.

"I gave him my heart."

"No," he shakes his head sadly. "You gave him love. He needs your heart, literally. He needs to take it out of your chest and place it in his own."

"Bullshit."

"I know it seems impossible, but this is magic we're talking about. Dark magic. It doesn't have to follow the rules of the human realm."

I cross my arms over my chest. "So, you're saying he's been grooming me to kill myself for him?"

"Not exactly." He opens another window. "From what we can gather, he has attempted this before, but the heart is never given willingly. If he takes the heart by force, it doesn't last. If the heart is given willingly, he will have unconditional immortality. And his power will grow."

"That fucking lying rat bastard!" White hot rage boils in my blood. "He's tried to get other hearts?"

"Wait..."

"Oh, when I see him again!" I pace around the table. I start plotting the ways I can make him suffer.

"You're mad that he's taken other hearts, not mad that he's been lying to you?" His brow furrows.

Jealousy–green and bitter–rises like bile in my throat. "No, I'm fucking furious that he lied! He told me I was the only one. Special." That motherfucker.

"He told you that he needed your heart?" He is having a hard time keeping up.

"No!" I throw my hands in the air. "He told me it was about blood! He needed blood and to take from my essence. I gave him that willingly. Now, I'm hearing that not only was that not true but that he's done this with other women?"

He doesn't speak. A look of absolute dumbfounded bewilderment has taken over his face.

"So these other women, they didn't give him their hearts willingly?" I tap my toes, trying to regain control of my rage.

"No," he says slowly.

"I want to talk to him." I roll my shoulders back.

"No." He immediately shoots it down.

"No?" I'm momentarily shocked.

"I can't allow that."

"I'm not asking your permission." I huff. "I need to talk to him."

"We can't risk it."

"What if I promise not to give it to him?"

"There is still too much risk, Sasi. He's very persuasive and patient."

I bite back the urge to throw hands. "I just said I won't give it to him. I'm not going to be persuaded. And I'm offended that you think I could be."

"He could decide just to take it. It won't last forever, but it's better than nothing." He shakes his head.

There is a silence, a pause, that passes between us.

"If he has a heart, he's more powerful–regardless of how he received it." His voice is softer. He's trying a different approach. Good cop, or whatever. "We can't let him get too powerful, Sasi. That would be bad for everyone. As it stands now, he is manageable. We can't let him become invincible."

How am I going to play this? I don't care what he's saying; I want to talk to Shade.

"Won't he come after me?"

"I'm sure he will. But we can protect you." He looks so arrogantly sure of himself.

"But I can't leave?" I tilt my head, studying his reaction. "I'm a prisoner here?"

"No." His brows shoot up into his hairline. "You're not a prisoner. You're here for your own protection!"

I hum, looking over the papers again. I smell his bullshit from a mile away. "Why haven't you killed him?"

"What?"

"If he's so dangerous. Why haven't you killed him yet? What are you waiting for?"

"We can't just kill him. It's more delicate than that. He is darkness. We are light. Balance between us is the most important thing. Without darkness, light is weaker. We don't want to completely eliminate the dark. Killing him would cause a ripple through the realms; it would be felt everywhere. If we take that step, we have to know that it's worth it."

"Interesting."

"There are still safeguards. There is a sword that is bound to him, created from his own blood. If he has that–then we would be really worried."

I roll my lips into my mouth to hold back a laugh. Should I tell him?

I'll hold on to that little tidbit, at least for now. It may come in handy later on. If information is currency, I consider that piece of knowledge a pretty sizable wad of cash. I'm not giving it away for free.

My body feels tired. Sliding into the seat he originally offered me, I stare at the information.

There is no way he's been lying about everything. I can't believe that is true. He saved me. He gave me a part of himself to keep me alive.

Possibly in the way we feed cattle, so we can slaughter them later.

Leaning forward, I rest my chin on my hand.

Something weird and sad weighs on my chest. I don't like this at all. I have to talk to him. His eyes will tell me everything I need to know. Once I see him, I'll know what to do next.

I'm not going to take Pretty Boy's word for it. He's probably a liar, too. He is a man after all.

I just need to figure out how. This place seems pretty well guarded.

I don't have the necklace anymore, but I still feel it on my neck like a heavy chain.

"Come with me." He stands suddenly. "I'll show you to your room. I'm sure this is a lot to take in."

A lot to take in? Is he serious?

I don't want to be shown to a room. But without any other option, I stand and follow him.

This place is a maze. I have an unnaturally attuned sense of direction, and even I can't figure this out. I'll never get out of here without someone helping me.

But I will find a way out of here. If it kills me.

CHAPTER THIRTY

it's back

THE MORE I think about it, the angrier I feel. I can't sit still. Pacing around my room, I let it fester and eat at me. Fucking Gordon.

And Shade.

And Thalora.

Fuck all of them.

Devious plans pop into my head. The things I could do to him. The ways I can make him pay.

I don't want revenge. I want justice. He fucked with the wrong woman. And he needs to know it.

Now, I am the woman scorned. And I won't go quietly. I want him to feel it.

I want him to bleed in the dark. He thinks he can lie to me and get away with it?

I'm going to burn his world to the ground.

He's taken other hearts?

My fingers twitch at my sides. I feel violent. It's in my veins.

"He's taken other hearts," I growl. The thought fills me with a jealousy so violent it makes my hands tremble.

"I can't believe you're focusing on that." Gordon gasps.

Spinning around, I scowl at him. I forgot he was here. "He's a lying, manipulative asshole!"

"Right, but–"

"And that pisses me off, Gordon." I point my finger in his direction, the volume of my voice rising with each word. "It's the betrayal. He and I were supposed to have something special. Something different. Turns out, it's exactly the same. He's the same as every other fuckboy!"

I need an outlet. I want to destroy something.

He pinches the bridge of his nose and takes a breath. "He's planning to kill you, Sasi."

"Technically," I grit my teeth, "he will only kill me if I don't give him to heart. If I gave it to him willingly, that would be consensual organ donation."

"What?" He looks bewildered again.

"That seems like a loophole." I shrug.

"You are–" he shakes his head, letting his voice fade instead of speaking whatever insult is on his tongue.

"I'm what?" I tap my toes. I'm in the mood to fight. He's the unlucky man standing in front of me, so my ire, whether he deserves it or not, is directed at him.

"I was going to say insufferable."

"And you're boring."

"I can see why he picked you." He rubs his hands over his face.

"Thank you."

"That wasn't a compliment."

"Well, I can take it however I choose." I roll my eyes.

He doesn't answer. Instead, he drops his head back and looks at the ceiling.

The walls of the place are so white. There is no color, no darkness, nothing to look at. These fucking light bringers are so straight-laced. All beige and morally superior.

"You're focusing on the wrong things here." He tries his futile attempt again. "It's not about the other women."

He has no idea what he's talking about.

"To me, that's all it's about."

"He is planning to kill you!" He yells, ripping at his hair.

"And that is less egregious than the fucking lie!" I shout back.

He closes his eyes and takes a slow breath. I think I've finally shut him up.

The itch is back.

It starts in my spine and moves up to the base of my neck.

My fingers, my ribs–everything twitches. My skin crawls.

It's been gone for so long, I almost forgot it. Shade buried it. He forced it into hiding. But now it's back.

And it's pissed.

It wants blood, too. And this time, I'm not going to hold back.

"You should rest." Gordon stands to leave. Finally. He's a hover-er. Just as I think I'm free of him, he stops, turning back to look at me. "I know that was hard to hear."

He's waiting now, like he expects me to say something.

His eyes are full of pity, which only makes me angrier. I don't want to be pitied.

"Right." I nod, looking at the door and hoping he'll walk through it.

"Right." He puts his hand on the doorknob but doesn't actually open the door. "If you need—"

"Jesus Christ! Get the fuck out of here!" I'm about to shove him out the door.

"Sorry!" He lifts his hands and leaves.

I don't miss the sound of the lock clicking. I assumed he would lock me in, but it's still irritating that he did it.

Now that I'm finally alone, I drop onto the bed and stare at the ceiling. My limbs feel heavy, and my lungs hurt.

Everything is quiet except for the screaming in my head.

This fucking sucks.

I can't cry. There aren't any tears. I don't feel sad. It's beyond sadness. This is the aftermath of a soul being torn apart. It's hollow. There is a place in my chest, an empty place, that didn't exist before.

He created it; he filled it with sweet lies, and now it aches without him.

I want to hurt him physically.

I want to break his heart. But that doesn't seem possible. He doesn't have one to break.

My mind drifts, ideas popping into my head like bubbles. I wonder if I could get my hands on a curse of some kind. I'm sure those exist in the spirit realm. I want to cast a spell on him. To leave him empty and aching without me.

I want my name carved like a rune on his skin. Each time he thinks of me, I want it to burn.

All the time he gains from his new immortality will be filled with suffering. He'll hear my voice in his head, taunting and laughing. He won't be able to escape from me.

Let his nights be sleepless.

Let every face he sees morph into mine.

Let the silence consume him.

I hope he never comes again. The image of him, writhing and on edge for the rest of his eternal life, is the only bright spot I can find.

But even that isn't enough.

No matter how much pain I wish for him, it wouldn't be enough to fill the hole.

He doesn't get to walk away while I'm left bleeding with invisible wounds.

Even now, with the bitter truth in my mouth, I don't believe it was all a lie. He showed himself to me. That couldn't have been a ruse, a cleverly designed attempt at making me feel bound to him.

I hiked a fucking mountain to get him a sword.

The look on his face when the ghoul bit me flashes in my mind. It was genuine fear.

But was it the fear of losing his immortality because the heart he planned to take was about to stop beating?

Everything swirls until I don't know which way is up or what was real.

I'm not this kind of girl.

I force myself to sleep. When I see him again, I refuse to look sleep-deprived and heartbroken. He can eat his fucking heart out.

When I wake, the clarity I hoped I would feel is not here. It's still the same. Heavy and slightly blurry. My eyes burn, and there is an ache behind them.

Someone is tapping at my door. I consider ignoring it, but I doubt they will go away.

"Yes?"

"Good morning." A few men walk into the room. Very military-drab and formal. One of them has a bandage over his nose. "We have clothes for you to change. After, we'll escort you to the dining hall."

"Can I take a shower?"

I would like to scrub him off my skin. The memory of his hands and mouth on me needs to be washed down the drain.

"Of course. We'll wait." He gives me a tight smile.

The one with the bandage doesn't speak. He looks familiar, though. He winces when I make eye contact with him.

Gasping, I take a step toward him, and he fully flinches. "You!"

He gives me a tight-lipped nod but doesn't say anything.

"Sorry about your nose." I have to keep myself from laughing. He looks miserable.

In the bathroom, I drop my dress and step into the cold shower. The water bites at my skin, but it feels good. It feels right.

I hate being rushed. But I'm hungry, and I know they're waiting.

The uniform is awful. Staring at it, I roll up the sleeves and opt to forgo the pants. If I only button the three in the middle, it looks like a cinched mini dress. That will have to do.

When I step out of the bathroom, both men have physical reactions. One coughs as his eyes bug out of his head. And the other takes a step back like I'm going to grab him and hurt him.

"Where are your pants?" He's trying not to look at my legs.

"I don't like pants."

"But–"

"I'm starving." I fold my arms across my chest.

"Let's go then." He looks unsure.

"Do you wear little berets with your uniforms?" I bounce down the hallways beside them.

"You want a beret?" He looks shocked.

"I think it completes the look." I gesture over my outfit.

"I'll see what I can do."

"I really appreciate that." I crane my neck to look at his name. "Holder."

We walk through the maze to a large metal box with tables.

"It's cafeteria style; grab a tray." Holder points.

"Thanks." I walk past rows of tables to the line. People whisper and stare.

"That's one way to wear a uniform, I guess." Gordon looks disapproving.

"Well, I'm not a uniform kind of girl." I take a plate of fruit from the line.

"Did you sleep well?"

"I did." I nod. "I think we should have a chat."

He looks as if he was expecting this. "Come sit with me."

I don't even look at the next few things I put on my tray. I don't care.

At the table, I still feel everyone watching me.

"I know you don't want me to see him, but I'm going to have to insist." I don't even wait for him to be fully seated before I blurt it out.

"Sasi." His lips pull into a thin line. "I explained yesterday why that wasn't possible."

"Right. And I heard you. But again, I'm insisting."

"And I'm overruling that." His eyes narrow.

Leaning back in my seat, I watch him, studying his face. "Listen, Gordon. I understand your position. But I am not one of your little soldiers here. You can put out a command, and I don't have to listen to it. So, there is no overruling here. I'm going to speak to Shade."

His jaw clenches. I'm getting on his nerves. "Right, but–"

"So, either you set something up so that I can speak to him, in a way that you deem safe, or I go out on my own. The choice is yours.

You have until tonight to come up with a plan." I stand, grabbing a slice of toast from my tray. "I'll be in my room."

I know people scramble behind me to follow me, but I don't care. Without looking back or leaving any room for his demands or excuses, I walk out of the dining hall.

CHAPTER THIRTY-ONE

poor fool

THE SHARP KNOCK on my door pulls me out of the mind-numbing boredom that has taken siege of my brain.

"Dinner time." A muffled voice comes through as the door clicks open.

"Wonderful." I stand, following him out with my head held high. If this motherfucker doesn't have an answer for me, I'm making my escape. He wasn't at lunch, definitely avoiding confrontation.

Everyone in here, men and women alike, looks so wound up it would take almost nothing to unravel them. It doesn't appear that sex is high on the priority list, and it shows.

"What was your name again?" I inch slightly closer to him with each step.

"Holder."

"First name?" I bat my eyelashes.

He clears his throat. "Jeremy."

"Jeremy," I whisper it, watching his face change.

I knew it would be easy, but shit, this is embarrassing. I actually feel bad for him.

"How long have you been a light bringer?"

"Forger." His jaw muscles clench. "I'm a Light Forger. For about six years."

"Wow. You must have seen some things." I look up at him through my lashes.

He lets out a huff of a laugh. "You wouldn't believe it if I told you."

"Try me."

"I wouldn't want to scare you." He smiles.

"I was bitten by a ghoul. I'm not easily scared."

"No way." He shakes his head. "A bite from a ghoul is fatal."

I wrench the collar of the shirt away from my neck and watch the color drain from his face.

"How are you alive?" His hands come down on my shoulders, pulling me close to inspect it. I let him see it, touch it.

"A little magic, a little moxie." I shrug, smiling up at him.

"Wow," his eyes are fixed on it. "I've only seen four ghoul bites in person, and none of them survived."

"Special. I guess."

"W-We should go." He releases me, taking a big step away.

"I'm starving." I offer no resistance. Be as agreeable as possible. They don't know me well enough to know that is a red flag.

I can tell before we sit down that Gordon has made his decision.

It's in his body language, the way he folds his hands at the center of the table like a judge ready to hand down a sentence. There is a slight smugness in the arch of his brow. He thinks he's in charge here.

Mistake number one.

"We've discussed it at length." He looks me in the eye, his voice neutral. "You won't be permitted to speak to the Umbramancer. We simply can't risk it."

I nod casually, tucking a strand of hair behind my ear. "I understand. Thank you for considering it."

He looks relieved.

Mistake number two.

Shade would have seen this coming from a mile away. He would know that my sweet smile and docile response were lies.

But he isn't Shade.

I look across the table at Jeremy. Sweet, naïve Jeremy.

He looks relieved, too. Poor fool.

I slide my foot out of my boot under the table and stretch my leg slowly. My toes brush the inside of his ankle.

He flinches, dropping his spoon.

Gordon doesn't notice. He's too busy talking about boring bullshit. "Containment risks" and something about Greenland.

I press my foot further, sliding up his calf. His breath hitches.

This is going to be fun. It has the added bonus of Shade's reaction when he finds out. He might be a dirty, rotten liar, but no one can fake that kind of possessiveness. This is going to bother him, if only for his own narcissism, that someone else got to touch his toy.

I eat slowly, letting my tongue cradle the spoon as I drift higher. His face is getting red.

I feel his eyes on me, but I don't look. That's part of the game. Confuse him.

By the time we finish eating, I've got him as good as collared. Wiping my mouth on my napkin, I throw him a glance.

He's already looking at me. Of course he is.

"Stasia, take her back to her room." Gordon barks, standing quickly. "We will come and get you again in the morning for breakfast. Sleep well."

"Thanks." I don't pout or fight.

I send one last, longing look at Jeremy before following Stasia out. She is just as tightly wound, but in a different way. She's a tough bitch. I'm not even going to try. With her, it could go either way; she would either beat me to a pulp or fall hopelessly in love with me.

I'll just wait patiently for Jeremy.

He'll come.

Jumping in the shower, I listen for a knock. It has to seem like a coincidence. "Oh, no! You caught me just getting out of the shower. All wet and naked!"

But this fucker is taking forever.

When I finally hear the tap, I have to fight my natural inclination to snap at him for keeping me waiting.

"Hi." I slip the door open, tilting my head to one side innocently. "Did you need something?"

"Um, can I come in?" He whispers, looking over his shoulder.

"Sure, Jeremy. Is everything alright?" I don't miss the way his eyes roam over the towel wrapped around my body.

"I shouldn't be here." He shakes his head.

"Then why are you?"

"I just wanted to check on you."

"That's so sweet of you." I step toward him, resting my hand on his chest. "I'm fine. But I wish I could go for a walk or something. I need fresh air."

He frowns. "You can't. It's too dangerous."

"I know." I pout my lower lip. Stepping away from him, I sit down on the bed, letting the towel bunch around the tops of my thighs.

"Sasi." His voice is hoarse. "I would take you, but–"

"Please." I look up at him. "I feel like an animal in a cage. You could watch me. I know you won't let anything happen to me."

He rubs his hand over his forehead. "We can't."

"Please, Jeremy." I let his name drip from my lips. "If we can't go outside, can we just go somewhere? Anywhere but this little room? I hate being cooped up."

He hesitates. Damn. He's got more backbone than I thought. Standing, I lean into this chest, coming up on my toes to press a kiss to his chin. "Please."

"Okay." He gasps, pulling away.

"Let me get dressed." I drop the towel. "You can watch if you want to."

He gulps and looks down at his shoes, but I feel his eyes on me as I turn around.

"We're going to have to be really careful." He looks like he might pass out.

"We will. I'm not trying to get you into any trouble." Cue big doe eyes.

He leads me through dark corridors and into a hidden door with a stairwell in it. "There aren't any cameras back here." He whispers more to himself than to me.

We walk down several flights of stairs; this thing goes on forever.

Finally, we creep into a hallway. "There is an outlook–" He freezes, his voice dying. "Shit, come here." He tugs me into a dark room and closes the door softly.

We wait in silence for a few seconds.

"They're probably gone." He whispers.

We're in a supply closet. Rows of shelves lined with canned food, uniforms, and blankets fill the space.

"We can hide for another minute." I press my chest to his. "Just to be safe."

He looks like a deer in the headlights.

Running my fingers over his crotch, I smile at the bulge already waiting for me there. "I'll make it worth your while."

He groans and melts into me.

"Such a good boy. Get on your knees." I squeeze him just hard enough to make his body jerk.

He drops down.

"I'll never get used to the sight of a big, powerful man on his knees in front of me." I run my fingers through his hair, stepping around him. "And you're such a big–strong–man." I punctuate each word.

My eyes dart around the room. There must be something in here I can use.

Like it's fate or something, my eyes land on a long, heavy flashlight.

Bingo.

Grabbing it, I swing it like a baseball bat, and it's lights out, Jeremy.

"Sorry about this." I use a sheet to tie his arms to his ankles. "That's going to be a killer headache when you wake up."

Opening the door quietly, I listen for a moment before running down the hallway. I test each door. Locked. Locked. Locked.

Unlocked.

It's the outlook. It's like a balcony on the side of the mountain.

Running to the edge, I lean over the railing and look in every direction.

"Shit." It's just a straight drop down into the water below.

New plan. I run on my tiptoes back through the hallway to the stairwell. No cameras.

I hesitate. Up or down?

If I choose down and it's wrong, I'll have to come back up a hundred flights of stairs. If I go up now, I have maybe fifty to reach the top.

"Fuck." I sigh. "Up."

I'm only halfway up the first flight when I hear yelling. Voices echo below me, and the sound of heavy boots on metal bounces in the air.

I try the first door I come to. It's locked.

"Sasi!" A voice calls, much too close for comfort.

Taking the stairs two at a time, I reach the next door. When I yank it open, Gordon is waiting for me.

"Oh, hi." I straighten my hair.

He grabs me tightly and yanks me out into the hallway. "Did you think we wouldn't find you?"

"I was hoping."

He doesn't speak for several minutes, through the hallway and into the elevator.

"You'll be confined to your room. Meals will be delivered, and you will have guards at your door round the clock." He growls. "Female guards."

I throw my head back and laugh. "Interesting that you think I can't seduce them, too."

His jaw clenches as we reach my door, and he shoves me into it.

CHAPTER THIRTY-TWO

swamp thing

WITH NOTHING TO do but sleep, I slip into bed and force my eyes closed.

I can't sit in the quiet with my thoughts. That's dangerous. As I lie here, his face is all I see. Devilishly handsome and dark. Images flash in my mind. The moments we've shared, the times he gave more than he took.

Sleep comes uncharacteristically easily. Too easy. I should have been suspicious of how fast I started to slip out of consciousness.

One minute I'm in my slightly uncomfortable bed, locked like a prisoner in a cell, and the next I'm standing, knee deep, in swamp water.

Thick fog presses against my skin.

It smells like moss and dirt as I wade through the sea of tall grass and gnarled trees with roots that bend and twist over the surface of the water.

He's here.

"Where are you?" I call to him.

"Right here, love." His voice comes from behind me.

I spin around, and sure enough, there he is. Handsome as fuck and as deadly as sin. That bastard. He has no right to look so fucking delicious right now.

That's fine. I can still yell even when my pussy is wet.

"What do you want?" I fold my arms across my chest. I have the high ground—righteous indignation.

"You."

I huff. "Right."

"Where are you?" He stands from the large root he's using as a chair.

"I don't know. Some mountain somewhere."

"Leave."

"I can't." I won't explain how I tried and failed.

"You aren't wearing the necklace."

"Yeah, the light brigade isn't as stupid as their name would suggest." I snap.

"Sasi." His eyes gleam in the moonlight. The same deep eyes that I stare into as I lose myself.

"So," I step toward him. "Is it true?"

His jaw clenches. No denial or question about what I'm accusing him of.

"You're planning to kill me?" I suck my teeth. My anger is growing. But something else is growing too, beneath the anger. Something I don't recognize. It's heavy and gray.

"I need your heart."

"You motherfucking, lying sack of shit!" I kick at the water.

"I didn't lie, not exactly."

"Omission counts, motherfucker!" I wade through the water as elegantly as I can to pass him. It's hard to be sexy when trudging through knee-deep sludge.

"I will cherish it forever." He has the gall, the audacity, to look sad. "I would hold it inside myself through eternity. You would be immortal–by my side."

I laugh, bitter, enraged, tired. "Well, fuck."

He steps close enough to touch me, but he doesn't. His hands flex at his sides; maybe he's really trying to hold himself back. Or maybe he's just putting on a show. I can't tell the difference now.

"Do I get a choice?" I look up at him.

He doesn't answer.

"How were you planning to talk me into this?" I truly want to know. What was his plan here?

"I wasn't." He pauses. "I was simply going to ask you for it."

"What things were true? From where I'm standing, almost everything was a lie, or at least it was wrapped in lies. Was any of it real? Or was every moment, right from the start, just a means to an end?" I felt it when he said he didn't want to hurt me. He wasn't lying. Somehow, he draws the line at hurting me, but killing me is fine? I can't make sense of it.

"When I told you your blood and essence were enough, that was a lie. And when I told you I needed Umbralius for protection." He inches closer, our toes touching below the murky water. "Those are the only lies."

A laugh bubbles up in my throat. "You had me steal the blade that you were going to use to cut my heart out. That's diabolical, Shade." I should have expected nothing less.

"It's the only blade that can remove your heart and the only blade that can open my chest. I wasn't lying when I said I couldn't go up and get it myself. None of us could. A dark spirit cannot enter that plane." His fingertips graze my arm. He's wearing the balloon animal cufflinks I got for him.

For some reason, a tear slips down my cheek. I wasn't expecting it. I think that the last time I cried, I was ten. I don't understand this. It hurts in a way I don't have words for. It's sharp and deep.

He watches the tear until it drips off the end of my chin. More than the actual act of crying, which I can now say with confidence, since I've done it, I hate that he's seeing it.

"I thought you loved me."

"I do. Not normal love. Not human love. But the way things like us can love, I do. With every part of me."

"I don't believe you."

He flinches. Just slightly. Just enough.

How dare he look hurt.

"It's you. The brightest light in my life." He comes down slightly so I can see his face better—so I can see the pain in his eyes. "It's you, woman. Always you. When I gave you the broken pieces of myself, I meant it. I want you to have them."

No. I don't believe it.

"I'm leaving." I rip my arms out of his grasp.

"Don't."

"I'm not staying here with you." I turn and start to walk away.

"I'll find you." He calls after me. A threat and a promise.

"Yeah, yeah." I wave him off without looking back.

He doesn't follow me. I'm not sure whether I'm happy about that or angry. He should be behind me, grovelling. I want him on his knees, begging my forgiveness. I want him raw, crying and pleading, screaming into the void.

I'm caught in a strange place, a place I've never been. Normally, I would just leave. That would be it. There would be no second thoughts, no internal crisis or longing. But walking away feels difficult. And not just because it's physically difficult to move here. It's as if we have a tether holding us together.

Just seeing him, being in his presence, fucks me up. The way his breath hitched when I said I didn't believe him–it makes me feel scrambled.

I want him to crack my fucking back like a glow stick. I want him to touch me like he needs me to survive. Then, I want him to kiss me and tell me I'm pretty until I feel better.

But he wants to cut my heart out.

Fucking selfish prick.

He's so concerned with his life, he's willing to throw mine away.

I cried. Like a stupid, emotional, ridiculous woman, I cried for him. How cliche.

Oh, god. I'm filled with shame.

Is this what it feels like to have your feelings hurt? I don't like it. It's humiliating.

I was faithful to him on the mountain full of naked, orgying hotties! I said no to them. For him!

Why am I acting like there is even a choice to be made here? Obviously, I can't let him kill me!

But there is a tug in my chest that's never been there before.

It hurts to breathe. It sears my insides, making my judgment questionable.

What a treacherous thing feelings are. I wish I never caught them.

CHAPTER THIRTY-THREE

my hate will keep me warm

I PASS between waking and sleeping multiple times. I don't know how much time has passed.

I wake, stare at the ceiling, then fall asleep again.

Eventually, breakfast is delivered.

Then lunch.

I don't have the strength to care.

My chest aches. I think it's a heart attack. I'm dying slowly.

The keys jingle outside; the door swings open. "Dinner."

"Neat." I don't move.

"You have to eat something. You didn't touch your other trays." She flicks the light on.

Hissing, I throw my arm over my face to block out the light. "Just let me die."

"You're not dying. Sit up and eat."

"When I'm gone, just throw me in the mountains so that I can be ravaged by wolves. I don't want a fuss made, just let them eat my remains."

"Holy shit. You're a drama queen." She laughs.

"You'll feel bad for that when I'm dead." I groan, sitting up to look at the slop they're trying to feed me. "Gross. No, thank you." I drop back and put my pillow over my face.

My existential dread aside, I've never been more bored in my life. Sitting in this white room with nothing but a bed is sucking the life out of me.

When the door clicks closed and the lock slides into place, I sit up and stare at the tray.

I hate it here.

I hate these people.

The only solace I find is in my violent fantasies. I imagine punching Gordon so hard that his nose breaks against my hand. I want to make him bleed.

He isn't at fault for Shade and his fucking lies, but he's the one who told me. It's a shoot-the-messenger situation.

If he hadn't kidnapped me and told me the truth, I would probably be bouncing on Shade's dick right now, in ignorant bliss.

"If I get my hands on that fucker, I'm gonna break his nose." I sing out loud.

I don't even know if I'm talking about Gordon or Shade.

Maybe both.

"Break his nose! Break it clean. His face is going to meet my fist. And—" I'm mid-harmony when a thud in the distance catches my attention. Then a scream.

This place is like a clock. Nothing happens. No thuds. And definitely not screams.

I sit up and listen to it.

They are as quiet as mice all day long. The only time I hear anything is when someone brings a tray.

Something is happening.

There is a slither, a whoosh. I know it well.

Folding my arms over my chest, I watch as shadows move outside my door.

It's colder, the air shifting. He's here.

There is a crack in the silence. My metal door splinters, bending like it's being rammed from the outside.

Darkness swirls in over the wreckage of my door.

He's ripping this place apart by the seams.

Stepping over it, I walk out into the hallway. Darkness hangs in the air like fog over water. The doors of every room are being blown out.

Thanks, Shade.

Alarms start to blare, red strobing lights flashing from the ceiling.

It's chaos.

Laughing, I walk through the hallway, retracing my steps to the stairwell. People are running in every direction. Light Forgers are putting on riot gear in the corners, rushing, panicking.

Somewhere deep in the compound, someone screams again. Loud sounds, booming, crashing, thuds–somewhere there is a fight.

I reach the stairwell. As I step onto the first step, the ground shakes. The entire building–the mountain–is trembling.

Running down the steps, I don't stop until I reach the bottom. My lungs burn, and my legs ache. There isn't time for that.

Pushing the door open, I burst out into the madness.

There he is.

The sight of him takes my breath away. Dark strength and raw power.

My body reacts to his. I can't stop it.

Through the smoke and flickering red lights, I see him like a god among mortal men

He's fighting with three Light Forgers, including Gordon. It looks like a scene out of a movie, light and dark duking it out. He's in the middle of it, with his arms spread out, a smile on his face. Darkness writhes around him.

Shadows swirl off him like smoke, tendrils snapping out and knocking them to the ground.

He loves it.

Then he turns, above the chaos, and his eyes jerk up to meet mine. He feels me.

We lock eyes across the room.

He grins.

Game on, motherfucker.

I won't give him the satisfaction of a dramatic stare-down. Eat your heart out. I spin on my heels and run.

Out into the cold.

Fuck him. Fuck him. Fuck him. My feet hurt after only a few steps. It's cold and dark. Fuck Gordon, too.

What kind of cheesy, melodramatic spy movie villain bullshit is this? Who actually builds their lair inside of a mountain?

Ducking down, I creep away until I can't hear anything but the sounds of the trees around me. It's too dark to see my next step.

The ground isn't just cold; it's rocky, with sharp stones and tree branches sticking up out of the dirt and scattered patches of snow.

But still, I would rather be here, cold and running, than trapped in that room for another second.

I'm not sure how long I've been walking, but the sun is starting to rise over the mountains. The river rushes in the distance. That feels like salvation. If I can just make it there.

Or maybe all that is waiting for me is hypothermia.

My feet are numb at this point, burning from the cold as I stumble through the trees.

Trying to keep myself optimistic, I plot revenge in my mind. I don't stop at Shade or Gordon. I scheme against everyone who has ever wronged me.

It keeps me going until I reach the water. Sweet, petty revenge.

After Shade and Gordon, Janie is at the top of my list. If she had never forced me to the carnival, I never would have met him.

My hatred keeps me warm.

I stumble through the trees, my lungs heaving and my legs on fire. The water cuts through the mountain, a treacherous white-water rapid that is impossible to cross.

"Fuck!" I scream into the stillness. I'm going to fucking die out here!

Leaning against a jagged rock, I sit down, giving my lungs and legs a break. My breath comes out in white puffs in the air. My lungs burn. My feet ache. My heart hurts.

That should have been my rescue. If he weren't a fucking liar.

A sound, something unnatural, not the wind or water, cuts through the trees.

Fuck. Now I'm caught. It's either back to a cell or the gallows, I suppose.

Hot pink flashes through the trees.

Thalora comes crashing through the trees on a fancy snow rover.

"Need a ride?" She smiles.

"To where exactly?" I arch my brow.

"I won't take you back," she cuts the roaring engine off. "To either of them."

"And why should I believe you?"

"I guess you don't have to, but you'll freeze to death out here if you don't."

She's right.

Pulling myself up, I throw my leg over the seat and scoot in behind her. It's heated. My ass starts to thaw instantly. "This thing is cute."

"Well, yeah." She shrugs, tossing her ponytail. "I only travel in style."

"Just so you know, I'm not a pawn. I know you're only helping me because you're mad at Shade. But I don't want to freeze." I straighten my spine.

"I know." She grins.

For a little machine, this thing packs a punch. She blasts through the trees and down the path until we're out of the forest completely.

We ride in silence except for the hum of the engine. I'm glad to have the time to warm up and rest before I have to speak or possibly fight for my life again.

She pulls into a crowded rest area on the side of the mountain. She cuts the engine and spins around. "So, what's the plan here?"

"I'm not sure." I run my fingers through my tangled hair.

"Can I ask you a question?"

"Go for it." I don't have the energy to be argumentative right now.

"Is there any part of you that wants to give him the heart?" I don't trust her, but she looks genuinely curious. Even if she is just gathering information to run back to Shade, what's the point now?

"Yes." I don't know why I tell her the truth. My throat burns, and my eyes feel watery.

I'm going to blame exhaustion.

"I wish I could give him mine." She wraps her arms around herself.

"Why can't you?"

She lets out a laugh, both sad and surprised. "I don't have one. Not like yours. It won't help him."

"I was honest with you. So now, will you do me the same courtesy?" I watch her face.

"Sure."

"How many hearts has he taken?" This information will only torture me, but I have to know.

"Since I've been with him, maybe three. It's hard to recall."

My blood boils. I'm just another. One of many. I don't relish the thought of being his number one girl out of four. I'm only one of one; otherwise, I don't fucking want it.

"Is that why you're angry?" She laughs. "Not that he wants to kill you, but–"

"But because he lied. He told me I was special to him, and it wasn't fucking true."

Her breath catches; she looks like she's been punched in the chest. "For what it's worth, I don't think he was lying about that part."

"Sure." I wave her off dismissively.

"He tried to protect you. He held me back from pushing. I think he wanted to keep you alive." She looks honest. But she's a good actress. And at the end of the day, she's Team Umbramancer all the way.

"He still lied." It doesn't matter that he didn't want to kill me or that he didn't want to lie. "He made me believe that I was curing some loneliness in him."

She looks at me with a kind of sadness, an understanding. "Men aren't lonely, Sasi, they're hungry."

"Sons of bitches."

She chuckles, sad and soft. "Sons of bitches."

There is a moment of silence between us.

"You know, I have a friend, someone who will let you stay with him for a while. At least until you decide what you want to do." She looks pale, as if betraying Shade is making her ill. "He's not a friend of the Umbramancer. I'm sure he wouldn't look for you there, not in a million years."

I have no options. I'm destitute.

I left my life behind to follow him across the universe.

"That would be great."

"His name is Mortimer. You'll love him."

"What is he?" I know her well enough to know that he's not going to be human.

CHAPTER THIRTY-FOUR

scorched earth

IF I WERE a Georgian-era woman from a Jane Austen novel, I would love this room. It's perfect for sitting by the fireplace and embroidering pillows while waiting for my beloved cousin-husband to come home from the war.

Alas, I am not.

The bed is narrow and hard, with too many frilly blankets that don't actually keep me warm. There is no central heat, so I have to tend a fire all night long like some Dickinson ghost. The windows let in a draft. And the whole place smells like dried lavender and mildew.

I think she brought me to Mortimer's house to punish me. It was a trick disguised as a kind gesture. She sent me back in time to suffer without a single modern luxury.

Mortimer is nice, though.

He looks like a handsome professor, always tucked into a three-piece suit. He looks like he might be just a few years older than me, but he acts like he's three hundred years old.

Honestly, he might actually be three hundred years old. He isn't creepy, and I never feel like he's trying to fuck me. He's a perfect gentleman, which is a shame.

Shade would hate it, and I could use the attention. I need a self-esteem boost. A harmless little nibble on my neck between friends.

I've been given free rein of the place. Yesterday, I looked through the dust-filled library for information.

The age of social media has made stalking an ex so simple. Anything I could want is right at my fingertips. It's all just a few clicks away. All I can do with Shade is look through ancient books for illustrations of him stealing other hearts. It leaves a lot to be desired.

Today, I'm raiding the closets. This house has thirteen bedrooms. I will be occupied for at least a day.

There was a woman here at some point with excellent taste in dresses. Some of them are moth-eaten, others stained with the passage of time, but I can fix them up. Cotton, linen, and silk, in every color and pattern. Deep royal purples, blood reds, and emerald greens.

I'm sprawled out on the floor with a pile of dresses beside me, working on a hem. The damaged pile is much larger than the ready-to-wear pile, but there are some really great prospects.

"Good morning, Sasi!" He peeks his head into the library.

"Hey, Morti! Good hunt?"

His mouth pulls into a thin line. "Stop calling me Morti. But yes, it was an excellent hunt. Would you like to come down for breakfast?"

"Sure!"

"I see you've found Amelia's old dresses."

"Who is Amelia?" I bounce down the stairs beside him.

"Oh, just an old friend, from a long time ago."

"A lover?"

"Hush." He hushes me a lot. He pulls out my chair at the opposite end of the table from him. He insists on our sitting this way. With twelve empty seats between us. Etiquette or something.

He sits at the other end of the table with a wine glass full of blood and his newspapers. New York and London.

"You know, they have this thing now called the internet. You could read papers from all over the place, right from your phone." I use a spoon to crack the shell of my egg.

"I like the feel of the paper in my hands." He smiles, his sharp teeth pressing into his lower lip.

"What will happen if the Umbramancer finds me here?" I take a sip of my orange juice. "Is this freshly squeezed?"

"Of course."

"You're a classy guy, Morti."

He lets the nickname slip this time, choosing to continue our conversation. "If he comes here, I have a friend across the lake. I'm sure she would help you."

"Where would I go?"

"In an emergency, she can hide you until it is safe for you to leave." He pauses, swirling his glass like a fine wine. "There is a place where you can go. But it's far away in this realm."

"Now I'm intrigued. Don't leave me hanging, Mortimer."

"There is a temple in Romania."

"Romania?" He wasn't kidding about the distance.

"There is a group; they are a cult, more or less."

"A cult?" I sit forward in my seat. "What kind of cult?"

"If you would let me get to it, I'll explain." He looks stern, but something twinkles in his eyes.

"Oh! I'm sorry." I grin. "You old-timers just take so long to get to the point. I wasn't sure there was one."

"Old timers?" His lips twitch. "You young people want everything so quickly nowadays. A little patience would serve you well."

I snort. "Are you going to teach me?"

"You would be a difficult student." He groans like the idea itself is exhausting.

"I would be your favorite student."

"My favorite student would listen when I talk." He shakes his head. "You're a menace."

"Oh, Morti. Don't bully me. I'll come."

He chokes. "Sasi!"

"Sorry. I forgot you're from a bygone era." I smirk. "Anyway, please continue. I'm all ears. A captive audience."

He sighs; I'm exasperating him. "They worship the Umbramancer."

"Oh, no fucking way!" I drop my fork. He has a cult of worshippers?

"There is a sword." He continues, ignoring my outburst. "Now this is where it gets complicated. The sword is–"

"Umbralius?"

"You know about Umbralius?" He looks stunned.

"Yes." I take a bite of toast. "I went to Greenland and stole it for him."

"He has Umbralius?" If he could possibly pale any further, he does.

"Yes."

"You went to Greenland and got Umbralius?" He speaks slowly, like I'm misunderstanding somehow.

"Yes," I respond just as slowly. "I did."

"This is worse than I thought." He leans back in his seat, slouching, very unlike him.

"What's so bad about him having his sword? Gordon was going on about it, too."

"The sword not only gives him the ability to take a heart and strengthen himself. But it also allows his power to go unchecked." He explains. "I am from the dark realm. I relish the darkness. But it must be checked. There must be a balance. The world would be thrown into chaos if one side had too much power over the other."

"And all of that comes down to Shade?"

"Not necessarily; there are other dark forces. And equally powerful light forces. But he will be toeing the line. He is an enigma. In all my years, I've never met another like him. He is reckless and careless, but also, somehow, careful. He cares for his family with a fierceness."

"I know he does." At the expense of my life.

"He's getting greedy, Sasi." He finishes his glass. "He could very well continue on forever, taking a heart. But he wants the power and permanence of a given heart."

"He wants the best."

"You know," he chuckles lowly. "I never thought he would actually find someone who might give him her heart willingly. But you are a rare breed."

Unlike when Gordon said it, I know Mortimer means this as a compliment.

"Thank you."

"I know you spent all day in the library yesterday. I have a special selection of books that might interest you. They are in the study. On the top shelf."

"Which room is the study?" All the rooms in this house have strange names. Places like the drawing room and the salon, which I've come to learn have nothing to do with hair care.

"The parlor off the conservatory." He's speaking in Clue again.

"Right, okay, Colonel Mustard. I'll find it."

"Who?" He looks appalled.

"I'm off to learn about cults. Thanks for breakfast and the titillating conversation." I wink and slip out of the dining room.

I think the conservatory is the sunroom. I should have played the game more; maybe this would make sense.

Through the foyer, past the kitchen, down the long back hallway, I come to a room of high glass walls filled with dead plants. Just past it is a closed door.

The ancient handle is stuck, so I have to push and pull and wiggle until the door finally opens.

It's dark and musty inside. A thick layer of dust covers everything.

Opening the thick velvet curtains, I work for ten minutes to get the window to open. Everything in the house is almost broken.

When the room finally has light and air, I climb onto the desk to reach the books on the top shelf.

Big, dusty, leather-bound books that don't look like anyone has opened them in a century.

The spine creaks as I open it, looking through the pages filled with words in a language I can't understand. With painstaking care, I turn through each page. I don't want to miss anything.

The first book has nothing.

The second somehow has less. Less than nothing.

By the third book, my nose is itchy, and I'm annoyed.

The fourth book is double the size of the others. The leather is cracked and peeling, and some of the pages have come loose from the binding. They're as thin as tissue paper as I turn them.

Page after page of absolutely nothing.

And then, there it is.

On page two hundred and forty-two.

Shade, holding a heart in his hands, lifted it up into the air.

The woman, discarded garbage on the ground, is barely added to the picture, a few pen strokes noting her form.

From here, it gets more interesting. Interesting and infuriating.

Page three hundred shows Shade standing in a black temple, surrounded by naked women on their knees. Their hands are raised, worshipping him.

He's obviously enjoying himself.

There are several pages of words again, then another picture, an altar of fire. It looks like the same temple. Tearing a piece of paper from the typewriter on the desk, I mark the page.

With the book pressed to my chest, I run through the hallways, searching for Mortimer.

"Sasi?" He calls when I run through the foyer.

"Where are you?"

"The veranda."

Rolling my eyes, I step out of the open front door; the screen slamming loudly behind me.

"Did you find anything useful in your search?"

"I did, as a matter of fact. Can you help me figure out what this is?"

He takes the book and opens it to the page. "Ah," he nods thoughtfully. "This is the fire that forged Umbralius. This is the only place where his power can be stripped away."

"The Umbramanceror the sword?"

"Both." He looks at me with a strange sadness. "If you go this route, you're choosing scorched earth." He warns.

"Good."

CHAPTER THIRTY-FIVE
blue flames

"BE CAREFUL, SASI." He looks down at me like a disapproving father.

"Thanks for everything, Mortimer." I throw my arms around him. "Who knows, when all this is over, maybe I'll drop in for a visit."

"I look forward to it."

With a flourish of the dark blue velvet of my skirt, I curtsey in the middle of the parking deck of the George Bush Intercontinental Airport.

In just under seventeen hours, I'll be in Romania.

I still don't know what I'm going to do when I get there. I'll just float until I find the Templul întunecat.

As I walk through the airport, I can feel eyes on me. Maybe this dress was a bad idea. For a person with a fake passport who is trying to lie low, this might have been the wrong choice.

The security line has half the state of Texas in it. My passport looks legit. But only time will tell.

For exactly fifty-three minutes, the line ambles slowly up to the agents waiting to pick our luggage apart.

When I reach the agent at the beginning of the scanning process, I flash him a smile and place the passport in his hand.

"Hello, where are you heading today?" His voice is bored and mechanical. He scans my ticket, then shines a light on my passport.

"Romania." I smile, small, subtle, disinterested. Polite but not suspicious.

His eyes flicker, but not at the passport. He tilts his head slightly, curiously. "What's the special occasion?"

"What do you mean?"

"Your dress. You look all dolled up for something." He gestures to my dress.

"Oh," I smile, a real one this time. "Me. I'm the occasion. So I figured I should dress like it."

He looks at me with awestruck wonder. He chuckles and shakes his head. "You're definitely making an entrance." Handing me my passport and boarding pass, he waves me through.

The other ticket agent looks at me with a big smile and something like admiration. "Have a great trip."

"Thanks!"

I would kiss Mortimer right on the mouth if he were here.

Picking up the flowing skirt of my dress, I kick off my shoes and place them in the bin before stepping through the metal detector.

The alarms immediately begin to sound.

Looking sheepishly at the agent, I step toward him, leaning in to whisper. "I have piercings." I gesture to my chest.

"Oh, right. We'll do a manual pat-down."

"Lucky me." I grin before waiting for the female agent to finish putting on her gloves.

With dead eyes and a frown on her face, the agent pats me down and quickly sends me on my way.

While this hasn't been the worst travel experience of my life, I miss moving between realms. The night train was and always will be the superior mode of travel.

Lines, gates, security–it all sucks.

It feels like it takes an eternity, but when I finally board my flight, first to Charlotte, then on to Romania, I'm exhausted.

The entire flight to Romania is spent tossing and turning. I can't shake this feeling that he knows where I'm going.

I imagine finding the temple, and he's waiting for me there with his band of dedicated followers.

I've never been to Romania, but in my dreams it's a shadowland full of monsters. I never see Shade, but I feel him lurking everywhere, waiting to reach out and grab me.

Over and over again, I jolt awake, only to find myself still sitting in my seat.

I'm not a nervous person. I blame the clothes. I've been overcome with female hysteria.

"Are you alright?"

"Yeah." I wipe the sweat from my brow.

"Not a fan of flying?"

"No, not really." I cringe.

"Is Romania your final destination today?"

"Uh, yeah." I finally look at the man speaking to me. "You?"

"Yes, I'm heading home."

"Oh! You live there?" I lean in. He could be useful to me.

We make agonizing small talk for almost an hour. He thinks I'm a nurse at Grey Sloan Memorial Hospital.

He was visiting friends for a wedding. Blah blah blah.

"Can I ask you a question?" I've waited as long as I can. We're landing in less than thirty minutes. We've already begun our final descent into Bucharest. I'm out of time. Hopefully, the small talk will have helped.

"Sure."

"I'm trying to find the Templul întunecat. Do you know where that is?"

His face pales, and he shakes his head. "You don't want to go there." He's pulling back.

"No, see. I really do. I need to go there."

"That is a bad place."

"I know." I let my eyes well up with tears. "My sister is there. I have to find her." My voice cracks perfectly at the end.

His lips purse into a flat line. "The Dark Temple is a house of witches."

"I can't leave her there! I have to find her and bring her home." I start thinking of another lie to add to the story. A dying family member whose last wish is to see her. "Please, help me!"

He looks torn for a moment before sighing. "Go to Old Town in the shadow of the Stavropoleos Cross." He whispers. "You will find a sign there. Follow it. But I have to warn you, be careful."

"Thank you so much, Alexandru! I can't tell you how grateful I am." Pulling a pen from my purse. "Can you spell that for me? Stavropoleos?"

The rest of the flight is torture. I got what I needed, but I still have to play nice. Small talk is the bane of my existence. Why does everyone feel the need to fill silence with frivolous talking?

It's moments like this when that painful tug comes back. The ache of missing him.

He could be quiet.

He didn't feel forced to fill the silence. And when he did, it didn't feel like a chore; I wanted to talk to him.

I can't focus on that. I have to stay angry.

By the time I finally deplane, my rage is back. He has a whole cult full of women who worship him. Why didn't he just get a heart from one of them? They would probably have given it gladly. Instead, he lied to me.

Roiling, boiling rage.

Good.

When I show the taxi driver the note, he smiles and nods, taking me exactly where I need to go. Horrible small talk for the win!

Bucharest is beautiful. The old and the new blended together in a way that takes my breath away. My eyes don't know where to land.

And just like clockwork, his face comes into my mind. Cold and beautiful–young despite all of his years. Standing in the middle of the ring with his arms open wide, with the wild glint in his eyes, makes my heart stop. I know he's smiling beneath the golden mandible. Is this an image that my mind conjured up, or am I seeing him in a vision?

I don't want to think of him. But my body does. My skin misses his.

My treacherous heart aches and tugs in a way that makes me wish you would just rip it out of my chest so that I don't ever have to feel this way again.

I could be here with him. The beauty of this city is exactly like something he would have wanted to show me.

In the dark parts of my brain, I wonder if I could give him my heart. He's broken down so many of the walls and barriers I built; I surrendered myself to him.

What's once more?

Shaking my head violently, I push the thoughts away.

The taxi comes to a stop, and he points me in the direction of a courtyard. It's smaller than I was expecting, just an unassuming little monastery in the middle of the city.

The sky is full of clouds, so there isn't really a shadow on the ground. Standing in front of the doors, I stare up at the cross. With careful steps, I walk out in front of it, searching for the sign I'm supposed to find here.

Then I see it.

A black stone pressed into the bricks. It's shiny, like a pebble from a fish tank. There is another one a few bricks away. Then another.

I follow them, a trail of shiny black breadcrumbs.

They lead me to a narrow alleyway between two very old buildings. I can already feel the shift in energy. A dark shadow is looming over me. I feel him here.

The passage dips down, long, shallow steps taking me into the heart of the city. Down and around corners.

Then, finally, a door. It's old, splintered wood and rusted hinges.

When I push it open, it gives immediately, with no resistance whatsoever.

Inside, another long, narrow corridor, lit by black candles in spiral sconces.

I follow the hallway down until I hear humming. It's many voices all together. It's beautiful. Sacred.

It sounds like Shade. An ancient language full of darkness and grief.

Around a final bend, light flickers.

I have to bite back the urge to laugh when I see them. I expected dirty, barefooted women in black cloaks.

This room is a cathedral of night—stained glass in shades of black, gray, and red. An altar with a shining obsidian stone, cut like a crystal, engulfed in blue flames, is at the center of it all.

The women are beautiful. All wild hair and silk dresses. Of course, Shade's followers aren't a bunch of raggedy women on their knees.

"Welcome, sister!" One of them stands. "If you have journeyed this far, it's because you feel the call." Her eyes are wet like she might cry, or she was just…

"Come." Another one reaches for me. "Do you feel him here?"

"Sure do." I groan. He's everywhere, like an itchy wool blanket trapping me.

"Where are you coming from?" She hands me a glass of wine.

"That's a long story." I watch her. She seems sweet, but there is something about her. She's not a blind follower. She is devout. And nothing will come between her and her lord.

"Are you here to worship?" Another woman steps up, too close. She has dark tattoos on her face.

"Yes." I nod, smiling.

"Do you believe?"

"In the Umbramancer?"

"In his power."

"Oh, absolutely." I know his power well. "How long have you been here?"

"This temple has been here for centuries." She looks around at the polished black glass.

"What do you do, exactly?"

Her eyes narrow, like she suspects me of being a reporter or narc. "We worship him."

"But why?"

"Because he is worthy of it. He is the darkness. And when the darkness is happy, the light shines brighter."

"Right." I nod. "Can I watch?"

"Of course."

Sitting on the stone pew, I watch as they join hands around the altar. They sing and walk in a circle, and one of them reads from a book that looks very similar to the one at Moritmer's house.

It could just be jetlag, but it feels like it lasts forever.

My eyes burn and beg to close.

"Does he ever come here?" I call out in a quiet moment.

"What?" She looks shocked. "No, he has–"

"He doesn't?" He has a cult of groupies, and he doesn't even bother to show his face?

"It has been decades since his last appearance here. But we guard the temple anyway, waiting for him. Whenever he chooses to return to us, we are here."

"You live here?" I actually feel bad for them. He's such a dick.

"Yes, we guard his temple day and night."

"Are you guarding the fire specifically?" I peek past her, looking at the strange flames.

"Why are you asking these questions? Are you a Light Forger?" The mood sours quickly. Everyone is turning on me.

"God! No! Honestly, I'm offended that you could possibly think I give off that energy. I just… I'm looking for information."

"Why?" Her fist clenches.

Because I want to kick his ass. "Because I'm lost. I thought maybe he was the answer." My chest is hollow.

CHAPTER THIRTY-SIX

horny, hungry & jet lagged

THEIR TEMPLE IS MASSIVE. A twisting labyrinth of dark corridors and hidden rooms. I'm sure we've passed the same painting twice before. They're leading me up, down, and around to confuse me.

Too bad for them, I am a master navigator. They're trying to trick me. Not possible. Every turn has been logged in my mental map. Unlike the lair in the mountains, this place has tons of landmarks.

The top floor has a glass ceiling; the sun is starting to set on the horizon. They really stayed down in the dungeon all day, sending him energy and love.

"You can stay in here. We all eat together on the terrace." She points toward the French doors at the end of the hallway.

"Great." I give an overly fake thumbs up. I'm feeling dysregulated.

The room is dark and cold; all the furniture and fixtures are black–go figure. It's very chic. Gauzy linens and dimmed lighting.

The four-poster bed has potential.

If only I had a tall, dark, and handsome to tie me to it. I sigh and sit at the end of the bed.

Stripping out of my dress, I stand under the cool spray of the shower. I wonder if he'll come here?

The girls would get the shock of their lives.

My soapy hand slips down over my stomach, pausing between my legs. I shouldn't do this. But I'm achy and tired.

And I miss him.

Rinsing and turning off the water, I fight the urge to make myself come while remembering the way his jaw clenches when he's close.

Horny, hungry, and jet-lagged is a hell of a combination.

Staring up at the ceiling, I allow myself to think about him as I drift to sleep.

I wonder if thinking of him opens the door for him to summon me to him. Because before I'm even fully asleep, it starts.

My body is left on the bed while my consciousness is dragged away.

"Come back to me." His voice surrounds me.

"So you can kill me? I don't think so."

"You miss me as much as I miss you."

"So what?" I wrap around myself, shielding my heart.

"Where are you, Sasi?" He finally comes into view. In all of his raw, dangerous glory.

I shrug, not trusting my voice not to tremble.

"I didn't want to hurt you; you must know that." His voice is softer now.

"Funny way of showing it."

He steps closer, into the light of this endless void we're in. When I can see his face, really see it, I see the weight of this.

He looks weaker. Tired. Sick.

"You look like shit."

He huffs a laugh. "Yeah, well, there's this woman."

"Let me guess? She left you?"

"I don't have a heart, but if I did, I'd guess this is what heartbreak feels like." He steps too close.

"What does it feel like?" My own heart aches.

"It feels hollow. I'm wandering the world without my best friend. Everything is too bright and painful. Too loud. I find peace in nothing. This world is rot and ruin without you."

"Without my heart, you mean."

"No. Without you." He grabs me, his fingers curling tight around my arms. "Come back to me."

"Are you still going to kill me?"

Before he can answer, a distant tapping starts to pull me from my sleep. I'm confused for a moment, blinking in the dark. Someone is at my door, knocking.

Cracking it open, I look out through blurry eyes.

"Are you coming to dinner?"

"Sure thing." I give the same stupid thumbs up. I don't know what it is about Elspeth, but she knocks me off my game.

It could be the fact that she is wholly and unshakably devoted to my man.

Following her down the hallway, I pass an oil painting that looks like it should be hanging in the Louvre. It's at least as long as my body.

"Who painted this?" I see bits of him. But it's wrong. The eyes. The lips. His fingers. I know them intimately. Biblically. I would know them by touch in the dark. These aren't his.

"Oh, her name was Temperance. She passed last year, joining the night." She smiles at the painting.

Out on the rooftop deck, there is a long table set with crystal place settings.

It's beautiful. It looks like a wedding.

"Is tonight a special occasion?"

"Every day that we get to honor him is a special occasion."

I don't mean to let my eyes roll. They do it completely on their own. None of them has ever honored him as much as I have. I've honored him in front of a dragon. On my knees in the center of the big top. In the sand dunes of Erb Chebbi.

We gather around the table, where big silver cloches cover trays of food.

I'm starving. This is the best part of today so far.

They talk quietly around me. I tuck in, keeping my head down, listening, and eating.

"The last carnival was in Lagos." One of them says quietly to the girl she's talking to. I perk up.

"Where is it going next?" I blurt out suddenly.

Elspeth narrows her eyes. "You know, we don't know that. Or you would if you were a follower."

"What do you mean?"

"It's impossible to follow the carnival."

"There isn't a schedule?" I was with him for all that time and never asked. Whenever I asked where we were headed next, he told me. I never realized that it was some big fucking secret.

"They just pop up. Then, like the night, they disappear."

"Oh, yeah. Right." Shit.

"Where did you say you came from?" Elspeth sets her gaze on me.

This jig is up.

"Look, I know him, alright? I've been to the carnival. I'm looking for him." I go with a bit of truth with a heaping side of omission. They don't need all the dirty details.

"You know him?" One of them barely whispers.

"She's lying." Elspeth hisses. "He doesn't interact with mortals at–"

"Fuck you!" I snap. "I'm not lying. I need to find him."

"What was he like?" The calm explodes into chaos. Everyone is frantically calling out questions, growing louder by the second.

But I'm focused on Elspeth. She's watching me like a bug that she plans to quickly squash.

It hits me suddenly. There must be levels here, a hierarchy. She knows the truth. She may not know him personally, but she has information–truth.

"Why are you really here?" She grits her teeth. "You say you're looking for him. What do you plan to do when you find him?"

I smile, a moment passing between the two of us.

"Ladies!" She shouts above the group. "We should let our guest rest. Come, Sasi." She holds her hand out.

Smiling sweetly, I wish them a good night and follow her through the double doors.

As soon as we're alone, the air changes. She slams me into the wall, using her forearm on my throat to hold me in place.

"You're with Gordon, aren't you?" She watches me closely. "As soon as you arrived, I knew there was something about you. You're lying."

Reaching around, I take a fistful of her hair and yank. "I'm lying, but not about what you think."

"You aren't a true believer in his power."

"See, that's where you're wrong. I know all about his power. I've felt it…inside me. You sit here in a fucking convent, dancing around a fire. I ride his cock. We are not the same."

To her credit, she takes me by surprise. I wasn't expecting her to haul back and punch me.

This starts a chain reaction. Hitting, scratching, biting, and hair pulling.

We stumble down the hallway, ripping at each other.

Crashing through the door of my guest room, I shove her to the floor, jumping on top of her.

We roll and wrestle.

In a moment of clarity, I think of how much Shade would enjoy watching us like this—beating the shit out of each other in his name.

She wraps her arm around my neck, squeezing until my vision blurs. I feel the pulse in my bulging eyes. Reaching blindly, I feel for something on the ground and use it to hit her face.

She lets up enough that I can slip free. Hacking and desperate, I grab the obsidian candlestick from the mantel and swing.

Maybe I was paying more attention to Clue than I thought.

Spinning on my heels, I run out of the room and down the hallway.

Turn here, then there, then down these stairs, then through this door. I retrace the steps back to the lowest level.

Running into the empty room, I stare at the blue flames. I don't even realize I'm walking toward it until I'm standing in front of the altar.

Holding my hand up, I don't feel any heat. The flames are cold.

Reaching into them, I squeeze.

I feel him. Wherever he is. It's like a voodoo doll. I grab and twist, his pain radiating through the flames.

Taking a handful of the fire, I cup it in my hand and run.

I can feel his scream in my chest. This is really why they're here. They guard the flames.

They failed.

CHAPTER THIRTY-SEVEN

open up and take it

WITH THE FIRE in my bag, I run out the door and into the alley.

I can only assume they will be after me. Shade knows where I am now, too. I don't know how long it will take him to recover from what I did, but I can only hope I bought myself enough time to get out of Bucharest.

The alley grew while I was inside. It was long before. Now it's unending.

When I finally burst into the courtyard, I look around in the dark. I don't know which way to go, so I pick a street at random and run.

It happens almost imperceptibly.

My pace slows. The air feels colder.

I feel him.

Stopping in the middle of the small side street, the hair on my neck stands on end.

"Hello, my darling." His voice echoes in the silence.

"Shade."

"Did you enjoy that?"

"I did actually."

He chuckles, and the sound is so close, I'm sure that he's right behind me. There is wrath–fire and fury in his voice, in his laughter.

His fingers brush my neck, the icy chain of my necklace touching my skin. "You lost this."

"I won't go quietly."

"I expect nothing less." I can hear the smile in his voice. "If you want to run, go ahead. You know how this ends. I love a good chase."

There's no use in it now.

I can't outrun him.

I'll save my energy.

"I'm not in the mood to play games." It doesn't matter that he can hear my heart beating; I make myself sound casual and unaffected.

His hand wraps around my wrist, pulling me along with him. He's angry.

Whatever happened to him when I stole the fire upset him.

Good.

He walks me into a portal. It's barely visible, just a ripple in the air, but what's on the other side is a different world.

Darker than black, the air is so thin it hurts to breathe it. We're in a void. Vast emptiness in every direction.

"Is this your favorite place?"

"It is."

He said he would bring me here. I wonder if this is what he planned all along.

"Did you bring me here so no one can hear me scream?" I'm only half-kidding.

"You know me well."

"Apparently not. It seems there were many things you neglected to tell me about yourself." I cringe. That was too vulnerable.

He hums, his fingers running along my shoulder to grip my neck. "Whose blood is this?"

"Elspeth." I roll my eyes. "Don't worry. She'll live to worship you another day."

"What did you think of my temple?" He has the audacity to sound amused.

"I've seen better."

"I had to have the flame guarded. Being a god is of little importance."

"So you're tricking women into wasting their lives in your name?" Shocking.

"Since when did you start caring if I trick people?" He runs his hand up my arm.

"Since you tried to trick me!" I jerk back, but he's on me.

"Not everything was a trick."

"Fuck you!"

"I'd love it if you did," he says, taking a fistful of my hair and craning my neck back, forcing me to look at him.

"I would rather fuck Gordon." I smile up at him despite the pain in my scalp.

"You wouldn't. He could never satisfy you."

"I'll let him try. He gives good-boy energy. I bet he would eat pussy like he was starving."

He growls, wrestling me to the ground before kissing me with such force that it breaks my lip against my teeth. "Give me the flames."

And just like that, I see it.

He's still in pain.

He'll find the flame; it's only a matter of time. I know he will, but at least I can get one more jab in.

Reaching down, I slip my hand into my bag and squish it as hard as I can. He crumbles, stumbling forward and falling into my chest with a strained groan.

"Fuck." He growls, his muscles trembling. "Give me that fucking flame."

"Take it, motherfucker." I dig my fingers into it again.

"Sasi!" His hand grips my throat tight, squeezing me as hard as I'm squeezing the flame. "Stop."

When I don't ease up at all, he roars, coming up on his knees and pulling me with him.

My vision blurs, and black creeps in at the edges. I feel my eyes bulging. He's going to break my windpipe.

I kick my legs out, but it doesn't do anything. Panic courses through me. I can't make a sound.

I release the flame and grip his hand, pulling frantically, but it doesn't budge. My fingers are weak; I can't grip his.

He screams, releasing me just as I feel my consciousness slipping. I'm vaguely aware of my body being lifted completely; he's holding me.

"Breathe, Sasi. Take a breath."

I heave, struggling even though his hand is gone.

"Get off." My voice is a hoarse rasp. I push against his chest, but not hard enough to move him.

He wraps around me tighter, holding me. "I can't fucking do it."

The rage in his voice rattles my bones. He jumps up, letting me tumble out of his lap and onto the ground.

"What the fuck did you do to me?" He paces in front of me. Manically ripping at his hair.

Holding my neck, I glare at him. It hurts too much to speak, so I let my eyes convey my fury.

"I need a heart. If you won't give it to me, I'll take it. That's what I do. That's how I survive." He snarls through clenched teeth.

The cords of muscles in his neck strain, and his body trembles. He unsheathes Umbralius, holding him in one hand, almost thoughtlessly.

Dropping to his knees, he looks up at me, his eyes dark and his muscles rippling beneath his skin as if something is trying to escape–to burst out of him.

He seethes, a kind of untamed, unrestrained chaos that I've never seen from him.

His fist hits the ground, sending a splintered crack like a fissure in glass beneath me, and up into the darkness. But it doesn't make a sound. There is no crunch or cracking, just his violent scream.

He grabs me, his darkness coiling around my limbs and dragging me behind him.

"Give me the heart."

"No," I hiss.

"Give it to me, Sasi."

"No."

"Fuck!" The darkness brings me up, holding me like I'm chained in shackles, my body sagging under its own weight. But he wraps around my waist, relieving the pressure.

I watch him, full of suspicion, waiting.

His nose presses into my cheek, his labored breathing hot against my skin. "You love this, don't you? Watching me struggle. Watching me fail."

"I don't," I whisper.

And I mean it. I really don't like to see him like this. But I'm savoring it because he deserves it.

"Then give me your heart. I'll hold it in my chest through space and time. I'll take you everywhere with me. Show you everything."

"You lied to me. You took other hearts before. It wouldn't even mean anything to you."

"I didn't try to get them to give it to me. I just took it. I didn't want them for eternity."

"Fuck you." I don't mean to, but a tear wells up and falls before I realize it's happening.

He watches it for a moment before leaning in close. He licks the tears away. "You're an evil woman." He growls. "A parasite. You wiggled in where you don't belong, and now I can't be rid of you!"

I don't feel fully in control of my body yet, but I'm able to move my hand enough to push it against his chest. "I hate you."

"You don't." He whispers. "I can smell it. You still want me."

"No." I shake my head. "Never again."

He hums, shifting around me, pressing his weight into me. "I want you. I always want you."

"Too bad you lost that privilege."

He scrapes his teeth against my neck, sending pain through the tender, swollen skin. Goosebumps roll down my arms and legs. "Need you…" He mumbles, rolling his hips against me. "I'll fuck it all better."

"No."

"I bet your little cunt is soaked. Isn't it?"

I shake my head. But I'm lying.

"I'm so hard it hurts. It aches for you. I have suffered in varying states of hardness since I last held you. I've fucked my fist over and over again, but it never helps. I need you."

I shake my head again, a feeble attempt to deny him.

"Stop shaking your head. Speak. Fight. You are not a weak, silent woman." He growls, anger flickering in his eyes again.

"You almost broke my fucking neck." I push past the pain. "Speaking hurts. And I don't think you deserve the effort."

A low rumble vibrates his chest. He steps back, grabbing Umbralius from the ground and making a cut on his chest. He reaches in, pulling out a drop of his blood, one single drop. "Take it. It's all I have left."

Before I can protest, he rubs it into my neck.

He rips my dress open, running his hands over my body roughly. "Look at you." His fingers spread me open, collecting the slick wetness. "Don't deny me."

"You'll never fuck me again." My voice already feels stronger.

"Oh, my wicked little darling. We both know that's not true. You're thinking about it right now, aren't you? How good it feels when my cock slides in, stretches you open, then fills you with cum. You're dripping."

"Let go of me." I don't know what comes over me, but my mouth moves before I can stop it. "I'm going back to Mortimer. I want a gentleman."

He lets out an angry laugh. "You don't want a gentleman. You want to be fucked like a whore–ravaged and used. Don't ever speak about wanting another man." He presses my legs open, pinning them to the ground.

"He was so–"

"Don't." He growls, shoving his fingers in with no warning.

My back arches off the ground. "His cock is–"

In a whirlwind, he pulls his fingers out and flips me around. Darkness holds me on my knees with my face pressed to the ground.

He slaps me so hard the sound echoes in this empty chamber. I feel the hand-shaped welt forming on my ass, the sting of it making my stomach clench.

"Don't." He smacks me again, on the other side.

Fuck. I clench again.

"Look at this pretty pussy. It's so empty. Clenching and gripping around nothing. You don't want Gordon or Mortimer. They would never satisfy your wicked little cunt." He slaps it, and I yelp.

Fuck.

Fuck.

Shit.

"I could do just as well by myself. I don't need you."

He chuckles, "You're dripping on the ground, Sasi. You want me so badly you can't fucking stand it."

I'll die before I admit it.

He slips two fingers in again, sliding in until his palm is flush against me. He curls them, and my eyes roll back.

I try to pull away, but the darkness wrapped around me is too strong.

"Fuck," I whimper.

"That's it. Grind against my hand." He whispers. "You're strangling my fingers, Sasi. Is this what you need?" He moves faster, massaging me right where I need it.

Despite myself, I start to unravel. I don't want to give him the satisfaction, but my pussy, that traitorous bitch, completely sells me out.

"Shade." I clench my fists.

"What is it, darling? What do you need?"

I need him to pound against that place inside me that only his cock can reach. "You don't get to come."

"Is that your condition?" He curls his fingers again.

"Yes."

His fingers slip out, and his cock rams in. "Deal."

I didn't even know his cock was out.

A scream rips through my chest and tears at my still-aching throat. "You might be mad at me, but you love my cock. Open up and take it."

I brace, spreading my knees slightly.

He slams forward, brutal, unforgiving, angry. I feel it in every thrust.

His hand wraps around my hair, tugging so hard my head jerks back.

My intention is to scream, fuck you. But all that comes out is a loud, throaty, "fuck!"

"Tell me how badly you missed it."

I bite into my already bruised lip to keep my mouth from betraying me. I won't say it.

He laughs loudly, out of his mind. "I'm going to fuck you until you admit it."

Harder and harder. My knees ache, and my back feels like it's one thrust away from paralysis. His filthy mouth is quiet now–too overcome to keep talking shit.

"Sh-Shade..." I whimper.

He slips out suddenly, dropping his face down onto my back and groaning. "Let me come, Sasi."

"No."

"Please."

"No, finish me off with your mouth."

He lets out a sharp, pained gasp, but the darkness lifts me up, trapped in this position, bound on all fours. His fingers pry me open wider as his mouth starts to lick.

My body is fine-tuned to his touch. He knows how to draw pleasure out of me like he designed me himself. He knows how to prolong it.

A master of his craft, he fucks me with his tongue.

I come once. And he gulps it down.

Then he flips me around, pinching my piercings hard, rolling them between his fingers as he slips into me again.

I lose count after three, my cock-drunk brain unable to keep up.

True to his word, he never comes.

After what feels like days, I'm dehydrated and exhausted. When he finally pulls out, I don't have the strength to push back when he holds me on his chest.

CHAPTER THIRTY-EIGHT

i should hate you

BEING SO SURROUNDED by darkness is strange. It's not what I was expecting.

This place feels endless, but somehow still claustrophobic. I understand why he likes it so much. There is a clarity in the dark. It's like, you can't see anything, so you can see everything. All the distractions, the lies, the illusions–everything is stripped away.

I like it. And I hate it.

My mind is tangled. Too many thoughts are wrapped around each other to make sense of any of it. I'm a knot of desire and hatred, fear and longing. I can't figure out which is which.

I want to hurt him and kiss him.

I could do both. He's here, asleep in the abyss beside me.

I can tell by the look on his face that he's weak. His skin is pale with a layer of sweat over it. He's not dead. But he's not well.

It's strange to see him in this state. I don't like it.

He's the dark, supernatural shadow. And I'm just a woman. But I feel protective over him.

He's not a god, no matter how many pathetic women he convinces to waste their lives guarding his flame, but he's not a man, either. He's something just beyond both. Something ancient and hungry. And last night, I thought he would finally devour me.

He tried.

But he couldn't do it.

That should count for something. But maybe it doesn't.

He doesn't deserve this much grace. He tried to kill me, just because he couldn't go through with it, doesn't erase the fact that he tried. He wanted to.

Who am I?

I don't give grace. I burn bridges. I take the path of most resistance. I scorch the earth.

But when it comes to him, my brain steps back, and my body takes over. And my body is a horny bitch.

I'm bruised and bloody. Every muscle aches, overworked from clenching and flexing for hours on end.

My hips hurt. My knees are bruised. My poor pussy throbs.

Just because he couldn't bring himself to kill me last night doesn't mean he won't be ready to do it when he wakes up.

Umbralius is lying on the ground by my feet, discarded without a second thought.

He should have thought twice. He shouldn't have assumed I wouldn't use it against him.

Rolling out of his arms, I grab the sword and stand.

"Sasi?" He groans, reaching for me with his eyes closed.

"I'm right here." I press the end of the sword against his cock. That is inexplicably still rock hard.

"Fuck." He gasps, shifting his hips.

"I should cut this off." I smile at him. I'm only partially serious about this.

"So, the orgasms didn't win me any favor?" He chuckles.

"Doesn't look like it." I press the sharp point a bit harder.

He hisses through his teeth.

"You're still very hard."

"Yes, well, I've gone without for days. And last night was torture. I should have gained points for not filling you with cum the moment my cock touched you. I could have come the second I felt you under me."

Stepping in between his legs, I move the sword up, letting the tip scrape over his stomach and chest. His muscles tense, but he doesn't move; he doesn't flinch.

The blade fits perfectly in the soft part of his neck above his collarbone.

Leaning on it, I let the weight of my body press into the spot. A beam of dark light shines out of the cut, just like when he cut his chest.

If it hurts, he doesn't show it. By the way his cock leaks, I think he likes it. Throwing Umbralius to the ground, I drop down, straddling his hips.

"I'm not going to keep myself from coming if you ride my cock, Sasi. It's impossible."

I sink down, taking all of his inches at once.

His hips buck up to meet me, and his hands grip my hips.

I'm too sore, but I'll deal with that later when I'm limping around and unable to sit. For now, I'm going to fuck him like it's the last time. Because it might be.

Setting my hand on his throat, I squeeze.

"I should hate you," I whisper, rolling my hips.

"I know." He lets me squeeze my hand tighter.

He watches me, his eyes never leaving mine as the pressure starts to build. Is it regret in his eyes or just lust? I can't tell the difference anymore. Maybe there isn't one.

His hands are gentle now, roaming over my skin, tracing the bruises on my thighs and the bite marks on my chest.

It's like he's memorizing the damage he caused.

"I'm sorry," he whispers so quietly I almost don't hear it.

I don't soften my grip. Leaning down, I press my forehead to his.

"I don't forgive you." It's simply not in my nature.

"I know."

He flips us suddenly, his strength returning. I gasp as my back hits the cold ground.

Our eyes meet, only for a moment, but he says everything he needs to say.

And then he kisses me. It's desperate and aching, filled with everything I feel.

I kiss him back. Because I can't stop myself. Even though he almost killed me.

For now, I'll let him in, because we're both still here.

This is nothing like last night. The rage and hatred are gone; we expelled them from our bones with violence. And now we're hollow and tired. But my body still wants his.

"My wicked little thing." He groans, pouring himself into me.

I hold him until he's asleep again, running the tips of my fingers over his skin.

Then it hits me. Like a lightning strike.

CHAPTER THIRTY-NINE

california state prison

I SLIP THROUGH THE PORTAL, walking out into the hot Texas sun.

I don't immediately recognize where I am. The lake. In the distance, across the water, I see Mortimer's house.

A small, ranch-style house sits on this side, and a tall, unruly garden grows all around it.

"You're trespassing." A silky voice calls.

"Sorry about that. I'm not great at moving through the realms on my own yet."

"Are you Sasi?"

"I am." I finally see her. Definitely a witch. Her long, dark hair defies gravity, standing in a halo around her head. She walks with bare feet through the dirt, all of her silver and turquoise jewelry clinking.

"I'm Elmyra." She smiles, her gold-capped teeth glinting in the sunlight.

"Nice to meet you. I was trying to get to Mortimer's."

"You look like you've seen better days." Her eyes bounce from bruise to bruise.

"Oh, I'm fine." I chuckle. "Not my worst Friday night."

"You have his blood in you."

I watch her, waiting for her expression to give something away. I do have his blood in me. His last drop. What's it to her?

She hums, giving absolutely nothing away. "Come with me."

"I'm sorry for crash landing on your property, but I really need to speak to Mortimer." I don't have time for witch things, as interesting as I'm sure she is.

"I might have answers for you."

Sighing, I look toward his house. "You're not going to harvest my organs or something, right?"

Her head falls back, and she laughs. "No."

"Fine." I don't trust her, but I follow her anyway. At this point, what's the worst that could happen?

The deeper into her yard we get, the stranger it becomes. Plants that look like something out of an alien movie grow everywhere. The narrow path through her jungle is overgrown on both sides. Tall grass, trees, bushes, flowers–she has it all. Windchimes with a soft, melodic bell-like sound clank in the air.

Strings of beads and painted glass hang from the trees, catching the light and reflecting it back.

The untamed madness grows right up to her patio, which is covered in what I can only presume is an illegal number of cats. There are laws about how many animals one person can have, aren't there?

"Move, babies. Let us in." She coos, and the cats separate, clearing a path for us to walk to the rickety back door.

Her house is something out of a manic, pixie, occult dream world. It's somehow both whimsical and unsettling. It's a kaleidoscope of curated chaos. The kitchen and dining room are one large, open space. Nothing matches, but it all somehow belongs. The walls are a faded sage green wallpaper, peeling to reveal hot pink paint beneath. Dried flowers and herbs hang everywhere. Taxidermy cats sit like statues all around. Eyes watching from every direction.

"Please, sit!" She pulls out one of the mismatched chairs at her claw-footed dining table.

It looks like she's been conducting experiments here. Little bottles and vials are all over it. Some are empty, others have strange liquids inside.

She switches on the light, a chandelier made of bone and crystals.

Humming quietly, she digs around on her bookshelf. "Ask your questions."

"What?" I snap my head away from the jar of frogs.

"You have questions. Ask them."

She starts moving jars from her shelf to look at the ancient books behind them. They have labels of masking tape stuck to them. "St. John's Wart," "Rosemary," and "Dead Sea Salt - Do not use!"

"Ah! Here we are!" She pulls a book from the shelf. Several pages fall out and scatter around the room. She either doesn't notice or doesn't care.

It hits the table with a thud, and she cracks it open.

"I had an idea."

She smiles, knowing.

"Do you have a way that I can call Thalora?" I just assume she knows her.

"I do." Her grin gets wider.

"Great! Let's call her up!"

She whistles. A long, high-pitched tweet that echoes around in my brain.

By the time she's finished, Thalora is standing in the kitchen. "You rang, darling?" She starts to smile, but freezes when she sees me.

"I need to talk to you." I pat the table.

"You look–"

"Yeah, yeah," I wave my hand. "I know. I'm beat to shit. He tried to kill me."

"Tried?"

"Yeah, couldn't go through with it. But that's not what this is about."

She slides into the seat, staring at me like I'm the weirdest thing in this room full of actual jars of spiders.

"Does it have to be my heart?" I dive right in.

"What do you mean?"

"He needs a heart to be given freely. What if I can get him a heart? If I can get someone to give it to me, can I give it to him?"

Elmyra smiles, sitting on the seat on my other side.

"I–" Thalora looks confused. "Where are you going to get a heart given freely?"

"That's not important yet. If I can get the heart and give it to him, will it work?"

"I-I don't know."

We both look to Elmyra.

"Let's see!" She starts flipping through the brown, tattered pages of the book.

While she searches, I feel Thalora's eyes on me. "You want to give him a heart?"

"Yes." I'm surprised she has to ask. "I want him to live. I just don't want to have to fucking die for that to happen."

She nods, her lips parted, her eyebrows pulled together.

"Plus, if I get him the heart. I'll own him forever." A giddy laugh bubbles up in my throat. "He'll be my monster."

She opens her mouth, then snaps it closed again. I've rendered her speechless.

I turn my attention back to Elmyra. She's flipping faster now, page after page. "Here!" She points.

"Behind the veil of dusk and dawn,
The Umbramancer, the wielder of
Darkness, whose name is lost to time
Shall not taste death if a heart,
Warm and willing is freely given.

No heart torn from rage or greed will do
It must be offered.
A gift.
A sacrifice.

For such a heart, the veil will part
Time will stop.

The Earth remembers this oath.
The wind chants it.

So it shall be."

"So?" I stare at them. "If I can get him a willing heart, will it work?"

"I don't see why not?" Elmyra shrugs.

"That's good enough for me. Let's try it!" I clap my hands together.

"Where are you going to get a heart?" Thalora still isn't convinced.

"I need to go back to California. California State Prison, to be exact."

She just blinks.

"I have a few inmates there. I can get a heart. Can you get Umbralius? We would need to figure out how to get him in. But I've got the rest of it covered."

The air ripples, and Shade walks out of nothing.

I jump up. "Sh–"

He grabs me and slams his mouth onto mine. A shudder runs through my body. It's not that he's ever been shy with his affections, but right here, in the open, in front of Thalora and Elmyra, he's ravaging my mouth.

My already broken lip cracks against the force of his mouth, my blood hits my tongue, and I push harder.

A cat hisses in the background, and I remember that we're not alone.

Pulling away, I wipe my bloody, swollen lips. "Hey."

He cups my face, his eyes searching mine. "I never thought of this."

"Well, yeah. You were too busy trying to kill me to think of another solution." Coming up on my toes, I lean in to whisper so that only he can hear. "Once I save you, I might fucking kill you."

He chuckles.

"You're mine now. Once I get you this heart, I own you."

"You already do." The honesty in it takes my breath away.

CHAPTER FORTY

bigdog

"IF YOU WOULD STEP OVER HERE, please." The officer calls me forward.

"Of course." I shimmy up to the plexiglass-covered counter.

"Who are you here to see?"

"Tony Dillon." I watch with a smile as his face morphs into shock.

"You're here to visit BigDog?" His voice goes up an octave.

"Sure am."

"Um, one second." He stands, taking my ID card with him.

Shit.

Act casual. This is fine.

When he returns, there is a woman with him. She has supervisor written all over her. With her glasses perched on the end of her nose so she can look down on me, she reads the monitor of his computer with a sour look on her face. When she finally speaks to me, there is an edge of irritation in her voice.

"Your name is on his visitation list." She frowns.

"Yes, it is." I hold her gaze. "Is there a problem?"

"No."

But it looks like there is. I tap my toes, the only outlet for my growing frustration. I can't let them see it.

It took a few weeks of writing letters and phone calls for him to ask me to come down and visit.

It's been months since our last letter. I had to make this believable.

Then it took another six weeks for the visitation application to go through. I waited in the lobby for two hours. Went through the preliminary patdown and bag search.

Now they just have to bring me back to him.

"We're going to have to search you." She says this like I haven't already been searched, like this is going to come as a surprise, and I might object.

"Right. Go ahead."

"Come around." She buzzes me into the hallway behind the desk.

I'm finally behind the plexiglass! Step one, a resounding success.

"Do you have any contraband on you?" She runs her hands over my chest.

"Nope." I smile sweetly, letting her touch.

"How long have you known Inmate Dillon?" She doesn't even try to hide the judgment in her tone and expression.

"Oh, he's my husband." I smile sweetly. "The marriage record is on file."

"He's never had a visitor." There is accusation in her voice, though I'm not sure exactly what she would be accusing me of. Being a bad wife to a man serving life for robbery and assault with a deadly weapon?

Yeah, okay.

"Then I'm sure he's very anxious for me to get back there." I don't let my irritation show. I can't give her a reason to send me away.

She sighs, "Let's go. I'll bring you back."

"Thank you."

We walk down the long beige hallway, and the fluorescent lights flicker above us. Her shoes squeak against the polished linoleum, and mine click.

"There is a call button in the room if you need to get out for any reason."

"I understand."

She stops at a door, unlocking it so slowly I wonder if my next birthday will come by the time I finally get inside the fucking room.

It could be my own impatience and nervousness, but everything feels like it's taking so much longer than it should. I just want to get it over with.

"You have three hours." She moves to let me walk inside.

We won't be needing that long. I smile. "Thank you so much."

When the door clicks closed, I start unbuttoning the shirt I'm wearing as a dress. The silky slip I'm wearing beneath it is the show-stopper.

Smoothing it out, I sit on the bed, waiting for him like a present.

My fingers fidget with the necklace. "So far, so good," I whisper to it. I don't know if he can hear me, but it's worth a shot.

When the lock clicks, I plaster on my best smile.

"You have three hours, Dillon." A gruff man's voice barks before chains rattle.

The moment of truth.

Then he walks in.

He's a big man. Bigger than I was expecting. His bald head, tattoos, and jacked arms look like they came from the prisoner stereotype handbook. He is a textbook definition inmate. Holy shit.

He licks his lips when he sees me. "You look even more delicious in person."

"It's nice to meet you after all this time, husband." I giggle.

"How did you forge a marriage license with a three-year back-date?" He laughs, but it's disinterested. He's here for one thing.

"It was pretty easy." I slowly move the heel of my stiletto up my calf. I watch his cold, hungry eyes focus on my exposed skin.

He's a predator. The kind of man who takes what he wants.

"You look exactly like your picture." He groans, taking a step toward me.

"You still have that?" Of course he does. That picture was some of my best work. I know my angles.

"I've looked at it all day, every day for 456 days."

"Is that how long ago I sent it? I think it's time for an update." I move my legs again, this time pressing the heels into the mattress.

"Why would a pretty little thing like you want to be pen pals with someone like me?" He takes two large steps forward, his knees touching the bed.

"Do I have to have a reason?"

"Yes." He smiles with his silver teeth.

"Well, if you really want to know. I do have a reason. I need something from you." I beckon him with one finger.

He leans forward, dropping his hands down on either side of my hips. "Anything."

His face presses into the crook of my neck, licking and sucking my skin. "You smell so fucking good. I bet your cunt smells better."

"Oh," I giggle. "I see why they call you Bigdog."

"You have no idea. But you're about to." He lets the full weight of his big body down on me.

I need to regain control of the situation. It's getting away from me.

"Go sit up against the headboard." I hold his face in my hands.

He grinds against me, ignoring me completely.

"Tony." I keep my voice firm.

"What is it, sweetheart? I only have three hours. Let's get to it." He buries his face in my tits, licking them with his slimy tongue.

How romantic.

I roll my eyes and push his head back. "I want to ride you."

This seems to catch his attention.

"Up." I point. "Sit back."

Slowly, he picks himself up, sitting back against the headboard with his legs stretched out in front of him.

I make a show of crawling across the bed, up over his legs.

His cock twitches in his pants as he fists the blankets by his sides.

When I'm straddling his hips, I run my fingers down his shirt, stopping at the hem of his prison-issued pants.

"Before we start," I grind down, letting him feel me just enough to keep his attention. "I need something from you."

"What's that, darlin'?"

"Your heart." I smile sweetly.

He smiles, lust swirling in his eyes. "You got it." He leans forward to try to kiss me.

I press hard against his chest, his back hitting the headboard with enough force to make it bang against the wall.

"I need it. Will you give it to me?"

"Of course, baby. You can have anything." He bucks his hips up.

"Now listen." I reach down, pulling his pants down enough to expose the tip of his swollen, leaking cock. "I need you to understand what you're agreeing to."

He groans.

"Tony, I need you to say it out loud." I pinch the tip between my finger and thumb, and he moans so loudly I'm sure Shade can hear him. "Say it."

"You need my heart!" He pants. "It's all yours."

He starts to move, like he might try to pin me down.

His patience is about to snap.

I wag my finger. "I need you to say, you can have my heart. I give it to you freely. Say it just like that." I inch back, pulling more of him out of his pants.

"You can have my heart. I give it to you freely." A shudder rolls through him.

"One more time." I stroke him in my hand, and he twitches.

"You can have my heart. I give it to you freely!"

The chain of my necklace jerks, and dark coils of smoke spill out of it. They curl in the air around us.

Tony's eyes jerk open, like he can sense it.

"Wait! What the fuck?" Tony screams, but it's too late. There isn't anything he can do now.

Umbralius is in my hands, and the tip drives straight into his chest.

His chest opens, a clean cut that I can reach into. It's so strange. I expected gore and violence, but this feels easy.

It's as if his chest opens up and welcomes me in.

My hand slips in, past the slick tissue.

Wrapping my hand around his heart, I feel it pulse slightly.

I pluck it out, soft and bloody, and hold it in my hands.

Tony's body slumps over in the bed as I climb out of it.

"He touched you too much." Shade growls. The fury in his voice makes my skin tingle.

"Oh, stop. I had to keep him interested." I set the heart carefully on the bed.

My hands tremble as I pick up Umbralius. I've seen how this hurts him. I'm not excited about being the one to do it. That's new…

"It's alright, just do it." He reassures me.

I press the blade into his bare chest, opening him up. It slides in so easily, like a hot knife cutting through butter; there is no resistance.

Blinding light bursts out of the cut. Dark and light at the same time.

I can see into him, to the empty, hollow place where a heart belongs.

"Almost done," I whisper, and my voice cracks. I drop the sword and pick up the heart, placing it gently inside him.

The heart glows, beating again inside his chest.

"Did it work?" I pull my trembling hands away.

He just smiles. The ground shakes, and the lights flicker as the wound closes, leaving behind nothing but a cut.

"Was that an earthquake or was that you?" I'm breathless as he takes me into his arms.

He just hums, slamming his mouth against mine.

CHAPTER FORTY-ONE

conjugal

WE STUMBLE BACK, stepping over Tony's body.

How did he end up on the floor?

I drop onto the thin mattress, locking my legs around his waist and pulling him in hard. I can feel the difference in him. I can see it.

His power radiates now; it shines behind his eyes. It's raw–like something has been unlocked in him.

Just looking at him, I can see why the Light Forgers are so afraid. He's a different beast. Bigger, harder, darker. It's all there.

I fucking love it.

"You–" He stops, his raspy voice fades. His eyes touch me while he studies my face. "I am in awe of you."

"Yeah, well." I brush it off and force down the lump in my throat. "Let's not get all sentimental."

He smiles, but doesn't stop staring at me like I'm some precious thing. He doesn't laugh or shrug it off.

Damn it, Shade.

His thumb brushes my cheek, slow, reverent.

My monster.

His lips meet mine. The need is there–the hunger–but he's softer suddenly. He doesn't immediately dive in.

I don't want soft.

I have no patience. I want raw, breathless heat.

My bloody hands fist in his hair, pulling him closer. He groans low in his throat.

"We don't have long." He grinds into me. "The Light Forgers will have felt the power shift."

"I want to feel the power shift." I arch into him. "We'll be quick."

"It's never quick." He grins against my teeth, locking his hand around my thigh.

"Are you going to make me, your savior, the woman who just risked it all to help you, beg? Ingrate." I keep my face steely.

"Ingrate?" He chuckles.

"If the shoe fits."

"Do you want me to brutalize you, darling?" He looks like a wolf, with predatory eyes watching me.

A shiver runs down my spine. "Yes, please!"

"You asked for it, Sasi." He grins, yanking his pants down so quickly it makes my head spin. Without a second of hesitation, he slams into me.

"Yes!" I arch into him, opening up to give him all the access he needs.

"You feel fucking amazing." He grits his teeth, and I recognize the dark concentration in his eyes.

He's about to fuck the soul from my body.

With a smile on his face, he sets an unforgiving pace right from the start. The bed creaks beneath us, slamming into the wall so hard the plaster cracks.

"I'm going to fuck you like this every day from here to eternity."

"Good!"

His hand finds my throat, wrapping tightly around it. "I'm going to keep you forever. Do you understand?"

My brain is soaked in sex, and I don't really understand. This feels like something I should be paying attention to. This is more than just talk. "Huh?" The sound slips from my throat, dazed.

"When we're done here, we're going to Elmyra. There has to be a way." His eyes roll back, and something dark and dangerous flickers on his face.

"A way to what?" I pant, spreading my legs further.

"Make you immortal." He smiles– a sinister, wicked smile that makes my toes curl.

The words sink into my skin like hooks. Deep inside me, in my bones, something tugs. Me? Immortal?

"Oh, I think Gordon will be very unhappy about that." My lips curl as I lift my hips up to meet him.

"Don't talk about Gordon while my cock is inside of you." He growls in a low, primal, possessive way that rips through me and makes my stomach tighten.

"Still salty about that?" I tease, my body jolting with the power of his next thrust.

"You wouldn't have fucked him."

He drives into me again, harder–deeper– the piercing on the crown of his cock hitting just the right spot.

"Say it."

I moan instead. I can't breathe, let alone speak.

"Fucking say it, Sasi." He pulls back, almost completely out, and stops there. "I know you're close. I can feel you squeezing me. I won't continue until you admit it."

Fuck. He's serious. I take a breath; the resolve in his eyes won't be cracked.

"Shade." I touch his chest, running my fingertips over the cut.

He inches back further, leaving just the tip inside. "Say it."

"I wouldn't have fucked him!" I groan.

He slams forward, hard. "I know." His expression morphing into a smug grin–victory and possession.

My body squirms beneath him, so close I don't know what to do with myself.

I suddenly notice Tony on the floor. "Oh, shit! I forgot about him!"

But just as quickly as I remember him, I forget him again. There isn't space in my brain for anything but Shade.

"Oh, god! Shade!"

"I love it when you moan like that!" His voice sounds more desperate, and his grip tightens. "Do you want to be mine forever?"

"Yes."

"Tell me why." The rhythm of his hips falters.

"You first." I can't.

He smiles, "I'm yours forever. Because I love you, Sasi, the only way a shadow can love. You can have all of it, for as long as you want it."

"I love you too," I whisper.

That does it. From that moment until he fills me with cum, he fucks me like an animal.

The bedframe cracks, the thin mattress sagging to the ground. Then he flips me around. "Bend over and open up for me."

With his hand on the back of my neck, forcing me down, he wrecks me.

When he finally comes, it's violent. He roars, and the lights flicker.

"We've got to get the fuck out of here." I grab my shirt.

Keys jingle outside the door just a second before it clicks into the lock. The door flies open, and several officers run in just as we disappear into the portal.

We're on the train, in our room.

"Holy shit!" I spin around to look at him, but he's already on me. "Bath. I need to scrub you clean every place that is fucking hands touched you."

"His mouth, too." I bend over, purposely lower than necessary to turn on the faucet.

"His mouth?" He growls. "Where?"

"Here." I point to my neck. "And here." I pout, trailing my finger down to my breasts.

"Come here." He lunges for me, throwing me over his shoulder before stepping into the tub. "I should come here," he rolls my piercings between his fingers.

"You're a brute."

"And you love it."

"Maybe." I settle into the place on his chest that was made just for me. "Where are we going?"

"I told you, Texas."

"You're serious about that?"

"Absolutely."

CHAPTER FORTY-TWO

she walks in beauty

STANDING IN THE WINDOW, I watch the train roll into the long, honey colored grass beside the lake.

It only takes a few seconds after the train hisses to a stop for the whole thing to be surrounded by cats.

He takes my hand, leading me out into the heat. It hits me like a smack.

"Well!" Her voice rings out of nowhere. "It seems congratulations are in order!"

Spinning around, my eyes land on Elmyra, a cat in her arms, and her long, velvet robe draped over her shoulders.

He tips his chin. "I have questions."

"I figured as much," she smiles, walking through her backyard jungle toward her back porch.

"What do I need to do to make her immortal?" He doesn't wait to ask.

She looks back over her shoulder, a sinister smile on her face. "Come."

Shade is completely calm, his hand on my neck, walking like he owns the fucking world. I guess now, he does.

Inside her kitchen, there are three teacups sitting on the table. She was expecting us. "Sit." She gestures.

Something moves in one of the jars on the table. Leaning in, I try to get a better look. "Is that a mermaid?" It's so small, it could fit in the palm of my hand. A tiny, perfect little woman with a fishtail.

"Oh, yes." She nods. "Very rare and difficult to procure."

"Look at her." I lean down, almost pressing my nose to the glass. She bangs her itty-bitty fists against the jar. "Wow."

Elmyra sits at the table, setting a copper kettle down. "They're vicious little things." She holds up her hand, bandages around every finger. "Catching them is a chore."

The little creature holds its middle fingers up to her, smiling with razor-sharp teeth.

"Here." Elmyra pulls my attention away, opening a big, heavy book. She points to a page.

From where I'm sitting, I can't see it. But if the look on Shade's face is any indication, it's not good news.

"What? No!" He looks up at her like she's insane.

"It is the only way."

"Is it guaranteed?"

"Nothing in life is guaranteed, Umbramancer." She grins.

Sliding the book across the table, I read the page.

"To make a mortal's life unending,
First, the heart must stop its beating
Then the veins must stop their bleeding
When every drop is dripped at last
To revive the heart that was expired."
An immortal donor's gift is required

"You have to kill me?" I blink at the page.

"There must be another way." Shade starts flipping through the pages.

"This is the only way." She shrugs.

"Elmyra." Shade growls, slamming his fist on her table, shaking all the jars. The water in the poor little mermaid's jar sloshes around violently. "There is always another way. We've learned that too recently to believe we would forget it."

She hums, "There might be another way."

His eyebrows rise–waiting, irritated.

"If you had more than one donor. It would all but guarantee it." She slowly stirs her tea.

"Would you donate?" As soon as the words leave my mouth. The looks on their faces make me feel foolish.

"I am not immortal." She cocks her head.

"Oh, shit. Sorry about that." I cringe. "What about Moritimer?"

"Vampires don't have blood." Shade is staring tensely at his tea.

"Well, god damn it! Who is immortal and has blood?"

"I know who we can ask." He almost looks worried.

"Who?"

Elmyra's head falls back, and she laughs loudly. "Oh, the poetic justice of the fates!"

"Shut up, sorceress, or I'll remove your tongue." He snaps.

"Who?" I'm getting impatient.

"Thalora." He sighs.

"Well, I guess that's that. I'm fucked. It was worth a shot." I take a sip of my tea, wishing it were something stronger.

"No," he taps his fingers on the table. "She'll do it."

"Right!" I laugh. But he doesn't.

"I'm serious. She'll do it."

"Shade!" I'm flabbergasted. He's not a stupid man. In what world does she say yes to helping make the girlfriend of the man she wants immortal? She's probably counting down the days until I bite it so she can slip into my spot.

"She will do this for me. Come." He stands, his chair scraping loudly against the ground. "As always, Elmyra, you've been very enlightening."

She winks and waves us off.

He takes my hand in his, leading me through her yard toward the train. "We're going to make a stop first. Then we get her."

"Where are we stopping?"

"The City of Houston Municipal Courthouse." He lifts me into the train.

"Why?"

He stops walking, finally, turning to me. "The way I figure it, we only have a short window to move freely in this realm. The authorities won't know who you are yet. We can go to the courthouse, get married before your wanted picture gets out. Especially since they will probably have your real information linked to it from the missing persons report."

"Wait, you want to get married?" I don't really care about the rest of it.

"Preferably, while you're still human."

"Why?" I never considered marriage.

"Because." His handsome face is stone-cold-serious. "When I call you my wife, I want it to be true."

That's good enough for me.

"Let's do it."

The train hums through the air as we get ready. I'm no virginal bride, so I opt for sheer black lace. It's perfect. It matches his three-piece suit. We look like a perfect couple, straight out of the underworld.

"Don't forget this." He secures the golden mandible mask around my face, then his.

Sitting in one of the chairs beside the fireplace, I watch him loop his belt through his pants.

No man has ever looked sexier putting clothes on.

If we don't arrive soon, I'm going to rip everything off him again.

"Ready?" He runs his tongue over his lower lip.

"Yes."

"You're gorgeous." He spins me as we walk out of the train into the blinding sunlight. The train station to the courthouse is a short walk, but in this heat, wearing all black, I'm regretting some choices by the time we reach the steps leading up to the door.

With our hands linked together, we walk into the crowded building.

"I'll get the paperwork."

There are signs posted everywhere detailing the need for an appointment and how to make one.

It takes several minutes, but he comes to meet me with a clipboard. I watch him fill it out, his fingers holding the pen carefully, concentration in his face.

It's such a mundane task, but I've never seen him write before. I like it.

"You're staring."

"You're filling out government paperwork."

"I am." He nods.

"Have you ever done it before?"

"I have not."

"How did we get in without an appointment?"

"Linda at the front desk is very accommodating."

"Lucky us."

When we're called back, I'm sure my feet don't touch the ground. I float.

Shade gives the judge a piece of paper.

"The groom has requested that we do not use traditional vows, but instead, this poem by Byron to pledge his devotion to his new bride."

With my hands in his, and his eyes locked on mine, he leans in, just for me to hear.

"She walks in beauty, like the night
Of cloudless climes and starry skies;
And all that's best of dark and bright
Meet in her aspect and her eyes:
Thus mellowed to that tender light
Which heaven to gaudy day denies."

He pulls a ring from his pocket, an etched silver band. It looks as old as he is.

"My wife. Until death do us part." There is a knowing smile on his face.

"My husband."

I hardly hear the judge pronounce us married. He kisses me like we're alone. As if a justice of the peace isn't watching us. Instinctively, my body relaxes into his.

The man clears his throat.

Shade gives him a wicked grin and a wink before lifting me into his arms. "Let's go."

I grab the marriage license, signed, stamped, official.

I'm Mrs. Shade Umbramancer.

The train is pure chaos. A full-blown rager is happening in every car. They've pulled out all the stops. Drinks and bodily fluids are everywhere.

A banner is draped above our door.

Just Married!

We sit together, watching the craziness swirl around us. Different groups come forward, singing songs and performing their acts.

I feel like the queen of the damned.

"I don't want to rush you, but the Light Forgers are coming. It will be better to do this now, quickly and quietly."

"I'm ready."

"That's what I was hoping you would say." His hand comes to rest on the back of my neck.

The train slows to a stop, hovering in the now black sky.

"We have one more passenger to pick up." Shade grins.

The room explodes–loud, excited cheering from everyone as Thalora steps into the car.

She is welcomed home with open arms.

I watch her cut through the crowd, making her way to us.

"Congratulations." She looks between us. It genuinely looks like she means it.

I nod, and she does too. An unspoken understanding. A truce.

"I need to speak with you." Shade leans in closer, pulling her in to whisper in her ear.

Her eyes go wide, and she jerks back to look at him. I wait, watching. I expect anger. Maybe a big display of rage.

But instead, she nods.

Acceptance.

The three of us slip into our bedroom unnoticed. I'm sure my death and resurrection would be wonderfully entertaining, but there is something too special about it for spectators.

"It's such a shame to let your blood go to waste." Shade runs his fingers over my neck.

"You could bottle it?" I watch a smile tug at his lips.

"My darling." He holds my head in his hands.

"We should have fucked one last time. Just in case it doesn't work."

"It will work." He's so confident. "Ready?"

"Yes." I nod. I am ready. Mostly. There is no half-assing this. Just dive in. "Maybe I should sit in the bathtub? Otherwise, it could be messy."

Darkness lifts me off the ground, holding me over the bathtub.

"Spread those thighs," he steps between my legs. A place he has been so many times before, but this time it's different.

Of course, that's where he is going to draw the blood from. I relax into the darkness, letting it cradle me as he bites into my thigh. It's tender. There is no pain.

I feel the warm liquid run down my legs, dripping into the bathtub below me. The wound itself doesn't hurt, but I know it's bad by the way my adrenaline spikes. My heart rate rises, and my breathing is faster suddenly.

"You're doing wonderfully." He runs his hands through my hair. His voice is soft and sweet, tethering me here for just a moment longer. "Almost."

I nod, feeling lightheaded. My vision blurs, and my head feels hollow. My fingers and toes are cold, but the wound feels warm–hot even.

"It's peaceful," I whisper, my lips tremble, and I let my eyes flutter closed. Even as my brain feels heavier, slower, I realize that this is the last time I will see the world through these eyes.

When I open them again, I won't be the same.

"Your heart is slowing." He presses his face against my cheek.

I can feel it. The rhythm is faltering.

He never leaves my side. I sense him with me, even as my half-drunk brain starts to slip into unconsciousness.

Darkness wraps around me. There is nothing. No pain. No fear.

When my eyes blink open, I'm lying on the bed. Shade is pacing the length of the room.

The world has shifted.

I feel it. Different. It's power and recklessness rolled together.

"Shade." I sit up.

"Sasi." He spins around, a wicked smile on his face and dark satisfaction in his eyes. "My wicked little thing."

epilogue

HIS LAUGHTER ECHOES through the air from behind me.

"Hurry, Sasi!" He ushers me forward, through portal after portal. He's so versed in it, his power is so strong, he can pull them open and closed while running through them.

When the shouting behind us stops, I let out a breathless laugh, spinning around into his chest. "I think we lost them."

"They'll be back."

"What is this place?" I look around at the galaxy surrounding us. Purple and black sky filled with stars and streams of misty orange currents.

"I'm not sure. I lost track." He wraps his arms around me.

"I like it." I pull away from him and walk through the air. It's harder than it looks to move through nothing. It's been a bit of a fake it 'til you make it situation.

"You're getting the hang of that."

I sway my hips wider since I know he's watching.

"Come here." The slight growl in his voice makes me shiver. Now that I'm not mortal, we're not bound by basic human needs. I don't need to eat or sleep the way I did before. We are free to fuck from dusk until dawn.

Pulling the little vials from my pocket, I spin around. "I have something for you."

"What's that?" He looks intrigued but suspicious.

"An elixir of shared senses. It was a wedding gift." I hand him the little glass tube.

He looks at it for a moment before using his thumb to pop the cork off and gulp it down.

Excitement courses through me as I follow suit. It burns slightly, like cinnamon whiskey down my throat.

"Shared senses, huh?" He tosses his empty vial.

"Mmhm."

"Who was this gift from?"

"Elmyra." I grin. A soft, warm feeling starts to spread through me.

"I should have known." He reaches for me, but I dodge him.

"You'll have to catch me first, husband."

"I love a good chase, wife. Try to run." His eyes glint with mischief, but beneath it, I notice the slightly glassy look. He's starting to feel it too.

Spinning on my heels, I bolt, running through the swirling stars.

With every step, I feel it more.

Beneath my own desire, something is taking shape. It's thick and heavy. And it's spreading. I'm not just me, I'm us. He's us. We're one.

This is different from my desire. That is ever-present. But this is something else entirely. It's hunger. His desire isn't a whisper; it's a scream.

I can taste myself; my mouth is flooded with it. "What are you thinking about?" I tease over my shoulder.

"Come sit on my face. Let me show you." He licks his lips.

There is something electrifying about being able to feel how badly he wants me. It's different from my own desires. His feels dirty, thick, and needy.

Spinning around suddenly, I stop, letting him grab me. He takes me with bruising force, wrapping his hands around my arms too tightly. He's straining against his pants; I feel the ache of where his zipper is pressing into him in my body. It's awful and wonderful.

"I want thunder and lightning. I want the whole world to know what we're doing." I bite into his lower lip hard enough to break skin.

He growls like an animal, and it vibrates through me.

Wind whips through my hair as we fall through this realm, through another and another until he stops us.

Hands all over, he holds me against him. We're so high above the world, I can barely see it. Far in the distance, lights flicker and move, unsuspecting people live their lives, completely unaware of us here above them.

His hands roam over my skin, not gentle or hesitating.

"I want you on your knees." He tugs the skirt of my dress up to my hips. "Spread your legs wide and open it up for me."

He doesn't have to ask me twice. I let his darkness hold me up, resting my knees on it and arching my back.

On his knees behind me, I hear his belt buckle clink.

"I want to tease you. To torture you. To make you beg until you cry, but I can't."

I can tell by the tight strain in his voice that he's clenching his teeth. He drags the head of his cock up from my clit and presses against my entrance.

A delighted shiver runs up my spine as I press back into him.

He slams forward, and I scream into the dark sky.

"Oh, *fuck.*" He grips my hips hard and rocks into me again. "Do you like it?" He groans. "Is this what you wanted? To feel how much I want you? Can you feel it, Sasi?"

"Yes!"

"I'm going to wreck your pussy. Can you feel how badly I want to?"

"Yes!" I feel it everywhere. It's in my veins, it's in my bones. He's aching for me.

He drags his cock out slowly, then presses in hard and fast. Something about this rhythm makes me feral.

He's doing it on purpose. He can feel exactly what he is doing to me—the effect it's having.

"Harder, Shade!" I'm already on my knees, I'll beg if I have to. My own hot need combined with his sharp, raw desperation is too much. He would burn the world down to get to me, to wreck me like this.

His hips roll faster, and the piercing on his cock makes me flinch every time he bottoms out inside me.

I arch my back, bowing until it hurts. He doesn't waste the opportunity to slam into me even harder and faster.

"Fuck, yes!" I have nothing to hold onto. His darkness is holding me in this position, but there isn't anything to grip to ground myself. I'm drifting away. Floating.

Bright orange light cuts through the dark, shooting through the sky on the horizon. Streaks of daylight break through the black. It's like we're in between time; there is no day or night, just this moment.

I come. Then he does. Then I do it again. Over and over again until the sun has risen over whatever part of the world is waking up below us.

The elixir hasn't worn off, nor has his longing for me.

He spins me around, holding my body flush to his. With my legs tight around his waist, I kiss him while we come again.

Just as I throw my head back and yell his name into the sky, there is a ripple in the air beside us. Light shines through it from the other side.

"Oh, fuck." He grunts, opening a portal for us to drop through. "They're back."

"Fuck! Don't stop!" I use my legs to push myself up and down against him as we fall through open doors in the universe.

He buries his face in my neck and groans loudly. His cock twitches inside me as he comes.

"We have to get back to the train." He nips at my skin.

"I know."

"As soon as we get there, I want you in the bathtub. I love to feel your wet, soapy skin sliding over mine." I can feel his wicked smile against my throat.

"You haven't had enough?" I don't need to ask, I already know.

"Never."

did you enjoy this?

Visit myrandaraebooks.com for more where that came from...

note from the author

Dear Reader,

I wanted to take this opportunity to thank you. Writing books is my dream, and knowing that you've taken the time to read them means everything to me. I can't express enough how grateful I am for your support. If you enjoyed the story, it would mean the world if you left a review. Your thoughts help other readers discover the book. Even a few words make a huge difference! If you're not able to, that's okay—I'm just happy you're here. Thank you for being a part of this journey with me. I appreciate you more than you know.

For more of my work, visit myrandaraebooks.com

With gratitude,

Myranda

about the author

A bonafide motha' to five kids under the age of eight, Myranda requires no fewer than 2 cups of black coffee (2 sugars) each day to support her habits and has finally built up the courage to publish her work. She enjoys noise-cancelling headphones and long waits in school pick-up lines and can change a diaper one-handed while blindfolded.

also by myranda rae

SERIALS

fantasy/shifter

Beyond the Ether

1 Blood of the Innocent

2 Blood of a King

The Fairytales series

1 Captivated, Cursed

2 Love You Anyway

3 Finding Iris

4 Sucker for You

5 The Lost Girl

The Playlist series

1 Fix You

2 Beloved

3 Cherry

4 A Warrior's Heart

Sons of Sorsha (The Playlist) mini-series

1 Jack

2 Lucas

3 Samuel

4 Asher

 **scifi / aliens**

Coiled Throne Series

1 The Coiled Throne pt. 1

2 The Queen Trials pt. 2

The Astrynian Warriors Series

1 The Destroyer's Little Pet

2 Havoc

An'eo Chronicles

1 Callisto

2 Proximus

3 Nyon

4 Kieran

5 Loide

Tribute to the Alphagods

1 Wrath

2 Pride

3 Envy

4 Lust

contemporary

The Underworld duology

1 What's Done in the Dark

2 Will Come to Light

3 Zion (bonus mini-short)

STANDALONES

fantasy/shifter

- Alpha's, Kings & Play-things

- BEAST: Destined to the Hellhound
- Mark of the Damned
- Bound: Mates at War
- The Queen in Shadows
- Suck Me Slowly

contemporary

- In His Bones
- Unplanned: A One Night Stand
- PINK
- Lewd & Lascivious
- The Other Side
- When I Whisper His Name
- Just the Two of Us
- Going for Gold
- The Void He Feels
- Bound to Break

* Indicates Work in Progress

www.ingramcontent.com/pod-product-compliance
Lightning Source LLC
LaVergne TN
LVHW091024080826
845145LV00002B/348